AGAINST THE ODDS

A passion for the country

a novel by

Michael Dundrow

I would like to dedicate this book to all those, too numerous to mention, who in my formative years in a Bedfordshire village gave me a love of the country life which I have cherished ever since.

Also by Michael Dundrow:
A Lasting Impression: One boy's wartime in the country
Adventure on the Knolls: A story of Iron Age Britain
Villa Below the Knolls: A story of Roman Britain

First published July 2003 by
The Book Castle
12 Church Street
Dunstable
Bedfordshire LU5 4RU

ISBN   1 903747 36 8

Typeset & Designed by CLE Print Limited, St Ives, Cambridgeshire
Printed by Grillford, Granby, Milton Keynes

Mike Service is a semi-retired farmer much concerned at this country's agricultural decline and turmoil.

After supporting a protest march in London he is confined to bed for a few days with influenza and whilst there begins a re-run of his life to date with the intention of enlightening his young grandson on his family's history.

Mike's career as a farmer is far from being the traditional one; for a start he was born in London's East End! As the succession of vivid life scenes are mentally reviewed, we see an amazing story developing – truly against the odds. Mike's loves and friendships, his personal tragedies, disappointments and final triumph all lead to the unique position he now enjoys; loved by and loving the woman of his dreams in a corner of the English countryside which is his own personal heaven on earth.

Contents

A Lasting Impression

One boy's wartime in the country

Michael Dundrow

Foreword

It has sometimes been said to me by those who have read "A Lasting Impression" that they wondered what happened afterwards to the young evacuee, what became of the lad who had come to love his adopted family, his friends and the whole new environment which he had taken to so enthusiastically.

My return to London in the final phase of the war was not an easy transition back into city life with the golden glow of those boyhood years in the country as a pleasant memory. On the contrary and beyond my ability at the time as a sixteen year old to take a calm, objective view of life, I was for long possessed by a fiercely burning discontent at the agony of daily existence in London's endless concrete sprawl. How I longed for the fields and the hillsides, the woods and the streams, the freedom in the bounty of nature that I had known in Totternhoe but knew no longer!

My suffering was made worse by the feeling of guilt engendered from knowing that by rejecting the city, I also rejected my own background and everything my family ought to mean to me. As I yearned so much to be elsewhere, to live completely otherwise, it followed that I could not be loyal to my home and my mother as I ought. For a long time I must have given pain as well as constantly receiving it, for my mother was the kindest, gentlest soul imaginable, who deserved my total loyalty.

Into this still seething pool of discontent National Service eventually cast its huge boulder of disruption. It whirled me away to distant parts, gave me plenty of other things to think about and when it was all over, by my twentieth birthday, I was, I suppose, more or less grown up and had wider views of the world and of my own prospects.

I eventually left London and never returned to live in it. Burned away was any love of large cities. I was now unchangeably cast as a true country lover, one who through the years has felt a firm bond of oneness with the English rural scene, its farmers and its farms, its genuine village life and its traditions. In the fullness of time I re-established my contact with Totternhoe and with the farm, and now when I visit that enduringly lovely spot I feel great affection for what it is today and I never fail to thank my lucky stars for the wonderful times I had there as a boy whilst receiving a truly 'lasting impression'.

This imagined sequel to my life as an evacuee tells one version of what might have been, what almost happened in the years that followed the war.

CHAPTER 1

A Nightmare Beginning

"Keep moving, keep moving," the harassed police officer shouted into his megaphone. "Keep moving, gentlemen, please. If you try and break through our ranks we'll arrest you. You have been warned," he concluded, his voice rising as the line of uniformed officers with linked arms pressed forward upon the slowing ranks of marchers who were peering with sudden fury into Downing Street, ready to make at least a ritual attempt at entering.

"What do we want?" came the renewed shout from one of the leaders way ahead of Mike Service in the marching column.

"Becket out," came the full throated roar from the marchers.

"When do we want it?" the leader yelled.

"We want it now," Mike and his colleagues all shouted, grinning widely as they shuffled slowly along, barging aggressively into the police line as they went.

"Clod hopping bastards!" yelled back one of the jostled policemen, out of hearing of his superior officer.

Angry shouts rose high above the general hubbub at this, fists were raised, tempers flared in a trice and for a moment things looked ugly until a steward came hurrying up. "Let's have no trouble lads," he called anxiously. We're going to keep it peaceful, remember. Think of the cameras."

The aggression died away amid much fierce muttering and Mike and the many hundreds of fellow Rural Alliance marchers continued on their way, chanting their slogans, their spirits in no way dampened by the steady drizzle that oozed upon them on that late autumn Sunday morning.

All around Mike his fellow farmers and village neighbours were airing their grievances, their cynicism over the government's attitude to the countryside, voicing to the air and to each other the despair they felt deep down about their future in an out-and-out urban nation.

It was a good natured march as these things go; the English middle class countryman finds it difficult to be anything but polite and considerate even in these outlandish circumstances, so the long column trudged damply along to Hyde Park preceded by dozens of horn-blaring tractors, to be addressed by national names in the countryside protest business.

Mike had heard it all before. He'd thought long and hard over the years about the worsening plight of villages, exemplified in his own, and about the general decline of just about every aspect of life in the countryside. He'd watched with growing unease then apprehension as the land he knew and loved tipped further and further down, away from the strong rural roots and traditions which were still healthy across the nation in his youth. Now nearing seventy, he stood there in the crowd next to his eldest son John as the words of impotent anger and hopeless wisdom washed over him. He was glad he'd come to this his first attendance at any kind of protest rally or march. It took a lot to rouse him to action but that point had at last been reached. It was important to protest, he now felt, even if in his heart he doubted if such manifestations would change anything, that whatever profoundly harmful hidden agenda the government had for the English countryside would be pursued regardless. Their coach got them back home late and exhausted but still quietly elated by the adventure, the 'standing up to be counted' that the occasion implied. Mike wasn't particularly surprised that he had a headache at bedtime nor that the couple of paracetamol tablets that his wife Mary insisted he took didn't help much. He had a mainly sleepless night, throat afire, sweating and freezing, head pounding, trying not to disturb Mary alongside him. In the morning she was all recriminatory. "You shouldn't have been there in that rain and cold at your age," she chided in classic 'wise after the event' wisdom. "You'd better stay in bed for a while anyway," she went on, "to see if you can catch up on your sleep."

"Stay in bed!" he echoed. The idea was anathema to him but, faced with Mary's determined look that he knew so well, he backed down and grumblingly acquiesced. He was at least thankful that he no longer helped with the morning milking; John and his younger brother Reg took care of that, had done for the last two years or so as Mike gradually left control of the farm in their capable hands. But it still came hard for him, and as a farmer somehow undignified, to be confined to bed.

Nevertheless, he had to confess that he wasn't feeling very good. He couldn't face any breakfast when Mary brought a tray up to tempt him, a situation which set alarm bells ringing for her, as her husband normally had an appetite second to none. "I'm going to call the doctor in a few minutes," she declared. "There's no sense in neglecting these things at your age."

"There you go again," he protested. "What do you mean, at my age? You make it sound as though I'm about to fall off the perch."

"Well, if you don't take reasonable care of yourself, that's precisely what you might do," she replied with a cheerful grin. "Anyway, I'm going to call him, say what you will."

The doctor came just before midday after Mike had slept fitfully for an hour then lay awake aching and sweating and feeling generally miserable. After a brief examination the patient was told that he had what looked as though it was going to develop into a severe bout of 'flu. "That's not really surprising after what I'm told you got up to yesterday," the doctor declared briskly.

"There's no regrets on that score, believe me," was Mike's reply to that.

"Let's hope you're right," said the doctor dryly. "As a matter of fact," he went on, "I have a lot of sympathy with your unease, if I can call it that, over the rural situation. I see a lot of farmers and far too many of them are suffering from chronic stress. Things have got to be bad for that to be so. Mind you," he added, "it's similarly bad in the medical profession. We're nothing but prime targets for litigation these days as you may have noticed. One wonders where it will all end."

Mike nodded in sympathy. "I know," he said, "my daughter who's in practice says the same."

"I'll be taking early retirement, that's for sure," the doctor stated firmly. "Anyway," he added, "I'd advise you to have a couple of days in bed then see how you are. I'll leave you these," he continued, passing over a tube of pills. "So just relax and make the most of a short enforced rest. It'll do you good. Cheerio."

"Bugger this for a lark," Mike said to the four walls. "What am I supposed to do in bed for a couple of days?" He sat up straighter and immediately regretted it. A stab of pain ran through his head followed by multiple dagger thrusts. His senses swam, all was fluid and floating in his head as with a sigh he sank back onto the pillow and closed his eyes against the heavy ache that oppressed them.

"Fall off the perch?" he muttered, his brain still active in its reposed position behind closed lids. "I suppose it will happen one day, it's got to of course. But not now, not like this surely? Once I've reached my threescore and ten perhaps, I might go more willingly, but I'm not there yet, not quite." After a few transitory funereal moments he snapped his eyes open. "Christ!" he exclaimed, "don't get so bloody morbid, you've only got a touch of 'flu, that's all. Nothing to worry about."

It must have been late in the afternoon that Mike surfaced again to find his grandson Paul at the end of the bed.

"Hi, grandad," said the youngster beaming broadly.

"What are you doing here?" Mike growled irritably, groping for his senses. "Haven't you got any mates to be playing with?"

"Sure," said Paul, his grin widening. "I just popped in to see how you were."

"Oh, did you," Mike responded with a scowl. "Well, you're looking at a none too happy grandad, that's for sure."

"I'll just pull up a chair for a minute," the youngster said, to Mike's surprise.

"So," said the old man, casting about for something more welcoming to say to his grandson, "What's going on in the great big world today?"

"Nothing special," Paul replied. "Do you know, grandad," he continued, "I don't think I've ever known you to stay in bed during the day before."

"No-o," Mike agreed. "The last time I had to have a day in bed was, let me see, way before you were born I should think. How old are you?"

"Thirteen," said the youngster.

"Well," Mike continued, scratching his chin thoughtfully, "now I come to think of it, apart from the time I fell off the rick and broke my leg, about twenty years ago I should think, the last time I was actually in bed with an illness, germs and all that, was in 1942 I think it was. In other words it was when I was about your age."

"Gosh," the youngster said with all the incredulity of one who couldn't begin to imagine his grandad as a boy like himself.

"Oh yes," Mike said with a smile, correctly interpreting the lad's difficulty, "We're all young once you know."

"1942," Paul said speculatively, "wasn't that during the war?"

"Of course it was," his grandad said severely. "Don't they teach you any history at that school of yours?"

"Nothing about the war," the boy replied. "Not so far, anyway. But I've seen it on telly."

"Of course", Mike said, "it's all part of the entertainment industry now, isn't it?"

"You weren't in the war, were you grandad?" the boy asked, his sincere eyes probing his grandfather's stubbly wrinkles.

"That's right, son," Mike said. "I was too young, fortunately." He paused for a few seconds then added, "I was too young to join the forces, that's true. But don't forget that was the first war that everybody was in. It was total war, old and young, soldiers and civilians. Especially if you lived in a city; especially if that city was London."

"But you didn't live in London, did you?" Paul asked.

"I most certainly did," Mike said. He paused with the thought that he'd never really spoken to his grandson about his own early years or indeed anything much about his family at all. Somehow the time had never seemed opportune and he'd never detected any interest from the boy anyway. He always supposed that Paul's father might have told him something. It wasn't a subject that cropped up much with them. They were all busy people dealing with the here and now and with little concern for things past. But now, could the boy be getting interested in his family history? If so, Mike reflected, he'd have to take him in hand himself so that he'd get the story, such as it is, right. One day he'd do it. Not now. He really wasn't feeling up to it.

Just then Mary came in with a cup of tea for Mike and a glass of squash for the boy, and the conversation swung away to Paul's parents who lived in a bungalow less than half a mile down the road.

"It was good of you to call in, "Mary said to her grandson as he drained his glass, "but perhaps it's about time to let grandad rest now. We mustn't overtire him, must we?"

Mike rolled his eyes at this but let it go. There would be other occasions when he could talk to the boy.

"Bye grandad," Paul said with a cheery smile and went off downstairs with Mary.

Mike lay back on his pillow and reflected. The ghosts of long buried memories and piecemeal recollections of times past were beginning to stir in the dim recesses of his brain. Things he hadn't heard from for decades began to murmur within his fevered mind. He relaxed utterly and let them flow, idly wondering where he could start in making of the jumble a coherent story which might just interest as well as inform his grandson.

The confused images in his mind continued circulating for a long time before beginning to settle around his memories of boyhood. Suddenly the mental stage cleared and Mike found himself gazing at a certain scene, hard edged and precise…

A warm September sun shone from a cloudless sky onto one of Poplar's mean and monotonous streets of poor terraced houses. Twelve year old Mike sat on the kerb, feet in the gutter with his pals, one foot nudging the battered tin can they had been kicking around. His glance rested on a coal cart which had just turned into the street. He noted without comment the old nag between the shafts, head drooping, a battered straw hat on its head with ears poking through, and watched whilst the black faced and waistcoated coalman jerked off a coalhole cover in the pavement and started to empty his sacks with a slithering roar into the void below.

"Gis a bit," Kipper demanded when Kenny took a farthing toffee bar out of his trousers' pocket by way of half time refreshment. Kenny hit the bar on the kerb edge but it only bent, it was warm. He grinned as he peeled the paper off then slotted the bent up bar adroitly into his gaping mouth.

"Greedy sod," Kipper muttered in disgust.

"What you doing?" Dickie August called, running down his steps to join them.

"Might go fishin' in the cut," said Kipper.

They might but it was hot, the canal was a good three minutes' walk away and inertia was in control.

Mike glanced up above the clustering chimney pots and started to count the barrage balloons. One was just then going up and he watched its silvery bulk swaying heavily about at the end of its cable like some desperate, harpooned whale.

"Wish we could go swimming," he said suddenly.

The others nodded in ritual sympathy. To cool off in water would be bliss but none of them had money or prospects and the pool in the Roman Road cost.

"How about painting our scooters?" Kenny suggested around his toffee bar.

"Got any paint?" Kipper demanded.

They all looked hopefully at Kenny but never did learn the answer, for the silence was suddenly shattered by the hysterical wailing of the air raid siren at the end of the street. In that summer's end of 1940 the wholesale restructuring of the East End was about to begin as at that exact moment scores of German bombers were droning in tight formation over the Thames Estuary, their crews eager to bring the first horrors of total war to ill prepared Londoners.

In his sick bed Mike's clear cut mental images became suddenly blurred; the air darkened and was filled with horrendous roaring, the ground heaved with stupendous explosions which went on and on for a seeming eternity. He saw himself prostrate with terror amid the nightmare. Never had he suspected such a baptism by fire could lie behind his boyish excitement at the war at last coming to life to banish summer holiday boredom.

Day after day and night after night the bombers came and, all around Mike's little family, Londoners and their homes were consistently blown to pieces whilst the survivors, crouching terrified in their puny shelters, were scarred for life. Never would he forget the sheer naked terror of that prolonged rain of death from the sky.

After many days of near miraculous survival Mike's parents decided their son had suffered enough. His father took him by bus on the difficult, slow and circuitous journey across the East End's awesome destruction to St. Pancras station where he was put on a train and told to get out at Luton. There he would be met by his Aunt Marjorie with whom it had been hastily arranged that he would stay at least until the worst of the bombing was over.

Mike's mental pictures recalling the rush of events paused at what he saw next in his mind's eye, a compelling pause at a significant and memorable development…

After a journey without tragic incident he'd woken up on the first morning in his aunt's cottage following the bliss of an uninterrupted night's sleep. His little whitewashed bedroom was bathed in golden sunlight and through the half open window he could hear birds singing in the branches of a tree that lightly brushed the glass. He sprang out of bed to look outside. Down through boughs dotted with red flushed apples he could see a patch of grass with flowers alongside, a worn brick path, a rioting hedge and the slope of a field beyond. Gazing long in wonder at these marvellous things, the like of which his city eyes had never before looked upon, something inarticulate but strong deep inside him was touched and activated. A feeling of pure wordless joy enveloped him, an inspiration that remained forever intact in his memory.

"Hello, auntie," he said brightly a few moments later when he had clattered down the narrow, dogleg staircase to the small, cluttered living room where she gave him breakfast. She was his mother's young sister, a cheerful, lively Londoner with short, wavy hair and steady blue-grey eyes, whom he knew quite well.

"You're obviously pretty bright this morning Mike," she said, watching him attack his bowl of cornflakes with great gusto. He smiled, nodded and went on crunching.

"It must have been pretty bad lately," she went on with concern.

"Yes, it was," he agreed laconically.

"You'll be all right here, anyway," she said. "You'd never know there's a war on." She paused, troubled at what she had to say next. "Unfortunately, I've got to go away tomorrow and I'm not really sure how long it will be for."

He looked up startled, yet ready for whatever was to follow. Life was in such turmoil already that nothing would have surprised him.

"It's Tom," she said. "Your Uncle Tom, you know. He wants me to join him in Glasgow for a short while before he's sent overseas. He could go anytime apparently. I heard just after I got your father's telegram yesterday. But it's all right," she went on with a rush, "you won't have to go back there. I've fixed it all up. Only -", she paused again, searching for the right words - "I've arranged for you to stay with some neighbours. They're nice people. Just till I come back, of course." She burst out laughing. "If you could only see your face!" she exclaimed. He grinned ruefully and went on with his breakfast as he digested his aunt's words.

She came and sat down opposite him and looked earnestly into his eyes. "I'm sure you're going to love it here Mike," she said. "It's real country. And this other place where you'll be staying is a farm," she finished triumphantly.

A farm! To his city ears the word sounded exotic. It summoned up, even for him, vague race memory images of cornfields and cows in meadows and a bounteous paradise quite beyond his knowing.

"It's a nuisance, I know, my having to go away," she went on. "It's the last thing I would want to happen really but that's wartime for you, nothing is normal any more. So we'll go along there and get installed this afternoon. Look upon it as a farm holiday. I'm sure you'll enjoy it. And before you know it I'll be back and you can come back here. How will that be?"

Mike smiled. He wasn't a small child. He knew that he had to play his part in difficult times. After breakfast he went out to the front path and surveyed his new surroundings from close up. His aunt's tiny cottage stood in a terrace of four old red brick cottages squatting low at the end of long narrow gardens which sloped up from the road. Across this road stood an ancient thatched and half timbered cottage, the stuff of picture books to his eyes and behind this stretched acres of venerable, sombre orchards in which he could make out splashes of plum purple and apple green. He walked down towards the road and as he did so a few more spaced out cottages came into view with a crescent of council houses farther away. Mike gazed at it all with intense wonder for it was his first close up view of any village scene. It felt so strange not to be entirely surrounded by buildings. People actually lived amongst all this open space!

Later, when the housework was done, his aunt, wishing to please him, suggested a short exploratory walk. He jumped at the idea and they took a track starting a short way down the road and which climbed up behind the cottages. They hadn't gone many yards before Mike noticed the ground had changed colour. From mud brown the ruts had become white.

"Oh that," his aunt replied casually to his question, "It's chalk of course. All these hills are made of it." She pointed upwards where a bend in the track just then showed grassy slopes rising steeply to a rounded top hundreds of feet above.

Mike just stood and stared at the great hill in wonder and delight at its tremendous presence. He felt immediately at home there. They walked across some of the lower flowery slopes from where his East End eyes gazed out in fascination over the meadows, orchards and arable fields that lapped around the base of the hill and stretched away into the rural distance to other hills bounding the horizon.

"Well, do you like it Mike?" his aunt asked as they paused on one fine breezy viewpoint to study the panorama spread below them.

"Oh yes, it's nice," he replied, totally failing to express the stirrings of strong feeling he was experiencing.

As they walked back down to the cottage Marjorie felt relieved that Mike seemed, in his usual undemonstrative way, quite favourably disposed to his new surroundings and she hoped that the same attitude would prevail when he went to stay at the farm.

When the appointed hour came they walked up the road together, Mike struggling with the battered old suitcase that contained his clothes. "It's only two minutes away," his aunt said as she slammed the cottage door behind them. "Now," she said as she bustled along beside him, "it's Mr and Mrs Colston you'll be staying with. They've got two children which will be more interesting for you I'm sure, There's a boy, Dennis, he's a bit older than you, about fourteen I should think and a girl who's eleven. She's called Mary. They're both very nice."

Plum trees hung their purple laden branches low over roadside railings as they walked past, helping to distract the surge of anxiety he was beginning to feel about the strangers he was about to encounter. "Here we are, Manor Farm," his aunt said pointing to the name board as they arrived at the slope of an open yard with a large grey-yellow brick house on one side and black, tar-boarded barns on the other.

Mrs Colston came to the door at his aunt's knock. "Come in, Mrs Southgate," she greeted them cheerily. "Come in, young man," she went on with a friendly smile at Mike. He liked the look of her straightaway. She had friendly eyes in a smiling face. She was only as tall as he was and was comfortably built with greying, tightly curled hair and was wearing a long floral apron. She showed them into a large room which she called the front kitchen. A huge blackleaded fireplace with oven at one side had no fire in it on that warm end-of-summer day, though logs were piled ready. A large table covered with a tasselled green cloth occupied the centre of the room, whilst a long and high varnished dresser took up most of one wall, displaying vast amounts of blue and white crockery, pewter and copper jugs and tea urns. A spacious old roll top bureau stood against another wall below a large etching of some bygone rural scene and next to a well worn treadle sewing machine. A gleaming copper warming pan hung on one wall, a collection of walking sticks and a double barrelled shot gun rested in a brass stand by the door, whilst several easy chairs occupied points nearer the fireplace, edging the carpet square.

"We're only too happy to do our bit, you know," Mrs Colston was saying to his aunt as they sat a moment around the table. "As I believe I mentioned yesterday, we did have an eight year old evacuee in the early days. A poor scrap of a thing he was really, as thin as a rail. From Finsbury Park if I remember rightly. He got on all right here I think till his parents took him home when nothing seemed to be happening in the war."

"I don't expect Mike will be staying long, as I explained yesterday," his aunt said.

"That's all right," said Mrs Colston, smiling warmly at him. "However long it is he'll be welcome. Poor thing, all that bombing. It must have been dreadful."

"Right then," Marjorie said, rising to her feet, "if you'll excuse me I'll get back and do my packing. I'm catching the overnight train from Luton so I'll have to get on."

Mike stood up too as the ladies wandered to the door in their leave taking.

"Bye then, Mike," his aunt called. "Don't worry, I won't embarrass you by a parting kiss. I'm sure you'll have a lovely time and I'll see you soon I hope."

Mrs Colston came back after a brief word at the door and took Mike upstairs to a little bedroom at the end of a long corridor decorated with more etchings on its blue patterned wallpaper. "I hope you'll be comfortable here Mike," she said. "I'll leave you to unpack and make yourself at home. Mary and Dennis will be home from school soon and they're looking forward to meeting you."

Mike approved of his room. Besides a single bed with a nice dark wooden headboard which was by the window, there was a small wardrobe and a chest of drawers with a chunky tilting mirror on it and a small stack of well used books. The cream painted walls had small framed pictures of warplanes on them and a central carpet square warmed the coolness of surrounding brown linoleum. It was all far superior to anything he had known.

Downstairs again after he'd unpacked, he found Mrs Colston at the back of the house in what she referred to as the back kitchen, where she was busy with saucepans over a glowing coal-fired range. "Come in," she called, as he stood uncertain in the doorway. "You're to treat this place just like home, don't forget."

He came in and looked around. A big old deal table, bleached and ridged with generations of scrubbing, occupied the centre, with rough benches either side of it and against one wall an impressive old mangle. A copper was built into one corner, its basin concealed by a large wooden cover and, not being Monday, its firebox was empty. Two big brass oil lamps for the room's only lighting stood on a long workbench. The floor was made of shiny stone setts and the walls were distempered apple green. Mike's eyes went up to the open roof space with painted rafters, but before he could look further there was a sound at the front door and in a second or two a tall, dark haired youth entered followed by a younger girl.

"Hello, Mike," said the young man, offering his hand. "I'm Dennis and I'm pleased to meet

Mike self consciously shook his hand and mumbled greetings.

"Hi," said the girl, dumping her satchel on the table.

"And this is my kid sister Mary," Dennis said with a laugh.

"Well, now that introductions are done, why don't you show Mike around the place?" Mrs Colston suggested. "I'm sure he'll find it all interesting."

As she spoke she was also taking a tray of buns out of the oven. She quickly loosened a few with a knife's edge. Mary and Dennis plunged immediately and

Mike did too after a nod from their mum. They all went off laughing as they tossed the hot cakes from hand to hand before breaking them up and eating them.

"I'm going upstairs," Mary said. "I've got homework to do."

The two boys wandered outside and through a little gate in the fence that shut the cattle yard off from the house. Edging the other three sides of the yard were old tar-boarded barns with mossy tiled roofs and in the centre of the yard was a monstrous strawy dunghill over and around which chickens were scratching. Mike was shown stables for the working horses, vast dark and straw-littered caverns empty at that time of day and the cow shed, also empty, its walls lime washed, its mangers worn and shiny with the rubbing of bovine necks. He was also invited to glance into various calf boxes and pigsties where he gazed in fascination at their inmates and sampled their smells. They climbed vertical ladders into dim lofts where he saw mountains of chaff and hay beneath dusty, cobwebbed roofs.

He didn't pester Dennis much with questions. Somehow he knew instinctively not to behave like many a naive and wide-eyed city ignoramus would have done. There were a hundred things he hadn't understood as they toured but you'd never have guessed it by his manner. And Dennis didn't load him down with lectures and dense explanations but just kept up a stream of friendly talk. By the time they had finished their round they were easy in each other's company as if they had been friends for years.

"That's about it," Dennis said as they leaned over a gate looking out onto an orchard which stretched away below the house. "Of course," he went on, "there's the land. You'll see it all gradually I expect if you're here long enough. There's another orchard along the road, a couple of meadows and about a hundred and fifty acres of arable. About two hundred acres all told, so dad says."

Mike had no idea what space an acre took up nor what arable was, but he got the general idea of quite a substantial farm. He was already experiencing a liking for what he saw around him, and began to feel optimistic about enjoying this brief adventure which had dropped into his lap, as it were.

Mr Colston drove into the front yard at that moment on his old tractor and came over and shook hands with Mike and put him at his ease immediately with his ready smile and friendly manner. Mike couldn't help noticing the strong physical resemblance between father and son. An almost razor sharpness of the jaw, the fine aquiline nose and lively blue eyes were very obvious, even though the father's dark hair was silvering around his flat cap and his neck was deeply tanned like wrinkled leather.

"We'll be ready for milking in ten minutes," his father said to Dennis. "Do you want to be let off today?"

"No, that's all right," Dennis replied. "I'll nip upstairs and get changed now."

Just then a dozen cows came into the yard, picking their way gingerly over the rough ground, their udders swinging, heavy with milk. They were being driven in by an elderly little man in boots and gaiters, waistcoated and flat capped.

"That's our Arthur," Dennis confided to Mike. "He works for dad, been here all his life. He's a great guy. Anyway, hang around if you like and see the milking."

With that he disappeared indoors and Mike wandered over to the cowshed, aware that serious work was about to go ahead and that he'd better not get in the way, yet wanting to see exactly what was going on.

After he'd chained all the cows to their places along the manger, Arthur was busy doling out cattle cake from a small bath he used as measure. The cows were waiting patiently, standing in clean straw, turning their heads now and again to lick their coats or toss their horns to disperse clustering flies, their chains sliding and rattling as Arthur moved quickly and easily between them with quiet words of reassurance.

Mr Colston came in with several stainless steel buckets just as Dennis turned up in old clothes. Arthur had finished dispensing the feed, so the three of them put on brown milking coats, greasy old flat caps, took their three-legged stools and set on with the milking by hand, Mike leaning on a post watching.

Paul wouldn't need all those details, Mike reflected, forcing a break in his reverie. All those events of that first day on the farm might well have been momentous and unforgettable for him but Paul had been born and brought up to farm life. It was all straightforward and unremarkable for him. Nothing to make a soap opera of.

What was it he wanted to get over to his grandson anyway? He was anxious that the boy would grow up loving country life in all its varied aspects, and understanding something of its deeper values in a sane and happy life. That was the core of it, he decided. It was an aim not unsurprising in a farming grandfather perhaps even if it was more easily stated than achieved. Yet with average luck Paul would grow up to be a country lover anyway, after all he did live on a farm so his chances of so doing had to be good. So, Mike mused, he needn't worry about basic things like that, he was sure the lad was not insensitive. All he needed to do was to tell the boy the simple facts of his own personal history - and he'd enjoy doing that - and in so doing he might even strengthen Paul's love of farming and country life anyway.

How had the love of the countryside taken root and started into growth in his own case, Mike wondered. He saw again the scene of his first formative days on the farm and in Totternhoe, that village that the war had propelled him into. After the novelty of the first day there was no more standing on ceremony, he was treated as an equal by Dennis and Mary. The fact that they all had their own rooms in the large old farmhouse and enough living space not to be in continual competition was important in avoiding friction, as was the adults' no nonsense yet kindly way of dealing with the youngsters.

As it was not thought right for him to hang about idle till his aunt's return, Mike was dispatched to school in nearby Dunstable on the bus with children from all the surrounding villages. Dennis' presence as friend and protector made things easier for Mike so he was able to settle into the new routine quickly.

Prompted by Mrs Colston, after a few days he'd written a letter to his parents and soon had a reply.

> Dear Mike,
> I'm glad to hear you like it on the farm. You are a lucky lad.
> Poor Marj, having to go all the way to Glasgow but still it's not a bad turn out for you, is it? Your dad and me are well. We're glad you're out of it anyway, it's not very nice here. Nearly all the children have gone away now. We'll come down and see you one day soon when your dad can get a weekend off.
> You're being a good boy I'm sure. Hope you find this sixpence useful.
> Your loving mum.
> P.S. Don't forget to thank Mrs Colston for all she's doing for you, will you?

In the bottom left hand corner of the page was a sixpenny piece stitched in with white cotton.

His integration into farming ways went ahead on his first full day, a spare day before starting school when Dennis and Mary had gone and he was alone and at a loose end.

"Fancy giving me a hand, Mike?" Mr Colston asked. "Arthur and I have to take a few steers down to Five Acres just through the village and we could do with a pair of young legs to help."

"Sure," Mike said, thrilled to be asked.

"Here, put on this pair of Dennis' old wellingtons," said Mrs Colston, "and I've looked out one of his old jumpers. You might as well wear it if you like."

So reasonably kitted out, Mike hurried out to the yard where Arthur was preparing to open the barn door to let the steers out.

"You come in front with me," Mr Colston said, and we'll block up lanes and gateways to keep them going straight."

It was a simple job but a great thrill to Mike, who waved his arms frantically and bellowed with great gusto and to his relief successfully at the spirited steers probing a tempting lane ending, then raced ahead again to block an open driveway.

He felt a new sense of pride and pleasure in a simple task as they soon turned the steers loose into Five Acres then, on his way back to the farm, he recognised the track that he and his aunt had taken and immediately decided to explore further. This time he determined to go to the top and experience the view, the day being clear and sunny.

As he walked upwards his feet swished through patches of long, pale gold grass edged with bright green turf. Flowers of many hues abounded and unnamed birds flitted about among the thorny shrubs that dotted the slopes. The sun was warm, the breeze fresh in his face and he was entirely alone.

The views grew wider as he climbed, the slope grew steeper and when he paused for breath he looked out over a vast tapestry of farming countryside. The simple fact of overlooking was novel, magical, something he had not known on such a scale and he revelled in the delight he felt as he surveyed the kingdom from his lofty perch.

The highest point was a small knoll stuck as it were on the summit from which he was able to take in the full circle of the horizon. High, open, tree studded grassland was revealed where the hill spur joined the main chalk mass behind it. Close at hand below was the huge gaping white chasm of a chalk quarry which held out the delightful prospect of future exploration.

He stayed awhile on top, peering into the distance, wondering about the far wooded hills, the nearer villages, the single track railway drawn ruler straight across the fields on which a tiny train puffed slowly along. Then, filled with deep inner wonder and contentment, he came down and spent the rest of the day cleaning out a chicken house, then exploring the stream which flowed at the bottom of the orchard.

The September evenings were still light enough for youngsters to want to get out of doors to enjoy themselves and Dennis often had a few friends up to the farm to play cricket on a levellish stretch of hard surfaced courtyard behind the house. Mike was invited to join in as soon as he showed interest. It was a very rudimentary set up. Stumps were drawn in chalk on the barn wall and boundaries were scored on the enclosing walls and fences. It could be comfortably used by the three or four friends who usually came, as there was a minimum of running about to do. Mike, although younger than the others, was agile and quick eyed and soon took to this concentrated type of game where fast reactions were essential, not least to avoid bruising as the tennis ball hurtled about that confined space at great speed and with uncertain bounce.

Occasionally, as he passed through the yard, Mr Colston could be prevailed upon to join in for a few minutes and then there was a period of heightened tension as he took the bat and thwacked the ball around the yard. Sometimes, too, there was the triumph of catching or bowling him out, for they all knew that in his younger days he had played for the county side. When the light became too dim for cricket they wandered out onto the darkening road, talking in low, confiding tones mostly about girls, crude and serious talk to go with the first stirrings of sexual desire that were beginning to complicate the hitherto unclouded waters of his life.

When the others had gone Dennis and Mike walked back together and the talk was of other things, sport and personal ambition after leaving school. A curtain began to rise, letting Mike look out onto a far different world than his street gang knew. They became closer as the days passed, always Dennis taking the initiative, admitting Mike into his confidence, showing him warm friendship.

It was after Mike had been at Manor Farm for nearly two very happy weeks that he arrived home from school one day to find a serious faced Mrs Colston in the front kitchen, hovering nervously, waiting for them. "You two go upstairs to change," she said to Mary and Dennis, "I want to have a word with Mike."

She ushered the other two out, closed the door and told him to sit down. There was a long pause during which he began to feel a growing apprehension. "I'm afraid I've got some bad news to tell you, Mike," she said at last. "I don't really know how to do it. You're going to have to be very brave."

His brain, already alarmed, was racing straightaway. He sensed what she was going to say. It must be the blitz.

"Well." She paused and lowered her eyes briefly from his. "I'm afraid your house received a direct hit and your parents were both killed. There, I'm so sorry I've had to be the one to tell you that." She came over and put her arm around his shoulder as he sat staring blankly ahead, his brain numbed as he struggled to make sense of her words. They must be true for she had said them with great seriousness, but how could his mum and dad be dead? He couldn't take it in beyond the mere sound of words and yet the blow was immediately overpowering and paralysing. Mrs Colston said nothing more, she just squeezed his shoulder and looked anxiously down at him, expecting and rather hoping for floods of tears. None came.

At last he stood up, his eyes looking out on a blur of strange white light.

"Are you all right?" she asked.

"Yes, thanks," he murmured in a daze, aware of nothing, just a strange numb feeling in his head. Mechanically he walked towards the door, instinctively seeking solitude outdoors. In a dream he passed into the orchard and walked unseeing alongside the hedgerows, his brain rehearsing over and over again in a tight circle Mrs Colston's words, 'and your parents were both killed.'

The power of those words set his mind racing in a black chaos from which there was no escape. He couldn't get beyond them though they were somehow devoid of reality. He couldn't conceive of his parents' death, of their no longer being. It was only words. By the time he had completed a few circuits of the orchard he felt able to go back indoors and even to sit down to tea with the others. But it was awful, it seemed wrong to eat and drink yet he did it, he had to. It seemed wrong to be there at all, it was all so wrong, so impossible, a living nightmare but one he had to endure.

The evening passed as a blur of indoor distractions pursued doggedly by Dennis and Mary, so it wasn't until he was by himself again in bed in the dark that the tears began to flow at last as the rawness of his dawning grief and misery forced an outlet and it continued there for many days as the force of those dreadful words Mrs Colston had uttered became increasingly his reality.

The next morning he wisely threw off the kindly intended offer to stay away from school. He somehow knew that distraction was the best way of dealing with bereavement and he was thankful that none of his friends and classmates knew, for Dennis and Mary had received strict instructions. No further reference was made at the farm to his loss for many days though they all went out of their way to be extra considerate to him and there was eloquence in the looks and tones of voice directed towards him.

One evening a few days later he was called in from outside to talk on the telephone. "It's your aunt from Glasgow," Mrs Colston said, then discreetly went out of the room and closed the door. He picked up the earpiece, the first time he had ever spoken on the phone.

"Oh, Mike," came the crackly voice, "I wanted to know that you were all right. I've just heard the dreadful news."

"Yes, I'm all right," he jerked out briefly.

"Good, oh good," she went on. "Look, I'll be back as soon as ever I can. I can't put a date on it yet for all Tom's arrangements are hush-hush. But it can't be long now. It could be any day."

"Oh, that's all right," Mike said helpfully.

"So you're really okay, are you?" she continued anxiously. "How is it on the farm?"

"Oh, I'm enjoying it," he said briefly, then lapsed into silence.

"Good, I felt sure you'd have a good time," she said. "Anyway, I must ring off now but I'll be seeing you soon. Bye for now."

"Bye," he said and put the 'phone down with a lighter heart now that his aunt was there, even at a distance, taking an interest in him.

Dennis took almost personal charge of Mike for those crucial days whilst the deepest shock worked through him, being with him in all sorts of jobs about the farm for distraction. They fed a new born calf with milk from a bucket each evening and Mike learned to help the calf by putting his fingers in its mouth whilst in the milk as if it were the mother's teat. Afterwards it staggered unsteadily around the stall watched by the two boys who were fascinated by that new young life daily becoming stronger and more assured. Later, as darkness fell each evening, the two boys rode bicycles down the lane to the chicken house parked on the stubble beyond the village. Mike loved those warm shadowy rides down between the hedgerows, with bats wheeling past his face and the dim ghosts of trees standing with upraised suppliant arms against the blackness. Dennis, beside him as they dumped their bicycles against the hedge and tramped across the stubble with the stars beginning to twinkle above them, spoke quietly to tell tales of what happened when the hens hadn't been shut in, of the next morning's scene of wholesale slaughter and of the times when he and his father had come shooting partridges at twilight across those same stubbles.

"And does anyone shoot the foxes? "Mike asked.

"The farmers do," Dennis replied. "There used to be a hunt out this way pre-war but that's finished now for the duration. But still foxes aren't really a problem at the moment."

"I've never seen a fox," Mike said. "At least only in a picture."

"But you will," Dennis said, "if you stay here long enough."

Mike reflected on this as he swished his boots against the stiff stubble. Would he stay there long enough, he wondered. Surprisingly, amid all the chaos and grief he'd been enduring it was the first time that thoughts of his changed future status had struck him with any clarity. Nobody had brought up the subject of what would happen to him now that he was an orphan. The very word 'orphan' rang in his head for the first time, a strange word to apply to himself; strange and somehow menacing.

"What will become of me?" he asked himself, finding a certain thrill in the uncertainty of his fate. He couldn't see beyond his aunt coming back in a few days time. All he knew was that he was content where he was. It felt good to be walking in the darkness over the field with Dennis and to hear the soft cackling of the hens as they approached the chicken house.

Mary and Dennis' parents gradually relaxed their anxiety for him as they saw with the passing days that he was containing whatever he felt of loss and was surprisingly quickly taking his usual interest in all around him.

Mike recalled hearing a conversation between Mr and Mrs Colston one night when he came downstairs from bed unable to sleep, to get a glass of water.

"What will become of the boy I wonder?" Mrs Colston was saying. Riveted by those first few words he'd stayed on the stairs and listened, curiosity overcoming guilt.

"I've no idea," her husband replied. "Some relative will take him no doubt, perhaps his aunt."

"Yes, possibly," she agreed. "Though I can remember her saying that they hadn't got many close relatives. It's a very small family apparently. But yes, I should think she'll keep him if she can."

"It's a damned shame it's happened like this," her husband commented.

"The family were very poor apparently," she said.

"Yes, of course, look where he comes from. But then, that's no fault of his."

"Agreed, but what it means is that he'll have nothing. Nothing left to him."

"I expect that's so," he said. "He won't have it easy, that's for sure."

"You know what's amazed me," his wife continued, "is the way he's settled in here. I know youngsters are supposed to be adaptable but he's nearly thirteen and we might easily have had difficulties. Yet he's taken to a whole new life here like a duck to water."

"Yes, it's surprised me too," he said. "And he gets on so well with our two. In fact it will be a shame when he goes. I shall miss him I know that."

"So shall I," his wife said. "Poor lad. When you think of him having neither home nor parents. It doesn't bear thinking about."

"No," he agreed, "that's true, it doesn't bear thinking about. Anyway," he concluded, "we'll give him as good a time as we can whilst he's here. That's all we can do."

Mike stole back to bed, his thirst forgotten, his mind soothed.

Mr Colston and Arthur had been busy all week picking plums and apples in the home orchard. On Saturday morning they were glad of Dennis and Mary's help and of course Mike was looking forward to helping too. Dozens of sturdy round wicker work baskets stood ready by the gate when the three youngsters came out of the house after breakfast, and several splay footed ladders leaned against the barn.

It was a fresh sunny morning and Mike was excited. This was to be his first big job on the farm, he was about to help in something really important. All the school week he'd seen and smelt the basketed fruit in the barn. Now he looked forward eagerly to being up a ladder in one of the big plum trees and to being able to eat however much he wished, straight off the tree.

When the two men came they all went down into the orchard and helped each other position the heavy ladders, one to a tree. Then they went up aloft with fruit baskets and S hooks for hanging on a bough, leaving their two hands free for picking.

Everyone enjoyed this work. Even old Arthur, who had done it for more years than he cared to remember, had a special glint of pleasure in his eye as he helped Mike with his ladder. Once up in his tree Mike's elation knew no bounds as he took up residence between heaven and earth. A new sphere of existence was his to enjoy as much as he wished.

As for the fruit eating part of the proceedings, that soon settled down after an early feast, his appetite was quickly satisfied. The plums weren't in fact particularly good to eat, being dryish and not very sweet and of all incredible things, so Mr Colston informed him as they worked, they were used principally for industrial dyeing! To think that hundreds of tons of perfectly good, even if not sensational, fruit were grown merely for use in factories in some industrial process far removed from the pleasures of eating. It was a bitter blow but Mike was still undaunted.

"Are you enjoying yourself then, Mike?" Mr Colston asked him after a while.

"Oh yes, it's lovely," he replied, his eyes narrowed in the search for fruit skulking behind clumps of leaves.

"I must admit this is one of my favourite jobs on the farm," Mr Colston said.

"Yes, it's not bad," Dennis called from the top of his ladder. "But I reckon harvest work is better."

"The only job I really like," came Mary's voice from the depths of her tree, "is taking horses to the blacksmith. That's really fantastic, especially that super smell when the hot shoe goes on the hoof."

"Oh, you and your horses, that's all you think about," said Dennis hotly. "But Mike, there's one job you want to keep well clear of, in my opinion anyway, and that's potato picking. If you don't want to break your back in two that is."

"Oh, I dunno about that," Arthur growled as he was stacking skips. "After twenty years or so your back gets used to it and you end up quite enjoying it."

Everyone laughed at that and Mike had the warm feeling of being part of a good natured team always ready for a laugh and a joke, even if it was to be but briefly. He felt so lucky. This was followed by a sudden mental picture of his home street in Poplar, sordid and grim. He had a vivid sense of its despairing poverty and a judgement, previously suppressed by grief and loyalty to his parents, jumped into his mind. He could no longer think of defending such a place, even to himself in his secret thoughts. He admitted that it was poor and mean, cramped and overcrowded and for the first time he articulated the conscious decision that he hated it, hated it intensely and loved this new found paradise of green open space of trees and fields, orchards meadows and cornfields.

He thought again of his mother and father. He supposed they were in heaven now. That place, golden and mistily vague in his mind, where people are forever happy. So it must be that his mum and dad were happier now than they had been in Poplar where he thought they were unlikely to have been happy. The thought was soothing and was a big step on the road of coming to a full acceptance of their disappearance.

The picking of plums proceeded steadily all morning and many round skips were filled with purple fruit and carried up to the barn in the pony trap which Mary made it her special job to organise. By dinner time they were all a little weary and ready to stop. Mike felt that his enthusiasm even for this divine task had been well satisfied for the time being and he was thankful that work ceased on Saturday afternoon, except for milking that is, which, it had been pointed out to him several times, had to be done twice every day of the year with no exceptions.

So in the afternoon they were free and it wasn't long before a couple of Dennis' friends wandered into the yard. Seeing them, Dennis and Mike went outside and found that Eric had brought along a kite, a large, flat home made affair with a long tail of red crepe paper with knots along it.

"Is there enough wind?" was Dennis' first question.

"It's not too bad," Eric said, "but I thought perhaps we should go up on the Knolls, it's bound to be breezier up there."

"Okay," Dennis said, suddenly keen. "I'll get mine as well. You'll come, Mike won't you?"

"Sure," Mike said, anxious to be included.

Dennis was back in a moment with his kite, a long purple and yellow box design, and soon the four friends were toiling up the steep slope opposite the house which marked the edge of the chalk and took them swiftly up on to the heights.

"How far are we going?" asked Mac, the fourth one of the party and who, like Mike, hadn't got a kite.

"It'll be best on top, I reckon," Eric said.

So they climbed up the steep rampart hill which brought them puffing to the top, except for the small top knoll which lay over the edge. The breeze was noticeably stronger there, tugging at the kites with a mischievous longing to set them loose. They went round the top knoll and over the large flat field that lay beyond, a clear space as big as a football field, just right for kite flying. There the four friends busied themselves with essential preparations of kite and line, after which Mike and Mac took on the role of launchers, heaving the writhing things into the air whilst the other pair tugged desperately in little jerking movements to get their craft airborne. The breeze was, if anything, a little too boisterous to be ideal and there were many abortive take off attempts and several thumping dives into the grass from which Eric's kite sustained some tearing of paper and cracking of frame struts. But Eric, ever the practical one of the group, had brought along some gummed brown paper and quickly repaired the damage. At last, after a lot of running about and much shouting and laughing, the two kites were up and away, soaring and diving magnificently in the sunshine, and after a while Mike took over Dennis' kite and Mac had control of Eric's. It was great fun letting those wild flying things dive and soar crazily about and they stayed there for a long time before at last, being well satisfied, they wound them in and finally trapped and tamed them on the grass.

"It's a super field this," Mike remarked in a quiet moment, surveying the flatness marred only here and there by anthills over which, with eyes on flying kites, they had often stumbled.

"Yes, it is," Dennis agreed. "Of course, it's not natural, it's been levelled."

"Oh, has it!" Mike exclaimed, seeing now that it was pretty obvious as it was the only flat area in all the hills around.

"You mean the castle," put in Mac, who had only recently moved to the village but who was learning fast.

"Yes," Dennis said with the air of a knowledgeable tour leader. "See that top knoll over there? Well, it's the remains of the mound that a Norman keep was built on."

"Is that so?" Mike marvelled, hastily gathering up in his mind the few things that he knew about Normans and trying to picture a great rugged stone castle on the puny knoll.

"And this field was probably the castle yard or something like that," Dennis went on. "They must have levelled it."

"Yes, but they reckon it was only a little wooden keep, don't they?" Eric said.

"True," Dennis reluctantly agreed. "Some robber baron or other built it, so they say. But still it is our very own castle. Not that there's anything left of it," he chuckled, "just the knoll and a ditch around it and this field."

Mike looked around him with even more interest and respect for his new surroundings. Fancy living in a village which had its own castle sitting on top of the hill, or at least did have once!

"They reckon there were Ancient Britons living up here before the Romans came, don't they?" Eric said.

"Were there really?" Mike said in amazement. He could scarcely believe his ears that this place sounded so interesting, so exotic.

"Yes, it's true," Dennis agreed. "You should try coming up here at night when there's a moon or when it's misty. I've done it several times and I'd swear I've seen ghostly figures moving about over this field."

"Brr, that sounds real creepy," Mac laughed.

"In a way it was," Dennis said. "But somehow there wasn't anything to be scared of. I can't explain it. It was just a feeling I had that the spirits or ghosts or whatever they were seemed sort of friendly or at least didn't bother about living people.

"Do you really believe in ghosts?" Mike asked uncertainly. It was a subject he'd never before encountered in serious debate.

"I've got to after what I saw up here," Dennis answered. "That wasn't imagination, I'd swear it."

"I've never seen one," Eric declared stoutly. "And until I do I don't believe in them." He picked up his kite and line ready to go.

"I don't see why there shouldn't be ghosts," Mac said thoughtfully as they strolled over the castle yard. "There's lots of things we don't know the answers to."

"That's true," Dennis agreed. "And an awful lot of people have seen ghosts. They can't all be potty surely and I don't believe they're all making it up".

There the topic of ghosts rested and the four friends made their way back around the top knoll with its deep ditch that Mike noticed with a new awareness and down the steep slope beyond and so down to the road. How much part of his new circle of village life he already felt as they came into the yard, all chattering eagerly, exhilarated by the afternoon's activities!

CHAPTER 2

The New Day Confirmed

Drifting in and out of his 'flu bound reverie, Mike recalled how Marjorie had told him years later something of how those days had appeared from her point of view when she was up in Glasgow and the coming home. He remembered many of her words as they'd sat in the cottage's cosily furnished living room one evening...

"We'd talked it all over thoroughly, Tom and I, and we'd quickly come to the conclusion that we would be your new parents, if you'd accept us."

Oh yes he'd been happy to accept them, happy and relieved. He listened again in his mind as she'd gone on...

"But you'll have to cope on your own," Tom had said with feeling. "Heaven knows how long I'm likely to be away, it might be years. Damn the war! I shan't be able to share him with you yet. If only I'd got a home posting!"

"And you've still got no idea where you'll be going?" she asked.

"Some joker in the mess has got it all sorted out," he'd replied with a smile. "The fact that we're to be issued with tropical kit tomorrow obviously means we'll be bound for northern Norway, according to this comedian."

"Hmm," was all Marjorie's response. "Come on, cheer up Marj," Tom had said, laying his hand on hers. "Let's go out and make the most of what might be our last day together for a while. That nice little restaurant in Sauchiehall Street should do the trick I think. To start with anyway."

"Okay," she responded brightly. "I'll worry about Mike later. For now let's live it up."

Their eyes met and impish smiles broke out and Tom put his arm around her shoulder and squeezed her into him affectionately.

Twenty four hours later on the train heading south, she wrestled with the prospect of having an adolescent boy under her roof permanently. It wasn't the financial aspect that concerned her. She was far from being wealthy but she had lived comfortably so far on Tom's pay and anyway wasn't averse to taking a part time job herself. In fact she'd been seriously considering doing so only recently in one of the big flower nurseries in Eaton Bray that had been advertising for workers. Besides augmenting her income a little it would be partly out of a sense of doing one's bit. However indirect flower raising might seem to the task of beating the Germans, it yet did something to preserve the state of normality and that was well worthwhile, she considered. Chiefly though, she wanted to work as an antidote to the sense of boredom and purposelessness that she had begun to feel at the cottage all alone and where a social round of tea and gossip failed to satisfy.

Well, she would be able to work part time and look after the boy, she felt sure, and she had already begun scheming and dreaming of the things she would do for him. She would buy him a bike, she decided. A boy needed a bike in the country if he was to get about adventuring. He'd need football boots too. All boys did, surely. And a cricket bat, these were all part of a boy's standard equipment. Then he'd need books. He'd scarcely had a book in the Poplar house, she knew that, thinking back to her visits. Well, she would change all that. Oh, he wouldn't be spoilt, there was no risk of that. He'd just be able to keep up with his friends, which was so important for a boy, she knew.

The guilt at being absent at the time of his dreadful loss rattled around in her head. "I should have been there for him in the time of his need," she acknowledged. "I should have come home. Tom could have managed without me. And yet -.

Well, at least I'm going to be there from now on. Let's hope I can make a success of it."

Without any experience of bringing up children she wondered what she could offer Mike. With no Tom in the house for a while it risked being a very one sided, female orientated household. Not exactly the atmosphere for an adolescent boy who should have a certain robust male element around him, she considered. "But there you are, one more thing to blame on the war. I'll just have to do my best."

The following day was Saturday and by about mid-morning Marjorie, having slept well after her long and tedious journey and having spent a little time in restoring life and shine and fresh air to the cottage after its weeks of standing empty, was ready to go to the farm and bring her nephew back. In Glasgow, prompted by guilt, she had fervently hoped that he was liking the farm, that he was enjoying himself even, in spite of everything. But now as she prepared to walk to the farm she was a little afraid that he might be enjoying himself so much that he could be less than enthusiastic about leaving. That life in her little cottage might seem dull by comparison with all the exciting things he'd probably been doing on the farm.

As she came into the gravelled yard and down to the front door she heard laughter from the rickyard beyond the square of barns and stopped a moment as she caught sight of Mike, pitchfork in hand on top of a rick, pitching straw bundles down to Dennis on a cart, with the horse having its nose rubbed by Mary. Marjorie's eyes lit up and her face creased with pleasure as she watched.

Mrs Colston had seen her coming and was at the door to greet her and soon the two ladies were sitting around the front kitchen table. "No thanks, I won't take up your time with tea drinking," Marjorie said. "I got back latish last night, so I thought I'd better come straight up this morning."

"I think you'll find he's in pretty good shape," Mrs Colston said, straight to the point.

"Yes, I'm sure he is," Marjorie said. "I just caught a glimpse of him in the rickyard and from that distance even he seems to be having a whale of a time. But how's he been? It must have been awful for you. I'm so sorry, leaving you to break that dreadful news. I can't tell you how guilty I feel about it."

"No, no, not at all," Mrs Colston protested. "Marjorie my dear - can I call you Marjorie? I'm sure we're good enough friends by now and please call me Emily. Anyway the truth is we've enjoyed having Mike. I mean that, I really do. All of us are of the same mind. I won't pretend it was easy dealing with that terrible episode. He should not have had to hear things like that from a stranger. But he's come through it all wonderfully well, he really has. Perhaps he's been a bit too good, too controlled about it. But there you are, we're all different, aren't we?"

"I've felt absolutely dreadful about it," Marjorie said." So far away and leaving you responsible for everything."

"You mustn't feel like that about it," Emily said. "It is wartime after all. These things happen, I'm afraid."

"Yes, but all the same," Marjorie persisted, "it was asking a lot of you to cope with our problems. Anyway," she went on, "I'm back home again now, so we'll be able to leave you in peace."

"Oh, my dear Marjorie, I do assure you Mike's been no trouble to us at all. As for our two, they've taken to him as to a brother. There's no doubt about it, they're going to miss him."

"At least he won't be far away," Marjorie said. "They'll still be able to see plenty of each other."

"Oh good, I couldn't help wondering what was going to happen to the poor chap," Emily said.

"He'll live with us of course. There was never any question about that."

"I'm sure we'll all be pleased about that!" Emily exclaimed. "Now, when did you want him to come?" she added somewhat disconcertingly.

"Well, I -," Marjorie began then paused, sensing the possibility of a delay.

"The reason I ask," Emily put in hurriedly, "is that it is Dennis' birthday today and he's having a few friends in to tea, that's all. Nothing grand but Mike was to be there, of course."

"Oh well, that's all right," Marjorie said with a relieved smile. "I wouldn't wish to upset a birthday party. Perhaps he could come after that? He'll need a little time to get his things together no doubt, and to be honest I could do with a little time to pop up to Dunstable to get some groceries in. I need to stock up a bit. So what time shall I come for him?"

"Why don't we send him down to you when he's ready?" Emily suggested. "Dennis will give him a hand with his things I'm sure."

"That's perfect," Marjorie agreed. "We'll leave it like that then." She stood up ready to go. Moments later Marjorie picked her way daintily across the rough cobbles of the cattle yard and out to where Mike and Dennis had just finished loading the cart with straw and had come down to the ground.

Mike came out of reminiscing over Marjorie's story while he saw in his mind's eye the scene as his aunt had come across the yard into his view and into his active life once more. He remembered how pleased he had been to see her, aware, even if not in so many words, that he might be about to become part of a real family again, his own flesh and blood … "Hullo auntie," he called as she arrived.

"Well, you're quite the farmer's boy I see," she quipped. "Hello Dennis, hello Mary. I'm glad to see you're keeping Mike busy. What's he like as a workman?"

"Dennis smiled politely but said nothing. Mary retorted, "Oh, he's not too bad for a Londoner, I suppose." They all laughed at that, even Mike.

"I'm afraid you've reached the end of your farm holiday, young man," Marjorie said, pulling a wry face. "Are you ready to come back to my boring old cottage?"

"Sure," Mike said, his eyes lighting up. He immediately took his aunt's words as her way of declaring his future home and this sent his spirits soaring.

"Whenever you like then," she said. "After the birthday tea, that is. Oh, many happy returns by the way, Dennis. How many is it now?"

"Sixteen," Dennis replied.

"Is that so?" she said. "Quite the young man now aren't we?" She ran her eye approvingly over Dennis' handsome bronzed features. "Yes, well," she went on, "as I say Mike, if you'd care to pack up and come along home sometime this evening that'll be fine."

"Okay," he replied, savouring the 'come along home'. "I'll do that."

"Bye," Marjorie called, as she turned and stepped delicately across the ruts. "I'll have something cooking at about seven, I expect."

The remainder of Mike's last day at Manor Farm seemed to pass very rapidly. He didn't have time for regrets even if he were inclined that way, which he wasn't. They'd still all be friends which was the important thing. In the afternoon Eric and Mac came up and the four decided as the weather had turned, to go to the cinema in Dunstable, generously financed by Mrs Colston, to see 'Sergeant Yorke,' the latest in a series of American war films. They returned covered with military glory to a back kitchen table spread with a gargantuan tea fit for heroes with hearty young appetites. Mary had wisely arranged to be out so the four boys had the room to themselves to make the rafters ring and be as boisterous as seemed fitting on such an occasion.

Later, after a stirring game of cricket in the sheepyard, Eric and Mac left and Mike went upstairs and quickly threw his things into a suitcase. He glanced around with breezy affection at the little room before leaving it, conscious of the good and bad times he'd had there over the past weeks.

His actual departure from the farm was very low key, much to his relief. He came into the front kitchen with his case packed and stopped in the middle awkwardly, not knowing what to say. Mrs Colston made it easy for him. "Well, time to go, young man."

"Yes," he said, "I'd better get along now."

"I hope your stay has been enjoyable," she added.

"Oh yes," he replied vehemently. "It's been wonderful, it really has."

"Good. We've enjoyed it too, haven't we Norman?"

"Oh yes," he said. "And we'll be seeing plenty more of you no doubt."

Mike nodded eagerly, then Dennis came in to help him with the couple of carrier bags of extra items he'd acquired during his stay.

"I'll be off then," Mike said. "So thanks again for everything."

Mary came out of the stable and waved as they walked up to the road in the fading twilight.

"Well, that's that," Mrs Colston commented, as she watched them pass the window. "We could have done far worse than that young man."

Mike lay in bed later that evening letting his mind run over the events of the past few weeks. He wasn't at all unhappy. "Mike's an adaptable boy, there's no doubt about that," he'd heard Mrs Colston say one day and he'd taken it as a compliment. Most of his adventures had been happy ones and he welcomed this new episode of living with his aunt. He liked her very much and he'd already had ample evidence of her intention of doing her best for him. Not only was there a delicious plateful of sausages, mashed potato and beans waiting for him when he'd got in, which in the light of the birthday tea previously consumed he'd had some difficulty in doing full justice to, but she'd brought back half a dozen interesting looking books for him from Dunstable and half a pound of toffees from her accumulated sweet ration. What more could a boy ask for?

Marjorie sat downstairs, knitting. She was already several rows into the jumper she'd chosen to knit for her nephew and as the needles quietly clicked she felt a warm glow inside at having Mike upstairs tucked up in bed, part of her life from now on. She had long been aware of how much she missed having children of her own. There had been for long an indefinable edginess, a restiveness inside her that was scarcely ever entirely absent but which on occasions, such as passing by a lively school playground, had forced itself sharply into her consciousness.

She loved the whole idea of family life, She, who knew she ought absolutely to have several children, had for years grieved over her failure to have even one. Now with Mike under her roof, her responsibility, the silence of the evening was no longer oppressive as it had been for so long but was full of life and meaning. Her agile mind ran on, envisaging his development into later teenage then adult years and of the legitimate pride and pleasure she and Tommy would feel in being part of his progress, in helping to shape and mould that boy who was partly, after all, her own flesh and blood.

He came home from chapel the next morning to a copious dinner that his aunt had spent much of the morning cooking. The ration-restricted cut of beef was compensated for by a superb Yorkshire pudding, crisply baked potatoes and the last picking of runner beans which the neighbours had kept going in Marjorie's absence.

They were cosily convivial around the robust circular table. She talked vividly about Scotland and in particular about one or two of the trips she had made with Tommy into the Highlands and backed this up with some photographs she had taken on her old Brownie box camera. Mike was fascinated to see and hear about mountains and was full of wonder at the grandeur of the landscape, a quality that stirred him even in a small snap.

"One day you'll go, I have no doubt," she said, sensing his interest.

She asked him about his stay on the farm and although, like most youngsters, he tended to the laconic, he told her enough for her to realise what a profound experience it had been. Although she didn't detect any deep sense of regret at leaving the farm, she was very relieved that it was all over, for she felt sure that the longer it went on the greater would be his difficulty in adjusting to her small cottage.

Whilst she took a well earned rest after her labours, Mike went up to the farm to call on Dennis and found him, together with Eric and Mac, lounging about on the rickyard fence, trying to determine what to do with the afternoon. Being Sunday, it was only a question of where they should walk and as Mike joined them they had just come to a decision. "We're going over to Sewell. Coming?"

"Sure," said Mike, all the more interested as he hadn't yet been there though he'd heard about Sewell as being an old chalk quarry nearby, long abandoned.

They walked down through the deserted village street, past Marjorie's cottage and on past the Duke's Head, the quarrymen's pub, over the level crossing of the quarry line with the lime burners nearby gently steaming and on further into the lane that ran along the foot of the chalk escarpment towards Sewell. Once they had passed the Duke's Head there wasn't a house in sight, the only buildings visible besides the lime burners being the squat tower of Tilsworth's church across the marshy clay fields backed by scrubby woodland where they sometimes wandered when in need of woods.

As they strolled along Dennis was talking about leaving school now that he was sixteen. "Mum wants me to stay on till I'm eighteen," he said, "but I'm going to leave next summer. Dad could do with my help full time I'm sure and there's no point in staying on at school if I've got to learn to run the farm anyway. The sooner I get into it the better it'll be for me, I reckon."

"I'm leaving when I'm sixteen next summer," Mac said. "I'd like to join up really but they won't take you before eighteen will they? I hope the war's still on by then."

"What are you going to join?" Eric asked.

"The air force," Mac said with assurance. "I'm joining the A.T.C. next week, Dad says that'll make sure I get into the air force when I'm called up."

"I don't suppose I'll be able to join up," Dennis said." Dad says there's no chance if you're a farmer."

"That's what my dad says about me," said Eric who lived on a smallholding which his dad ran single handed. "It's just as well as far as I'm concerned. War is just plain stupid in my opinion."

"No it's not," Mac retorted heatedly. "We wouldn't like the Germans coming over here telling us what to do, would we?"

"No," Eric admitted. "But didn't they say the Great War was the war to end all wars? So what went wrong? Why have we got another one now?"

"Don't ask me," Mac said. "Ask the Germans, they started it."

"So millions will get killed and they'll still say it's to stop all future wars," Eric said. "And so it goes on. It's crazy."

"One day perhaps the League of Nations will be strong enough to stop wars," Dennis said thoughtfully.

"Maybe," said Mac. "But until then we've got no alternative but to fight. At least that's my opinion."

Mike was aware that he already knew something at first hand about the horrors of war but he didn't venture an opinion.

Then Eric saw a hare loping casually across a stubble field. "It knows we haven't got guns or a dog," was his comment.

"Of course it can't tell that," Mac countered in ongoing argumentative vein. "It's too far away for one thing."

"Don't you believe it," Eric said. "It knows all right."

"It's only got a tiny brain," Mac pointed out.

"Well, rooks have even tinier ones," Dennis put in, "but you walk by a flock of them with a gun under your arm and they'll take off, but with no gun they'll just go on feeding. I've done it many times."

A kestrel hovering over a hedgerow some way ahead next attracted their attention and led the conversation on to hawks for some time allowing Mike to absorb more country lore.

They came at last to Sewell's abandoned quarry, a huge scar in the chalk escarpment, and wandered about for some time eagerly searching for signs of former activity but there was very little. The old tramway tracks that almost certainly covered the quarry floor were all gone without trace. The sheds and other buildings were gone too, save for vestiges of foundations. All was grass covered, even the banks and heaps of chalk spoil had reluctantly allowed sparse vegetation to overspread them. As with all abandoned sites of human activity there was a certain subtle nostalgia to be sensed, bringing imprecise thoughts of the long departed workers and how all their efforts and industry over many years had now come to this almost nothingness.

Leaving the old quarry at last, they sat down on a grassy bank above where a spring of crystal water trickled from the hillside behind them. The day of mellow autumn sunshine and the rural peace and beauty of the vale before them were conducive to a general feeling of well being and optimism which was in stark contrast to what they knew in a different part of their brain was the nation's dire situation. News of military disasters filled the papers and the airwaves, invasion was talked about as an imminent threat, yet the four friends lounged comfortably without a serious care in the world save their own preoccupations.

"So it's sweet sixteen and never been kissed, is it Dennis?" Mac asked with a mischievous smile, leaning back on his elbow.

"Mind your own business, you cheeky sod," said Dennis, coolly.

"Oh, go on tell us." Mac insisted.

"Why should I?" Dennis protested. "You started it, you tell us."

"Tell you what?" Mac asked.

"All about your wide experience with girls, of course", Dennis said with heavy sarcasm.

Mike was all ears. Was he going to learn something really useful? The trouble was he knew already that you could never tell with Mac whether he was making it up or not. His glib imagination ran on like wildfire whatever the subject.

"All right then," he said smugly. "I'll tell you about the girl I had at my last school before we moved here. She was called Martha and I used to kiss her on our way home every day."

"That's not much," Dennis said scornfully. "Anyone can do that."

"Yes, but this was for real," Mac said. "And we touched tongues."

"So what," was the withering comment.

"I bet you've never done it," Mac said heatedly.

"Course I have, lots of times."

"Who with?" Mac persisted.

"I'm not telling you," Dennis replied.

Were they both lying, Mike wondered, as his brain raced at the exciting images conjured up. He went on to imagine getting his first girl, any day now, and he feverishly enjoyed the vague form he embraced as they all sat silent, wrapped in their own lascivious thoughts.

When Mike got back indoors an hour or so later he found his aunt all agitated, a case half packed on the table and clothes strewn about. "Ah, thank goodness you've come," she said. "Something terrible's happened, I've got to go away at once." She picked up a telegram from the mantelpiece and thrust it into his hand. "It's Tom," she said. "Read it."

His eye ran swiftly over the brief message. 'Lieutenant Southgate severely injured - stop - Ward Two West Cornwall Hospital Penzance - stop - Advise immediate presence.'

CHAPTER 3

Marjorie's Agony

'The English rural landscape in August has a mature beauty about it,' Mike read in the Sunday broadsheet lying on his bed, 'which is, or used to be before the blight of suburbia and its pervasive values escaped from the bottle, deeply embedded in the national soul. A chequer board of fields it was typically, where ripening grain stood heavy eared, girdled by green hedgerows in which larger trees cast pools of noontide shade. Today, harvest work is completely mechanised. It is therefore brief, hectic, industrially noisy and terribly efficient with almost no emotional connection to the earth and to nature in general. In the forties it was still labour intensive, much less efficient, still firmly connected to nature and the soil, full of natural sound and with strong touches of the romantic.'

How true that is, he thought. And what wouldn't we give to be able to paint a similar word picture of British agriculture today? Instead of the disaster and despair which is now farming's lot. He slipped easily back in his memory ...

Just after the start of another of those old style harvests where even boys could play a valuable part, Mike sat on the front of an empty cart, the cool black leather reins loose in his hands as Dolly the young chestnut mare stepped briskly out along the lane down to the harvest field. As they approached the gateway he sprang up, slowed the mare down with a strong pull on the reins, alert and ready to guide her between the posts which, with an anxious but accurate tug he accomplished neatly.

They bumped off across the stubble to where Dennis stood leaning on his pitchfork, waiting for him among the oat shocks. Mike pulled up with a flourish between the rows and threw the reins down to Dennis, who looped and hung them on the horse's collar.

"How are they getting on up at the yard?" Dennis called.

"Okay. Harry Blake's turned up so they're getting on faster."

"Good," said Dennis. "Though that means we'll have to load quicker or they'll be waiting for us."

"I'm ready when you are, "Mike responded.

Dennis dug his fork into a couple of sheaves and hoisted them onto the cart where Mike manoeuvred them tidily into the corner with his hands. Then he quickly slipped on a pair of old leather gloves, for a palmful of blisters had speedily taught him what the occasional thistle and the chafing of the bands could do.

Dennis forked the sheaves on steadily, sending the horse on between the rows with clickings of the tongue and stopping her with a loud 'Woah!' Mike arranged the growing pile into an orderly load, ears always inwards, filling first the bottom then gradually rising above and out over the frames to front and rear to make a solid, high load. This was something he had very recently been taught to do. It gave him the great satisfaction of knowing that he was a much more valuable member of the team now than when he was just leading the horse as he had started off doing.

Mike recalled, from his great age of almost seventy, with undimmed clarity how happy he had been as his thirteenth birthday approached and how he could have wished the harvest work to go on for ever in spite of that telegram which had called his aunt away.

The immediate result of the receipt of that telegram had been that they both went rushing off to the farm and, although Mr and Mrs Colston must have been astonished at the turn of events, they did what was requested without the slightest hesitation.

"That's quite all right my dear Marjorie," said Mrs Colston. "Mike can of course come back here if that will help you."

Mr Colston nodded his agreement.

"Oh, thank you," Marjorie said with sincere gratitude. "That will be one worry off my mind. I'll have to go at once obviously and I can't really take Mike with me. What I'll be confronting I don't know."

"No, of course you can't," Emily agreed. "Luckily I haven't had time to do anything in Mike's room, even the bed is still more or less made up. So you see it won't be putting us to any trouble. As for the telegram, try not to worry too much my dear. Telegrams always give a nasty shock, I know. My heart turns over whenever the boy brings one, which isn't very often I'm glad to say. Let's hope your husband may not be so bad after all."

"I do hope and pray that may be the case," Marjorie said, though her expression indicated that she feared the worst.

So she went off almost at once, very anxious to get down to Cornwall, having overseen Mike's packing. They left the cottage together, she to the bus stop, he to the farm.

Of course he'd settled in to life at the farm again without difficulty. It was a bonus really. Dennis in particular was pleased to have him around again. It wasn't until more than a week after his aunt's departure that he had a letter from her, enclosed in the same envelope as one for Mrs Colston. He came in from school and she gave it to him. He read it in his room.

> Dear Mike,
> Just a quick word to let you know how things are here.
> I'm afraid Uncle Tom is very seriously injured. I won't go into details now except to say that his ship was torpedoed at night off Land's End and I'm afraid he's had to have a leg amputated besides having other serious injuries and he's still in a bad way. So of course I shall stay on here for as long as it takes. I hope all is well at your end.
> Remember Tom in your prayers please.
> Your loving aunt,
> Marjorie.

Mike sat on the bed, staring at the wall but seeing in his mind's eye the dire images that his aunt's words conjured up. Though he didn't know his uncle quite as well as his aunt he'd been fun to be with and was kind and generous and the thought of what he must have gone through was very painful. The grisly horror of having a leg off didn't bear close thinking about.

Over the next few days he was forced to live with scenes of carnage on the sea at night, of graphic life and death struggles and all the rich luxury of horror which youth is subject to. Inevitably though, and fortunately, the passage of time and the press of life at school and farm began to dull the sharpness of that first knife-edged shock. The nightmare images played themselves to a standstill then left him increasingly free.

A week after that first letter came a second. As he glanced at the familiar writing he was immediately back in the sadness of the first one while he unfolded the single sheet and read:-

> Dear Mike,
> I'm afraid Tom isn't any better. The doctors are increasingly worried about him in spite of their best efforts. Yesterday in a brief period of consciousness he talked a little and one thing he said makes me write this. "I'd like to see Mike," he said several times over. "I'd like to see our adopted son." I just had to say you'd come. Will you come Mike? It would give him such pleasure I know. I'll phone with the details of the journey one evening soon. It will probably only be for a few days.
> I'm explaining all this to Mrs Colston in a separate letter. I wouldn't ask this of you if it wasn't desperate but it is desperate Mike so I know you'll understand and try to give some pleasure

to Tom in his hour of need. I can't write more at the moment.
      Your loving aunt,
          Marjorie.

So it was that a few days later Mike left the village for Luton on the early bus then took the train down to St. Pancras. From there he negotiated his way along the Underground to Paddington and was eventually sliding out through grimy brick suburbs on the long journey to Cornwall.

Penzance station was crowded with servicemen, sailors mostly with kit bags on shoulders milling jauntily about, but Mike found his aunt without difficulty. She smiled and pressed his hand as they walked off into one of the little side streets near the station where she was staying in a modest guest house. After he'd put his bag into the single room which was to be his, he came and sat down in her larger bed sitting room.

"How is Uncle Tom?" he asked, bringing up the crucial subject for the first time after waiting in vain for her to say something. There was a long pause during which her face became taut with emotion.

"He's bad," she said eventually, her voice almost choked. "If you don't mind," she went on in a low voice, "we'll go up to the hospital to see him in a minute. I know you've had a long day but -" her voice faltered and she turned away.

"That's all right," he said, anxious and trying to be helpful, though at a loss as to how to react to his aunt's tragic air.

So, after she had plied him with orange squash and shop cake, forcing herself to chatter a little about her adventures in Penzance, she picked up her coat. "If you're ready we'll go now," she said.

"Mike," she said quietly as they moved toward the door, "I must warn you -" She took a deep breath. "Tom's -, try not to be shocked. It's asking a lot of you I know. He does want to see you so much." Her eyes avoided his. "I hope it's not too late." He had never known her so solemn.

They walked up Market Jew Street where the high granite pavement was thronged on that fine evening surveyed by Humphrey Davy on his lofty plinth. Mike was scarcely aware of his unfamiliar surroundings, his mind pre-occupied with strange intimations of circling angels of death which were his only possible interpretation of Marjorie's words.

Through swinging hospital doors and bare corridors they passed and eventually entered a small side ward, where Marjorie leaned over the inert figure of her husband almost buried in bedclothes. "He's asleep," she whispered to Mike who stood awkwardly at the foot of the bed. He came slowly up and stood opposite his aunt and looked down at Tom's face, peacefully relaxed in sleep.

A nurse came in. "Oh, Mrs Southgate," she said softly, "the doctor would very much like a word with you. Could you come please?"

Marjorie motioned to Mike to stay, then slipped out. He stood there for a while looking down, mesmerised by the pallid features of his uncle, awed by his knowledge of the horrendous injuries and by the almost palpable presence of death in that silent, impersonal little room. He sat down on the bedside chair and watched and waited, his mind a blur of imprecise sadness as the minutes ticked slowly by.

Suddenly Tom stirred, sighed deeply and opened his eyes, staring up at the ceiling. Mike stood up, his eyes riveted on his uncle just as Marjorie came back into the room and went swiftly to her husband and grasped his hand. A weary smile spread over Tom's features, then he swivelled his eyes and saw Mike standing there. His lips moved, though no sound emerged, but his eyes were alight with something of their old intensity.

He raised his hand slightly from the bed and Marjorie whispered, "Take it." Mike did so and they were all three linked in line. He could feel Tom's eyes boring into his own and his lips moved, but again no sound came. The pressure on Mike's hand increased and Tom's eyes rolled round to Marjorie and he tried desperately but in vain to raise his head. Suddenly Marjorie thrust out her hand to Mike. He took it and a smile spread over Tom's features and he relaxed on the pillows as they were all three joined in a silent circle. Joined forever, Mike mused, a lifetime later, as he felt the force of that living bond still acting upon him.

After a few moments Tom had given another profound sigh and lapsed into unconsciousness; the circle was broken. Marjorie sat down holding Tom's hand, her head bowed. Then she looked up with a tear stained face and said in a low voice, "We'd better go now, we mustn't tire him too much."

The nurse came in again and felt Tom's wrist. "Yes, he's deeply asleep," she said.

Once outside she led Mike away from the crowded street down to the sea front as daylight was fading. "A breath of sea air will do us good," she said. As they passed by the street's heavy granite villas she said, "I think we were in time, he recognised you, didn't he?"

"I think so," Mike said. He dared not say more. Whatever Tom had tried to say to him Mike felt that the essence of it was in that look of strong, vital recognition deeper than words and in the joined circle.

"At least he had that satisfaction," Marjorie said. She paused a long minute, during which their steady footfalls on the empty pavement were the only sound. Then she continued in a low, flat voice, "The doctor said there is no hope and it will only be a matter of hours or a day or two at most." Mike felt his flesh creep and the hair at the back of his neck stand on end at those words, that sentence of death.

They turned onto the promenade where a high tide was hitting the sea wall and sending clouds of spray upwards. As they walked along in the near darkness of the blackout, Mike puzzled over the imminent death of his uncle, awed by the prospect and trying to grasp the depth of his aunt's suffering because of it.

Later, as they ate their modest evening meal in the half empty guest house, Marjorie, whilst eating practically nothing, did her best to lighten the mood for the youngster. "Well now, young Mike," she began brightly as they sat down, "I think you've had your fill of hospitals for the moment, don't you? I'll go in as usual tomorrow but I suggest you have a free day before we put you on the train home. There's not much fun to be had in wartime Penzance perhaps for a young man on his own but you might like to see some of the local sights. You could catch a bus to Land's End perhaps or St. Ives or have a look at Newlyn harbour with all the fishing boats. I wish I had the time to come with you, there's some grand sights around here."

She relapsed into serious vein once more. "I'm going to stay here for as long as it takes. And afterwards, well, I expect I'll go north. Tommy came from Maryport, you know, a little town you've probably never heard of. His old mum still lives in Maryport in a council house. But there's no need for you to be part of all that. You go back to the farm and I'll come home eventually."

Behind her smile Mike could see she was near to tears but he could think of nothing to do or say to change the mood, to whisk away the air of tragedy. It was too heavy a load of sadness for a youngster to lift. They were early in bed.

Mike, reliving those far off moments of his own life and dwelling on them in an attempt to discover the essential influences that led to his transformation from city gutter snipe to country lover and how to tell some of it to his grandson Paul, paused at this point - the previously unknown deep anguish of his aunt. He remembered waking the next morning in Penzance. A message had come from the hospital for Marjorie, a message of whose contents he did not get, nor need, an explanation and which had Marjorie packing him off home straight away, her eyes streaming with tears yet still regretting the fact that he was going to miss seeing his sights.

It was when his aunt had finally come home some ten days later, after Tom's funeral in the north, that there almost occurred a bizarre shift in his fortunes - one that didn't come off, couldn't have come off, but which he often thought about in later years when in 'What if' mood. They were in the cottage the same evening of his aunt's return which had, not surprisingly, been very quiet and low key, she being dressed in black and sombre grey. After they had finished eating and the dishes were waiting to be cleared, Marjorie had suddenly said, "Do you think we can settle down to life here in the cottage now Mike, just you and me?" She paused, looking at him earnestly, seriously expecting some response.

"Yes, I do," he said, wondering.

"Because," she went on almost sheepishly, "I did wonder if you'd rather stay on at the farm - oh, for various reasons."

He looked her in the eye, his mind working rapidly on the 'various reasons', trying to grasp why she was speaking to him like this, so out of character. "No," he said slowly, half sensing her still vulnerable state and the inadequacies she probably felt afflicted by. "No, I'll be quite all right here, don't you worry. I'll still have the farm close by in any case."

Her worried face broke into a smile. "I'm so relieved to hear you say that," she said, laying her hand upon his. "You've no idea. I only want what is best for you but I think you do mean it, what you've just said, don't you?"

"Yes," he said simply, "I do." He saw no reason for pessimism over his future.

They said no more as they cleared the table. "Have I done the right thing?" Marjorie still wondered that night in bed. She had to admit she'd been in a highly emotional state when she had taken the decision to offer to give Mike up and had even briefly broached the subject with Emily on the 'phone. Having no Tommy to share the lad with, she had clearly seen that she couldn't offer him nearly as full and rich an upbringing as he could get with the Colstons and which he would obviously enjoy so much. She had been in that depressed mood in which self denigration can come strongly to the fore. Not only did she feel that he could do much better at the farm but had even persuaded herself that the Colstons would be happy to take him on permanently. Emily, bless her, had gently declined even to discuss the subject, realising it was but a passing aberration of a deeply shocked and bereaved mind. But now Marjorie took great comfort from Mike's uncomplicated attitude and fell asleep, strengthened in her resolve once again to strive to bring the boy up to the best of her ability and to make him as happy as she could.

So there he was in the harvest field months later, coping with the problems of building a stable load of sheaves that wouldn't fall off the cart and block the road, a minor disaster which Dennis told him happened most years.

"That'll do," Dennis called, as he pitched the last two sheaves as high as he could reach. He unfastened the rope which hung at the back and hurled it upwards. Mike pulled it tight on top whilst Dennis pulled from the front, then fastened it to bind the sheaves securely on their journey to the rickyard. As they were doing this another cart came into the field and they made out Mary driving it. She arrived and pulled the big gelding Captain up alongside them, then jumped down with a basket on her arm. The golden brown tan of her legs and arms was pronounced against the pale lemon yellow of her shorts and blouse.

"Ah, great!" Dennis cried, grabbing the lemonade bottle of cold sweet tea that Mary held up. "Can we do with that!"

Without a word she handed Mike a bottle too. He unscrewed the top and swigged down a great gulp, whilst she stood half smiling as she studied him with her clear blue eyes slightly puckered against the sun. Then she handed out a couple of rock cakes each, which the lads dispatched with eager speed. "There are times," Dennis said with studied humour, his mouth half full of cake, "when it is a pleasure, almost, to see one's little sister."

"Oh, charming," said Mary disdainfully. "What do you think, Mike?"

"Er - well," he began. "I er -".

"Yes, quite," she interrupted. "Well, I can't stand here swapping compliments. Dad says, by the way, he wants you two to carry on down here through milking. He's got Tommy Holland coming up to unload."

"Oh has he!" Dennis exclaimed. "Poor old chap, he's way past it."

"Yes, it's all old men and boys nowadays," Mary called as she pulled Dolly into motion with the full cart.

Dennis and Mike looked at each other a moment before exploding into laughter.

"She's getting uppity, my kid sister lately," Dennis said thoughtfully. "Have you noticed?"

"Mm." Mike mumbled in agreement through the cake crumbs, as he stood watching her urging the mare across the stubble. There was certainly something different about Mary these days. She was no longer the simple, uncomplicated girl he had first seen a year or so ago.

"Ah well, back to business I suppose," Dennis sighed. "Do you want to pitch this one?"

"Okay," Mike replied. "We'll see how it goes." He had never done the pitching before and was keen to try, though he was pretty sure it was much harder work than loading.

It was no problem to start with. He just forked the sheaves two by two onto the empty cart. "This is a doddle," he thought. They went along at a steady rate mopping up the shocks, chatting as they went. He had time to glance out across the fields where he loved the view of the many tall elms around the neighbouring pastures and beyond them the slopes of the Knolls rising pale green five hundred feet above. It was when the load grew higher that he had no more time to think pleasant, leisured thoughts. He soon found that pitching two sheaves at a time way above his head was no doddle. It was hard on arms and shoulders - though Dennis managed it - and he had to revert to one, to his chagrin. The sweat ran down his neck in rivulets and dripped from his brow and his arms grew leaden, but still the load had to grow.

Work went on steadily, cart after cart, till early evening after the cows had been milked and the sun was entangled in the tops of the western trees, until Mary finally brought word that this was the last cart of the day. Mike was deeply thankful, for he had long been tiring until all the novelty and pleasure of harvest work was quite evaporated. Along with the romance of harvest and the interest generally of the farming life, he was beginning to experience the toughness and even drudgery of some of the work some of the time. So it was with great relief that he heard Dennis call up that the final load was big enough. They tightened the rope and Mike sat relaxing on top of the bumping, swaying load as Dennis led it across the field and up the lane to home.

When they arrived in the rickyard Mike was able to view the other side of the harvest operation, seeing what happened to the loads of sheaves that he and Dennis despatched from the field. Arthur had with great skill built several oat ricks and was just finishing off the latest one as they arrived, carefully placing a line of sheaves along the ridge as Mr Colston, unloading beside the elevator, slowly sent up the few more sheaves required. Mike watched Arthur working. As one who was himself relishing mastering the lowly art of loading sheaves into a cart, he could dimly appreciate the skill of one who could build these house-like ricks to stand solid and secure for as long as required.

He seemed such an ordinary little chap, did Arthur. But he must have been part wizard with all that knowledge and skill inside his unassuming frame. And here he was bustling about as active and energetic as at the beginning of the day, as he came down from the rick and with the big rake cleared the loose straws from the sides of his latest creation.

In bed in the cottage at night after those long days of hard but healthy work in the harvest field, his body toughened and glowing, his hands calloused, before he slipped smoothly off to sleep he sometimes thought about his East End life. That boy, as he thought of himself looking back as he used to be, who had known only the streets, now loved only the fields. It was very puzzling that he could contain those two so contrasting worlds so intimately. His last waking thoughts were often of the harvest field, he and Dennis working down by the brook, of forking golden sheaves amid the jingle of harness and the cart creaking as it moved across the stubble. It was a paradise of pure delight. His dreams were serene.

CHAPTER 4

A Proposition Accepted

Mike's freely running review of his earlier days leaped suddenly forward over years of settled contentment. They were years when he now realised he must have been, bit by subconscious bit, acquiring and consolidating his love of the countryside, gaining a new foundation for life, one of which, at his great age now, he was inordinately proud and to which he was fiercely loyal. The leap forward brought him to the time of his first major separation from his home in the village - national service...

"You 'orrible little man, you," growled the sergeant. "Call that a shave? You're a downright disgrace to your squadron. Name and number!"

"Service, sergeant. 19077660."

"Report squadron office 0700 hours tomorrow, shaved," barked the sergeant, making a note on his pad.

"Yes, sergeant."

The wave of fear that swept over Mike as he was submitted to the sergeant's wrath quickly subsided and left him feeling annoyed with himself for chancing what he knew was a poor shave before going on guard duty. And now he seemed booked for jankers, spud bashing or some other tedious punishment. The rest of the guard was inspected then handed over to the lance corporal who marched the file through six inches of snow and out into the partly cleared road. After three or four minutes they reached the huge vehicle parade ground flanked by workshops almost as large as aircraft hangars which they were to guard for the night. After they had fallen out and clattered into the large wooden guard hut furnished with a few battered easy chairs and half a dozen bunks, Mike's mates crowded around to commiserate with him. "He's a bastard, that sergeant," growled Lofty, Mike's closest pal, to which the others readily assented.

"No, no, no," said the lance corporal with a laugh. "It's your own fault, mate," he said pointedly to Mike. "You know he's a bastard, that sergeant. You know he's likely to be on guard inspection, yet you turn up with a day's growth. You asked for all you got."

Mike ran his hand reflectively round his face. It was rough, he had to admit it. "That damned water," he grumbled, "it was freezing. How the hell do they expect you to have a close shave in that?"

"You'll learn," grinned the lance jack. "Get in quick next time before all the hot water goes. Now listen to me, you lot." The chatter subsided and the lance corporal, who wasn't much older than his charges, looked down at his papers a moment before going on. "You're going out there," he said," to guard those workshops. Now I know you're all rookies but you've got to learn. You might soon be out somewhere where there's real guarding to do. Not here in peaceful Catterick but somewhere where they take pot shots at you. Right? So you've got to learn to stay alert. Now, it's two hours on and two off. That means you'll get two spells of duty each and you'll be in pairs. And remember," he added, raising his voice as the hubbub re-started, "the sergeant will definitely be round during the night, maybe several times. So God help the trooper who isn't alert."

Mike and Lofty took their first turn on duty at nine o'clock. Leaving the warm interior of the guard hut with its glowing stove, they found themselves out in the starry blackness of a freezing winter night. A mean wind whipped over the snow, a new fall having recently covered the old tracks. This was going to be quite a memorable first guard duty, a toughening up feature they had all been dreading. It might be just playing at guarding but the army took it seriously along with the tank driving, gunnery and wireless operating and had to be gone through even in sub zero temperatures.

They could move about as they wished as long as they patrolled the perimeter of the workshops, Lofty down one side of the vast tarmac space and Mike down the other, coming together frequently for a cheering chat.

Mike was resigned to serving out his National Service time. He and his mates had so far been kept too busy to have much time for grumbling and some specific things were interesting. He was learning to drive, to shoot and to read maps properly, though now the war was over he wouldn't have to do any of these in anger, for which he was thankful. 'But Catterick in a bad winter isn't exactly a picnic,' he thought grimly as he stamped his feet in a corner of a workshop out of the icy blast, peering across the snow, very uninterested in possible intruders.

Instead, he was looking back homewards and seeing once more in his mind's eye the warm interior of that big old stone barn with straw bales down the sides for seats, its naked bulbs suspended from beams and the whole seething mass of dancers moving rhythmically to the gramophone music and the caller's instructions.

They had gone over to Edlesborough, he and Dennis and Mary and their friends and most of the youngsters in the surrounding villages so it seemed, for this barn dance, part of the final victory celebrations and just before his call up which he was expecting any day.

As he set off again through the snow, driven by fear of the sergeant, Mike was in imagination back amongst that crowd of dancers, swinging his partner, promenading arm round waist, laughing, cheeks flushed, eyes bright. He danced with many partners that night but had thoughts for only one.

Mary at seventeen glowed with open air good health and vitality, her dark hair lustrous, her blue eyes twinkling with mischievous intelligence. She was as near perfection in beauty as makes no odds, Mike knew. He certainly had no criticism of her that night in her simple candy-pink and white cotton dress. He wanted, no, felt impelled as the days for the dance had drawn on, to try his luck with Mary, who over the preceding weeks was occupying his thoughts more and more. The years of his knowing her at fairly close quarters seemed, in retrospect, to have provided an inexorable, slow build up in his feelings for her. Yet it was only recently that he'd suddenly become aware that he was obsessed. He could call to mind the actual day, hour, minute of the revelation, the blinding flash that told him she was everything he could desire. She had been walking across the yard from the stable, carrying a bulky saddle as he came in at the corner gate. She turned her head and smiled and that was it, he was as if pole axed by her beauty, her radiancy, her utter comprehensive appeal. He stopped in his tracks, didn't even offer to carry the saddle for her as sensations of desire welled up in his brain and from that moment he was thoroughly aware that he was hopelessly in love with her.

It was true that neither before nor since had she given him any sign of anything other than friendship, yet he could almost convince himself at times that there was something more if only he had the courage to declare himself. 'Faint heart ne'er won fair lady,' was his oft repeated maxim as the self appointed hour approached when he felt he had to know the answer to his great question. Every time they met in the dance that evening he felt the electric thrill of her presence whilst contact of hand and arm was sheer bliss. It was strange, he mused, as they whirled and parted, how living so near and seeing each other so often, they never had more than friendly contact, nor would anyone suspect that his feelings for her were any more than a friend's, certainly not as consciously strong as he was experiencing in the dance.

The music died away, he could hear the fading notes still in his head as he stolidly tramped the North Yorkshire snow, gloved hands deep in pockets, greatcoat collar turned up, rifle over shoulder. He could see the youngsters thronging the bar at the barn's far end, soft drinks only. Many were in pairs. Mac, home from the R.A.F and Eric had picked up a couple of local girls and Dennis had Mary's riding friend Joan hanging on his arm - they were pretty inseparable by then. Mary stood by her friend, looking around. "Fancy a coke, Mary?" Mike asked and drew her away to a corner of the bar out of the crush.

As the music struck up again they chatted and sipped that one out, glad of a rest. She was watching Joan and Dennis dancing. "Are those two serious?" he asked, sensing her interest.

She shrugged her shoulders and laughed. "I can almost hear the wedding bells, can't you?" she said. "The trouble with Dennis," she continued, "is that he is lazy as far as girl friends are concerned. Joan's the only one he's ever had."

"That's true," Mike agreed. "And how about you, are you lazy too?" he asked jokingly, daring to say almost anything in the way of provocative banter that was along his desired route.

"Me?" she said, giving him a searching look. "Oh, I wouldn't want to get too serious yet anyway. Though I don't think I'm lazy in that way."

"No, not too serious maybe," he agreed lightly, "but a little serious perhaps?"

"And how about you," she went on with a sparkle in her eye, "you haven't had any girl friends yet, have you?"

"No," he admitted a mite reluctantly. "At least, just a little flame at school once."

"Oh yes, I remember," she said with a giggle. "And they all teased you unmercifully about it."

He grinned sheepishly then straightened his face. "But there is someone -." He faltered, his courage failing in the frank gaze of those clear blue eyes.

"Oh, is there?" she asked, slightly teasingly, he thought.

"Come outside," he said impulsively, "and I'll tell you. You can't hear yourself think in here."

They slipped off their bales and headed out of a small side door into the cool, clear darkness of the autumn evening. He stopped with Mary beside him. It was too dark to see her features clearly and this gave him confidence. "It's you, Mary," he heard himself confessing, "as you probably guessed."

She giggled. "Well -" she began, but left the rest unsaid as he lay his hand on her shoulder. He felt her come to him and in a second both his arms were around her and she was close up against him.

"I know," she whispered and turned her face up to receive the kiss that he tenderly pressed upon her lips. He squeezed her even closer and felt the firm pressure of her breasts through his shirt and they kissed again, long and lingeringly.

"We'd better go back in," she whispered after a few moments, "the others will miss us."

"Must we?" he pleaded. He could have stayed there like that for ever. And did it matter if the others did miss them? He kissed her one last time of pure bliss before they returned to the dance.

Back in the noise and light he scanned her face a moment for proof that something of what had just transpired was written there. He read what he wanted to read. His love for Mary had been declared and sealed with kisses and that long affectionate embrace. He felt as one dancing on air, his eyes only for her wherever she was in the snaking, twisting lines of dancers. When the dance progression brought them together, what bliss it was to take her hand, this superb, heavenly being whose eyes flashed and sparkled at him and whose lithe, seductive body he had held within his arms only minutes before.

When the last waltz struck up in the small hours he made sure she was his partner. Held close together, they shuffled over the packed floor cheek to cheek, his whole being in ecstasy. At the end with most lights extinguished and dancers all around them locked in firm embrace, he kissed her again to end the most romantic evening of his life.

In the arctic cold of his guard duties those warming mental pictures brought him cheer and consolation to offset the miseries of the military regime, miseries of becoming a mere number, of being at the mercy of ignorant, brutish authority. Fortunately guard duty passed without further hitch for him. The sergeant, sensible fellow, slept soundly and without interruption in his bed and the young recruits soon made up their loss of sleep and put their first guard experience easily behind them. The misery of 'jankers' wasn't quite so quickly and painlessly wiped from Mike's consciousness. The three days of fatigues, to which the lenient duty officer sentenced him for his heinous crime, consisted of snow clearing with a shovel, which would have been unremarkable if it weren't for the bad luck of his hut having several jabs that very first morning after duty against a cocktail of diseases said to lie in wait for soldiers in the tropics, to which areas he, of course, was never posted. With arms like lead he did not enjoy the experience of carving pathways through deep snow when all his mates were resting and recovering on their beds. At least he learned the hard way that army life was safest with a close shave.

It was in June with the six month period of training over that Mike's troop lined up at the squadron office one morning to be issued with rail passes and sent off on weekend leave. It was common knowledge that they would be embarking for Germany when they came back and Mike was well pleased - B.A.O.R. was considered a cushy posting. Life there, according to some of the old hands who loved to impress the youngsters, consisted mostly of exciting and realistic manoeuvres with live ammunition on Luneberg Heath and, equally exciting for some, of having the pick of the German women for a few cigarettes and a bar of chocolate, luxuries undreamed of by Germans groaning in immediate post war deprivation. All this whilst being comfortably stationed in superior barracks and living off the fat of the land.

Mike was looking forward tremendously to his leave. Much of the way down to King's Cross in the crowded train he was thinking about it, anticipating what he would do, guessing it would be hay time and picturing the scenarios - he and Dennis in the hay field loading, the faithful Captain pulling the cart, the chalk hills behind in smooth green splendour. Or perhaps he would be helping Arthur on the rick, all sweat and hayseeds and perhaps Mary driving the cart. Yes, Mary - there weren't many of his waking hours when he didn't think of her and of the barn dance. He'd had no more time alone with her after that and their brief day to day contact had been no different. Their eyes had met of course though he could read nothing special in that but was content to put it down to her discretion.

He didn't write to Mary from Catterick, nor she to him. Or rather, he wrote several letters hot with passion but didn't post any, not trusting himself to have struck the right note in his choice of words which did, he had to admit, look rather ludicrous in the cold, clear light of day. Having thought about it he decided he would rather wait the short while until his leave so that he could tell her those intimate things as he held her hand. He also didn't wish to risk appearing to instigate a subterfuge against her parents, of writing behind their backs, as it were, before he could bring the situation out into the open with them as he hoped he might soon be able to do. How they would react on learning of his affection for their daughter he wasn't sure, though he was troubled by the awareness that she was a farmer's daughter whereas he had a less than desirable background and only pious hopes of a future. On the whole though, knowing them as well as he did, he wasn't too pessimistic about the outcome.

He often tried to look beyond National Service to what direction his life might take, though so far without any firm idea. He realised that conscription was a sort of enforced breathing space, a time for taking stock. At the time of call up, in spite of Marjorie's best efforts, he'd been left school for six months without any worthwhile paper qualifications, just one or two certificates in favourite subjects and had been quite happy helping out at the farm for what he knew was a short period before call up.

His aunt however, took a lively practical interest in his future and often spoke about it. On the last Sunday before his call up, as they had sat at tea, the prospect of Mike in the army inevitably brought thoughts of Tom to the surface, for although the war was over there was a very real sense in which it would never be over for her.

Fighting back the smarting of the eyes as she looked through the young man soon to be in coarse khaki to the ghostly image of her husband in his smart officer's uniform, she said lightly, "So you're off tomorrow, "as she poured from her best Blue Nordic teapot. "It's come at last."

"Yes," he said, going over it once again. "Down to Maidstone for initial training, six weeks. Then they decide what outfit we get sent to, whether it's the pbi or the Pioneer Corps or whatever."

"Let's see, your father was in the artillery, wasn't he?"

"Yes," Mike replied. "The Horse Artillery, I think." He saw again in his mind's eye the black shrapnel scars in his father's back that he'd often seen when he was washing. He'd never had the story of those wounds and, now that he never would, the thought suddenly grieved him. "I might try to join them if I get the chance," he went on. "Of course, from what I hear about the army they'll probably make me a cook or a redcap if I put down for the artillery."

"Yes, I know," Marjorie said with a giggle. "Tommy used to say the same. He was an expert motor mechanic, so what did they do? They put him in signals, mucking about with field telephones."

She could at least talk about Tommy easily and naturally now. The sharpness of grief, though never perhaps healed entirely, follows an inevitable dulling process over the years, often in spite of our wishes to the contrary.

They went on eating in silence for some while. Mike's thoughts dwelt on the stability and continuity of life in that cosy little cottage ever since he had come there in the early days of the war. And now, although that would continue, he it was who faced change and upheaval. It was exciting, this preparing to fly the nest. Doors opening, all sorts of opportunities to be taken; action, adventure, exciting times. But a sizeable part of him was momentarily sad for what he was leaving behind.

"And when it's all over?" his aunt asked, not for the first time.

"I don't know," was his answer. "I can't see that far ahead. Two years is an eternity, too far off to consider."

"You'll see, they'll soon pass," she said with an indulgent smile. She appreciated that Mike loved helping on the farm, but farm labouring was no job for an up and coming young man with any ambition at all. No, he would be sure to turn to something worthwhile eventually, especially after being two years away rubbing shoulders with all sorts of young men. Something well paid and with prospects of salary and pension it would surely be. He would need to remedy his education unfortunately but that was quite feasible these days at night school. Perhaps he would become a civil servant or go for a job in the City as she had done. Anyway, we must obviously wait and see, she told herself, until this next little chapter is over.

So now, on his last leave before being posted to Germany, Mike arrived back in the village. It was still only late afternoon when he jumped off the bus as it stopped on the corner. He felt the old magic as soon as he glimpsed the plum orchards stretching away down to the cornfields and the familiar cottages ahead as he walked up to his aunt's terrace.

He walked in through the open stable door and was met by a beaming Marjorie who gave him a big hug and sat him down at the table which had been laid in readiness for him. "My, don't you look smart in your uniform," she enthused. "You'll turn the heads of the local girls, that's for sure."

Mike laughed at the flattery in a self deprecating way and asked how everyone was and what was going on as he ate his way through the corned beef salad placed before him, in a welter of happy chattering. He had a similar welcome an hour or so later when he strolled up to the farm.

"They're all still at hay work, of course," Emily said. "They hope to get finished tonight. I just hope Norman's not overdoing it," she went on, anxiety suddenly invading her voice and features. "The doctor told him to slow down if he wants to make old bones. You didn't know he's been having some heart trouble, did you?"

Mike almost gasped in astonishment. "Yes," she said, "he'd been feeling really done in several times lately after a normal day's work. Really thoroughly exhausted, much more than he'd ever been before, so he called in the doctor. He gave Norman a thorough examination and told him in no uncertain terms that he'd have to take things easy. Which of course will put more on Dennis' shoulders. To make matters worse," she continued, "he went to see a heart specialist in Luton last week and he confirmed what our doctor had said, that it's vital that Norman gives up all hard physical work straight away and probably permanently but in any case for the time being. But of course, it's not as simple as that, life seldom is. He's still out there working whilst he thinks what's best to do, so he says."

Mike's face registered his amazement. He had never known Mr Colston ill for even a day so it wasn't easy to imagine his life threatened, especially remembering he was only in his early fifties. "And Arthur's not getting any younger," he commented, thinking aloud.

"No, indeed he's not," she agreed. "In fact he'll be thinking of retiring before too long, I'm sure. It never rains but it pours."

Somewhat stunned by this news, Mike wandered out to the rickyard whence came the telltale sounds of work going on. Mr Colston saw him first from the cart which he'd almost finished unloading into the elevator and waved and shouted a greeting in so lively a way as to make Mike incredulous that he could be ill. Dennis looked round from the almost completed rick where he was forking the last few mounds of hay to Arthur and waved the old cap he was wearing. Just then Mary came out of the stable behind a couple of horses she had unharnessed and was turning out into the orchard. She waved and Mike waved back, his apparent equanimity belying the sudden surge of emotion he felt at his first longed-for sight of her.

Gradually, over the next few minutes as Mike stood watching, the work was finished off. Quiet came to the yard as the pony was stopped in its treadmill path, turning the rattling elevator, and Mr Colston came off the cart and led it away. Mike felt uncomfortably detached from the activity around him. He couldn't get involved as he normally would have done, standing there in his shining black shoes, the creases in his trousers like knife blades, his tie and carefully pressed shirt immaculate. He trod carefully, avoiding the ruts which were still muddy and altogether felt rather alien and wished he'd changed into old clothes.

Dennis came down the ladder from the rick and slapped him on the arm as they greeted each other warmly. "I thought we might go up to the Memorial Hall for a game of snooker this evening," he said as they wandered back over to the house. "You didn't know they've started a club up there, did you? It's quite good really. There's darts and shove ha'penny and table tennis as well."

Mike readily agreed to go. So, while Dennis went to wash and change Mike strolled about for a while looking at familiar things with sharpened pleasure now that he'd been away for months. In the deserted sheepyard he brought to mind the games of cricket they used to play. Now Mac had signed on in the R.A.F. and was overseas somewhere he'd been told and Dennis seemed to have moved on to snooker and serious courting whilst Eric had probably grown into other interests too. No more cricket in the yard.

Mike leaned over the orchard gate and reviewed his own prospects. One thing went without saying really, he would never make the army his career. He couldn't become a mere name and number, his individuality meant everything to him, he had little else. "What is open to me?" he wondered yet again, but at that moment he was so enthralled with the rural scene he was surveying that his newly conceived concern was how he could respond to its call which he now heard so clearly. How to translate a powerful but generalised love of his surroundings into a specific means of earning a living and, more importantly, earning enough to make getting engaged to Mary a possibility. Was there such a possibility open to him? He would like to think so but so far couldn't imagine what it could be. The clip clop of hooves on concrete interrupted his reverie and made him turn to see Mary astride her pony coming into the yard. She was still in her working clothes, sleeves rolled up, shirt wide open at the neck, her hair tousled. He ran his eye appreciatively over her, sitting easily in the saddle a few paces from him.

"You're looking very smart," she said. "How long are you home for?"

"Only till Sunday," he replied, letting her first comment pass without reply save for a smile of pleasure.

"And then?" she went on.

"Off to Germany."

"Oh," she said, her lips pouting, her eyes fixed on his in disappointment.

"Didn't you know?" he asked, feeling sure she did and liking the evidence that she didn't want him to go.

"I wasn't sure," she countered. "I suppose you'll be away a long time. A brother of one of my friends is in Germany and she says he's having a whale of a time."

He was aware of his heart pounding with the enormous desire to kiss her. The pony was an effective barrier to that but, as he patted its neck with his left hand, he rested his right daringly on her jodhpur covered knee.

"Is there a dance anywhere tomorrow?" he asked with a mischievous smile to see her reaction to being reminded of the previous occasion.

She chuckled and looked away a second, then met his gaze with twinkling eyes and slightly flushed cheeks. "Not that I know of," she said.

Just then Dennis came into the yard ready to be off, so Mike swung open the orchard gate to let Mary pass out among the trees for her ride.

They walked the tree lined road for half a mile or so, their talk mostly consisting of Mike answering Dennis' questions about army life and the forthcoming adventure in Germany. Mike had long ago realised that Dennis had been unhappy about not being able to join up - he occasionally still spoke about his unrealised ambition to be a fighter pilot. Now Mike sensed that perhaps Dennis, at twenty, was torn between what he could see as his predestined path in life of inheriting the farm, staying in the village to continue the settled, unexciting life of a farmer, prosperous though it might be; and a young man's innate love of adventure, of going out into the world to take his chance seeking fame and fortune. Whilst he envied Dennis his assured future he was aware of having something which maybe Dennis longed for, the wider world to operate in, the knock-about camaraderie of the army, the prospect of serving abroad and a future which was not already cut and dried.

When they came to the Cross Keys with its thatched roof, beams and whitewashed walls Dennis suddenly suggested they call in for a drink. "It's been thirsty work up on that rick," he said. "I could just sink a pint of bitter shandy."

Mike concurred. He wasn't a great frequenter of pubs, he couldn't afford to be on army pay, but he was partial to a half of cider now and again.

"Have you got a girl friend yet up in Catterick?" Dennis asked as they sat themselves at the bar.

"No, there's not a hope in hell of that up there," he replied. "There must be hundreds if not thousands of blokes for every local girl and anyway we don't get any free time for that sort of thing, it's not at all in the army's scheme of things," and he chuckled at the mere thought of it.

"Too bad," Dennis said. "You'll have to see what you can find round here to brighten up your leave."

"It's only a weekend, you know," he said. He idly wondered how much, if anything, Dennis guessed about his feelings for his sister. Though tempted, he hadn't had much opportunity to speak to Dennis about it and he'd certainly not taken any one else into his confidence. After a moment he asked, "How is it with you and Joan these days?"

"Oh, pretty good, "Dennis said, His eyes lighting up with enthusiasm. "To tell you the truth we're thinking of getting engaged soon. Don't mention it to anyone yet though, for I haven't so far said anything to mum and dad."

"Great, "Mike said. "Congratulations then for when you do come out with it. I hope you'll be very happy," and he drained his glass to that.

"Thanks," Dennis said. "Look, will you have another one? There's something I want to say to you, hang on a minute."

While Dennis was organising the drinks, Mike pondered on what he might want to say. He couldn't imagine, unless - a numbing thought struck him forcefully - unless it was something to do with Mary, something difficult, even unpleasant to say, needing extra Dutch courage?

"Cheers again," Dennis said, returning with Mike's cider, sitting down and taking a long draught of his own pint. "Did you know dad has been ill lately?" he began.

"Yes," Mike replied, his nerves taut, ready for the bombshell to come. "Your mum told me. I must say I was very surprised. I hope he's not too bad. He looked all right in the yard I thought." He turned his head away from Dennis, awaiting the verbal blow.

"Well," Dennis continued, "it's not too bad yet apparently but he's got to take things easier." He paused, appearing to study his drink closely whilst Mike longed for the worst of whatever was coming to be over. "I reckon he's going to have to take things very much easier," Dennis added. "In fact, it may well be that he'll have to consider giving up farm work altogether. He said as much to me once when mum wasn't about. Something about having to consider semi-retirement soon and how would I feel about taking on more responsibility for running the farm. Since then the specialist that he saw last week backed up what our doctor said."

They both studied their drinks carefully. Could this all be a lead up to something about Mary? Mike wondered. Perhaps that wasn't the point after all? He could of course understand Dennis' concern for his father's health. Physically, Mike felt sure Dennis could manage to run the farm okay, he was a fit and muscular twenty year old at just under six feet in height and there wasn't likely to be much work on the farm that he hadn't both the strength and skill to tackle.

"I reckon I'll be all right to run things if I have to," Dennis went on, after a lengthy pause which had Mike puzzling over what could be coming next. "So long as dad's around to advise," he continued. "But what I wanted to ask you was -" he stopped and looked quizzically straight into Mike's eyes before going on in a low voice, "How would you feel about joining me when your national service is finished? What I'm trying to say is," he added in hasty clarification, "coming into partnership with me."

Mike just returned Dennis' gaze with blank astonishment. This was nothing to do with difficulties about Mary! He was so taken aback he couldn't for a few moments properly take in what Dennis had said.

"Into partnership!" he echoed, trying to grasp the fact that he seemed to be being seriously offered a substantial share in running Manor Farm. Though not well up in these matters he felt sure that was what a partnership must mean.

"Will you think about it?" Dennis went on. "I haven't said anything to dad yet about it but I'm pretty sure he won't object. On the contrary, he'll be pleased and relieved, I'm sure. You see, apart from the fact that he's obviously considering at least semi-retirement, Arthur's definitely retiring in less than two years, he said so only the other day, so something's got to be done soon. I can't run the farm single handed." He paused again and left Mike a few moments in which to try to make sense of what he had been hearing.

"Of course," Dennis went on eventually, "I could just look around for someone to work for me, someone to take Arthur's place and I will have to do that if you decide not to team up, though it won't be easy, not many who are any good want to do farm work these days. But I reckon this way will be much better. Farming's changing fast. We're going to need to be more adaptable in the future, more mentally supple. There's going to be a lot of technical advances for one thing, I'm quite sure, and I'd much rather work with someone like you who's got a modern flexible outlook and yet who really feels for the place the same as I do. I think you'll be able to contribute a lot."

He paused again, putting his thoughts in order. "What's more natural after all," he continued, "than us two joining forces. We get on pretty well working and as friends, don't we?"

Mike nodded gravely in assent.

"We're near in age and we're more or less two of a kind, you and I," he continued. "So although it might seem at first a bit eccentric of me, I've given the matter a great deal of thought and I've come to the firm conclusion that a close business partnership would be the best thing for the farm and for all concerned. Now it's up to you. You'll be finished with the army in eighteen months just about, won't you? So it's just as well to make plans now. The time will soon pass."

Mike took a long, deliberately slow swig of his cider. His head was still pretty much in a whirl really, inebriated, not with alcohol but with Dennis' bombshell proposition. Dennis was waiting for him to come up with a reply and didn't seem disposed to say any more. So he took a deep breath, steadied himself as much as possible and listened to himself as he sought to make an adequate response.

"I don't quite know what to say," he murmured, keeping his voice conspiratorially low against being heard by the couple farther along the bar. "It's about the biggest surprise I've ever had, I don't mind admitting. But I don't really need time to think about it. Provided your parents are agreeable, I know that I'll accept."

"Good," Dennis said quietly. "I'm a hundred per cent sure they'll approve, otherwise I wouldn't have considered it. Let's shake on it, shall we?" They gripped each other's hand warmly and solemnly. "Leave it to me to sort out with mum and dad sometime fairly soon," Dennis said. "There's no particular hurry but I would like to get it all settled before too long, especially now my mind's quite made up and with all this business about dad's illness. I daresay there will be legal papers to draw up and sign and I'll work on all that, so that by the time you're demobbed we'll be ready to go. Let's drink to it, shall we?"

They touched glasses and drained them in quiet celebration of their future partnership. Mike couldn't and didn't try to give expression to the confusion of thoughts racing through his brain. Above everything perhaps at that moment, he was very, very flattered, to put it mildly, that Dennis so valued him as a friend and fellow worker that he was prepared to be so amazingly generous. He had never, even in his wildest dreams, considered such a fairytale possibility.

As they left the pub and walked on along the road to the Memorial Hall he was fairly buzzing with suppressed excitement. "So that's how big events are decided," he thought. "As seemingly casually as that."

It was no wonder that the rest of the evening went well for Mike. He exuded a greater than usual air of bonhomie, rendered all the sweeter by his pact to keep the matter secret until it was all settled. He was happy to lose at snooker, never having played before anyway and was very happy to play darts and table tennis with boys he had gone to school with and who were now grown men. He told himself that he was going to settle there with all these friends. This was home now in an even deeper sense than before. He would be able to come up to the Memorial Hall and play snooker and everything for as many years as he wished.

Determined to make a good impression in Dennis' eyes, before they parted Mike had offered to help with the morning milking. So, having tossed and turned in bed for hours and to Marjorie's amused surprise, he got up and turned up at the farm in good time. He had derived great satisfaction in finally learning to milk in the period between leaving school and going off to national service as he'd learned many other jobs on the farm. This time it was different, however. He felt a new man as he looked around the yard, seeing everything through the sharper eyes of partnership. He had the feeling that in spirit he had already crossed the thin but hard dividing line between being an employee, with its limited responsibilities and limited rewards, and partnership with its total, wholehearted commitment and its heightened rewards. He felt a warm glow inside thinking that he would soon have a share in these old barns, cowsheds and stables.

Dennis was already about, tying the cows at their mangers and feeding them, and they greeted each other warmly, conscious of the previous evening and of the different footing they were now on. "Dad doesn't do the morning milking now," Dennis said, as they took their stools and prepared to start, "though mum has a hard job keeping him in bed."

The air that morning in the cowshed's whitewashed interior was warm and heavy with the distinctive sweet odour of the cows' breath as they chewed their cattle cake whilst being milked. Now and again a chain rattled, but mostly the hiss and froth of milk into buckets was the only background noise, punctuated from time to time by snatches of talk or an oath as a tail flicked across a face or a cow shifted its position heavily. It was a time for quiet thought as the milking progressed and Mike was happily savouring the awareness that this, in the not too distant future, would be his daily lot. What was it Dennis had said about his contribution? A flexible modern outlook? Yes, he would bring that, and with enthusiasm. He wasn't young for nothing. They'd have to look at milking machines for instance, to assess their financial impact, their efficiency and other benefits such as improved hygiene. A boom time for farming was coming, he fancied, and he recalled the combine harvester he'd seen on Church End Farm, a giant red machine crawling around the fields, eating up and disposing of the corn in one smooth operation and, he'd thought then of the huge revolution that such machines must bring about in harvest work. Everything done by just one or two men, not the large gangs of tradition, and so much more quickly too.

Mike's bright pictures of his youthful days on the threshold of farming were interrupted by the power of their incongruity with the present confused and depressing farming scene. What went wrong, he asked himself for the thousandth time? As a young man, he acknowledged now, he had been as ready as any to embrace every opportunity for technical progress. He loved the horse and cart scene but felt it was his duty to sweep it all away if that was what efficiency required. And it was required, everybody from the government downward said so. That elevation of efficiency as farming's crowning achievement was a damning indictment, he now believed. It was also a disaster for the environment which should have had at least equal status with it. 'You can't put the clock back, you can't ignore progress' was everywhere at that time. Yet look where so called progress, efficiency as goal and the wholesale promotion of agri-business has led us.

Was it all inevitable, he asked himself now? Did it all stem from that enthusiasm for machines, for profit, for progress? No, surely not. Wisely led from the top, things could have been different. It was however, a very complex problem, this decline of agriculture and one which governments and ministers, ignorant of and indifferent to the needs of farmers and country life generally, had been making worse for generations. No wonder farmers had to march out of desperation for their livelihood and way of life.

Thus pondering, the pictures in his mind slipped back again to those early farming days of his, the times, he admitted ruefully, when the rot was beginning to set in …

By the time milking was finished that morning he had settled in his mind his basic attitude to his new position as partner designate at Manor Farm and felt quite calm and confident about the future and desired only that his national service might be over as quickly as possible. How was he going to put up with the tedium of it knowing what was waiting for him at home?

Dennis and he went in to breakfast with appetites honed to ravenning by work but were immediately confronted by plates of food quite able to match those appetites - eggs, fried bread and bacon followed by fresh bread, home made butter and marmalade. Everyone was up and seated around the table. Mr Colston was his normal cheerful self as far as Mike could tell.

"It was very good of you to help with the milking," he said to Mike.

"That's all right, I enjoyed it," he replied.

"Yes, I suppose you're used to reveille by now," Mr Colston went on. "What time does it go nowadays.?"

"Seven o'clock," Mike said. "So yes, it's about the same time as for milking but I wish the breakfast was as good as this one."

Mrs Colston beamed at the compliment. "Ah, we know how to feed the farm troops," she said.

"Well, I must say he's not looking too bad on army grub, is he?" Mr Colston declared.

"You're not looking too bad either," Mike said. "How do you feel? I didn't get the chance to ask you before."

"Oh, I'm not so bad," Mr Colston replied. I daresay you've heard about my little turn from one or another?" He looked around the table for confirmation.

"Yes," his wife said, "I filled Mike in when he came home."

"So there you are. I've got to slow down apparently. It must be a family failing for my father was just the same. I can remember him many a time reaching up for the sal volatile bottle in that same cupboard there when he came in from doing some job he'd no business to be doing. And needing the medicinal whisky from time to time too."

"Yes, heart problems are in our genes, I daresay," put in Mary who was taking advanced biology at school. At least on the male side."

"All right, if you say so, dear," said her father.

"She just means it's inherited," said Dennis, putting his sister down with a smile. "Actually," he went on, "genetic knowledge is being used at the present time to develop breeds of cattle less liable to abortion."

"Is that so!" his father exclaimed.

"Yes, but it's in human characteristics that the most amazing potential lies," Mary said, determined not to be pushed off her favourite subject.

"What do you mean?" her mother burst in. "The creation of a master race like Hitler tried?"

"No, of course not, mother," Mary replied. "But our biology teacher was telling us about something called genetic engineering which is beginning to be talked about in scientific circles."

"Ah, it all sounds to me rather like Huxley's 'A Brave New World' coming true," her father said. "Not a world I wish to be part of I think."

"There's nothing in this genetic engineering about it controlling the way you think, is there?" Mike asked lightly.

"No, it only deals with the physical side of things, I believe," Dennis said.

"So there's no gene to account for a love of the country suddenly developing in a city bred person?" Mike concluded with a smile.

"No, I don't believe thought patterns are genetic," Mary observed. "More like romantic perhaps."

He glanced at her, searching for recognition that her use of 'romantic' was more than accidental. Her eyes smiled at him for a second.

"Genes or not," said Mrs Colston, "it is amazing really how you've taken to country life, Mike. I wonder if it will last or whether you'll go back to the city one day?"

"No, I don't think I could ever go back," he replied coolly, yet acutely and deliciously aware of what he and Dennis knew of their future plans.

"I'm prepared to bet on that," Dennis said with a twinkle in his eye.

At this point conversation became fragmented and relatively sparse as serious eating got under way. Mike, left to his own thoughts, became very aware of how carelessly ravishing Mary looked opposite him, with her unblemished complexion, open necked shirt above gently swelling breasts and hair tumbling about her ears. He was also painfully aware that he wouldn't be seeing her for a long time and not all the attractions of his posting to B.A.O.R. could compensate at that moment for the coming lack of her.

Suddenly the galvanising thought struck him that perhaps Dennis, after all, knew how he felt about Mary. Could it be that was the reason why he had offered him the partnership? Mary and he and Dennis and Joan could form a strong, close knit group to own and run the farm between them and keep it in the family. Mike glanced at Dennis busily consuming bread and marmalade and wondered if that was the way of it. If it was, he was full of admiration for the intention and of course, all in favour of it coming about. But was Mary party to Dennis' plan, if plan there was? He would like to think so but on consideration decided it was unlikely. No, Dennis, he felt sure, would have said something to him in the pub about any such plan. Wouldn't he? But of course, Mike reflected, his brain leaping ahead. it might come about like that anyway. It would, hopefully, come about in just that perfect way if things with Mary evolved as he fervently desired that they should.

With breakfast over, the family split up and went various ways. Hay work had finished with the completion of the rick the previous evening, so Mike's hoped - for session in the field did not materialize. He went back to the cottage and found Marjorie busily doing her housework in the living room which seemed to be full of carnations, their scent disguising the liberal use of furniture polish. She discarded her duster and sat him down in a chintz covered chair to talk awhile and enjoy each other's company.

"Is the job still going well?" he asked, prompted by the mass of flowers. She had started her part time job at the nursery in Eaton Bray soon after Tom's death and it had been a good move, for it kept her busy over that very difficult period and she came to enjoy the work, dealing mainly with carnations under glass in all stages of their growth and marketing.

"Oh, yes," she replied. "They want me to go full time as manageress and I'm in two minds whether to accept or not. I think I could do the job all right and the extra money would be welcome, but I wouldn't have much time left to myself. But enough of me, tell me a bit more of how things are going with you. Have you got some good friends in your unit?"

"Yes," he replied with a grin as he pictured some of his mates. "There is for example, Colin from Rotherham. He's a good pal of mine and he invited me to his home a few weeks ago. There was washing hanging on lines all down the street. I'd never seen that before. And when we sat down to Sunday dinner we had this huge Yorkshire pudding served first on its own. It was amazing. They are a lovely family, really friendly and with a terrifically broad Yorkshire accent. Colin's sisters went out with us to a dance in Sheffield. It was great."

"It sounds as though the army these days is all fun and games," Marjorie said with a smile.

"Not exactly," he said. "But it does have its lighter moments fortunately. Now our training's finished it should get better. The trouble is we're all going to be split up and posted to different armoured regiments so I'll lose a lot of friends, most likely."

"Will you be over in Germany for the rest of your time?" she asked.

"Yes, as far as I know I will," he answered. "I certainly hope so, for everyone says army life is much better abroad than it is at home. We really are all cheesed off with Catterick."

"So we shan't be seeing much of you for a while," she said.

"No, that's one disadvantage, no home leave." He would very much like to have told her all the details of his discussion with Dennis which were buzzing in his head and longing to get out but he did just manage to restrain himself, thinking that it would be all the more satisfying anyway to reveal and discuss when it was all settled and he was back home and finished with the army.

She went to make them both a mug of coffee whilst he sat back and glanced around that room which held his earliest memories of his time in the village. He loved its small, square windows set in walls of great thickness and considerable unevenness, its stable door, its blackened oak beam you had to duck beneath and its low doorways.

The sun shone strongly through the front window onto the yellow patterned walls, bathing the room in golden light as they sat comfortably sipping their coffee. "And apart from work," Mike said, picking up on his interest in his aunt's activities, "is life here still okay?"

"Oh, yes," she replied, slightly amused at his serious enquiry, "I like it well enough here. I certainly don't intend to move back to London. Why, I've even joined the W.I., so you can tell I'm pretty keen on village life. Actually, it's the best thing I could have done, for I've found a couple of good friends and the monthly meetings are usually very interesting. Now, to change the subject, what are you doing this evening?"

"Nothing much," he said, taken by surprise. "That is, I'm not sure," he added, realising that he had vague hopes of arranging something with Mary.

"Well," Marjorie said, "if you're doing nothing special I'd like to invite you to the theatre in Luton. I've got a couple of tickets for a variety show at the Alma. There's the Luton Girls' Choir and Bernard Miles telling his comic Chilterns stories - I love them on the radio. And there are several supporting acts. It should be good."

"Fine," he said, realising there was no way out without disappointing her and being unwilling to do that, especially as she'd already booked. "Yes, good, I'd love to come."

"Oh, lovely," she cried. "We'll have some tea about five and catch the six o'clock bus."

"I don't think I've ever been to the theatre," he said.

"Haven't you!" she exclaimed. "Well no, I suppose it's not surprising really. You'll enjoy it. It's a totally different experience from the cinema, especially those flea pits you're used to in Poplar. The Alma is all red plush and gold paint. Real Victorian it is with boxes and master of ceremonies and all."

"There's nothing like that anywhere near Catterick as far as I know," he said. "Mind you, even if there were I don't suppose we would go. All I've been to since I've been up there is the NAAFI Club in Darlington. That's not too bad actually compared to the camp; it's nice to be properly warm and to have some decent grub.

Oh, and I've been to a football match in Middlesbrough once, that's about the high spot of our entertainment. Catterick is so remote and we've so little time off."

"Isn't there anything going on in Richmond?" she asked. "I've heard that it's a nice little town. It's got a castle, hasn't it?"

"Yes, it has," he agreed. "I've seen it from a distance. But, you know, a bunch of squaddies on their afternoon off aren't likely to appreciate the finer points of a little town like Richmond, especially in the winter. We tend to make a dive for the nearest pub or cafe to get out of the rain or snow which always seems to be falling up there."

"You brutes," she said, laughing.

"I suppose we are," he agreed. "It all comes from being out of our element with very little cash. We get by, I suppose, where survival is the prime objective. The ones I feel sorry for are the married men. We've got several and they don't seem at all happy drifting around with us single chaps."

"Yes, you're better off as a bachelor gay in the army," she said lightly.

When he reached the farm later he found Mary was out riding somewhere in the fields and Dennis had gone with his father to look at some heifers with a view to buying. So it seemed the obvious time to go for a walk over the hills, a treat he had looked forward to and which he was determined to fit into his leave somewhere if it was at all possible.

As he tramped up the lane after hailing several well known village faces, he was thinking about the coming evening and of how difficult to accomplish even the simplest things often seemed. He'd hoped to arrange an evening with Mary, now he was hoping she would understand why he couldn't. He told himself that no harm would come from it, she would understand when he explained the circumstances, but he was still uneasy about it, feeling he was open to the charge that he hadn't got his priorities right, he'd somehow made a mess of things. 'Ah well, che sara, sara,' he told himself and looked round calmly as he topped a prominent hillock.

The scene before him was a thoroughly familiar one but was as thrilling as on the day he'd first seen it - familiarity does not necessarily dull the vision. In fact he felt that his appreciation of that lovely view had grown over the years as he had acquired knowledge of the individual parts. He sat on the grass and from that eyrie viewpoint ran his eye out over the flat chequerboard of fields below that spread in a wonderful variety of shapes and colours across the extensive vale - westwards to distant wooded hills purple in the haze, south to bare, pale green high downland with Ivinghoe Beacon dominating the horizon. Villages that he now knew well stood out, studded with trees; the distant chimney of Pitstone Cement Works smoked lazily and he strained his ears but in vain, to catch the sound of a train on the Euston line passing the level crossing at Mentmore. Close by, below him, were some of the fields of Manor Farm where many of his best moments had been passed and he looked out over them with a thrill of pleasure that he would soon be a partner in their management. Here would lie his future and whatever of happiness he might know and his thoughts ran on to Mary and pleasurable thoughts of setting up house together and raising a family.

He scrambled to his feet and turned to face the high escarpment rising steeply nearby, clothed in a mantle of mature beech trees on one shoulder. He stood contemplating this well-loved scene for several minutes. It had nothing of the air of the Yorkshire Moors' vast mournful solitudes which were the only heights he knew to compare it with. It had none of their dark menace and supreme indifference to man either. These chalk hills with their green turf vivid in the sunshine and carpeted with harebells and self heal, their dazzling white gashes and the occasional hawthorn bush, were friendly and welcoming alike to man and natural life. Their slopes and heights were more to the human scale of things, their wildness satisfying but not severe.

After a hugely fulfilling review of his old haunts Mike returned to the farm in time for lunch to which he had been invited. In the course of conversation around the table Emily asked him if he had any plans for the rest of the day. He told them about Marjorie's invitation to the theatre, glancing at Mary as he did so, wondering if she would react in any way, but detected nothing. After the meal he watched and waited until he saw Mary go across the yard to the stable then sauntered over, determined to say something to her and hopefully to reactivate the sentiment they had shared at the barn dance. She looked up and smiled as he came into the stable. "Can I help? " he asked, taking hold of the tin of dubbin and indicating the pile of harness she was starting to clean.

"Sure," she said. "I can always do with some help on this job."

"Sorry about this evening," he said as he dabbed at a bridle.

"Oh, don't bother about that," she said rather brusquely. "I daresay Joan and I will go to the cinema anyway. We often do on Saturday."

"Oh," he said, not sure how to take that. "I could have wished it to be otherwise," he ventured.

"What do you mean?" she demanded.

"Well, I would have liked to invite you out somewhere."

"Oh," she laughed. "What, somewhere posh?"

"No, of course not. It's just that -" He paused, feeling at a loss for the right words - "Just that I wanted to be with you this evening."

"Hmm," she said grimly. "It looks as though you've arranged otherwise doesn't it?"

"I know," he murmured ruefully. God, how had he managed to be such an indecisive fool, he thought. He went on, "The trouble is I couldn't really get out of it."

"Oh, is that so!" she said tartly and shrugging her shoulders. "Well, don't bother about me, I'm sure. I've always wanted to see 'Random Harvest' anyway."

"Mike!" came Dennis' voice from the yard and seconds later he appeared in the doorway. "I've just had Tom Gurney on the 'phone," he said. "We're going to be a man short today because of urgent hay work and I said perhaps you'd help out."

"Okay," Mike said, pleased to be asked but regretting the interruption. "Providing you don't mind if I leave at four thirty."

"Sorry to take your help away, Mary," Dennis said. "We'll have to go straight away, the game begins at two." Mike met her gaze and raised his eyebrows in eloquent resignation then went briskly off with Dennis to play cricket.

The evening trip to the theatre was very enjoyable, all the more so for the uniqueness of the occasion for Mike. His aunt provided lively and amusing company and they got back on the last bus, tired but happy.

The last hours of his leave on Sunday morning passed very quickly. He went up to the farm at mid morning and found that Mary was out riding. When she got back he only had a brief moment with her and that, in retrospect, gave him no comfort at all. She was unsaddling her pony in the stable as he crossed the yard. He paused in the doorway as she straightened up from undoing the girths.

"I hope you enjoyed the film," was his opening remark.

"Couldn't get in," she said with feeling. "They were queuing all down the High Street."

"Oh, I am sorry," he said, sensing the ground suddenly opening at his feet. He decided to enquire no further. "Anyway," he said after a considerable pause, his voice falling soft, "you know I'll be thinking of you, don't you, all the time when I'm away."

She shrugged her shoulders and bent to release the girth. "If you say so," she said from behind the pony, "but I don't know that I believe you."

"Look, Mary," he began, alarmed, taking a step into the stable, only to stop when Dennis' voice rang out across the yard. "Ah, Mike, I wanted to show you this."

"I'll write to you," he called softly to Mary. "Okay?" Then he turned to see what it was Dennis was talking about.

"What do you think of it?" Dennis asked proudly, holding out a very nice looking twelve bore.

Mike looked it over, admiring at once its elegantly chased twin barrels glinting blue black in the sunlight. Dennis offered it and he tucked it snugly into his shoulder as he sighted into the sky-blue distance. "Very good," he declared enthusiastically, gently clicking back the hammers, then breaking the gun and peering down through the bore.

"I got it from George Pratt up at Church Farm," Dennis said. "He's just bought a new one so I made him an offer for this."

As they walked out into the orchard to stroll the hedgerows for a flock of crows or pigeons to try the gun on, Mike pursued his niggling anxiety over Mary. "Was I in the wrong?" he asked himself and had to admit that he probably was, but unintentionally. She had probably wasted her evening and was understandably peeved over that, but -. 'What a mess!' he thought and wondered how he could clear the matter up so that all would be healed for their long parting. He tried to convince himself that he was probably worrying needlessly.

When they got back it was time to say his goodbyes before going off home to lunch after which he had to catch the bus. Mary was nowhere to be seen, much to Mike's consternation, but there was nothing he could do about it at that late hour. "I'll write to her and it'll be all right, I'm sure it will," he told himself.

Dennis walked down the road with him. "I daresay you'll have a great time over in B.A.O.R." he said, as they strolled past the orchard.

"Maybe," Mike agreed, "but what I'm really looking forward to is getting back here."

"Good," his friend pronounced, smiling.

They arrived at the cottage gate. "Well, partner," Dennis said, shaking his hand firmly, "look after yourself and don't entirely forget us on the farm, will you?"

"Don't worry, there's no chance I shall forget," he said. "And look after yourself, too." He swung the gate open and strode up the path.

CHAPTER 5

Foreign Service

Half a dozen tanks in a well spaced line careered drunkenly down the scrub-covered hillside, spewing clouds of dust and stones in their wake. They plunged through the rocky stream at the bottom, bucking and slewing alarmingly, then accelerated with a mighty roar as they climbed the long slope towards the high, rounded summit.

In the lurching, swaying interior of Tango Two, Mike was taking down the message in Morse as it came dit-dit-dahing over the radio. "Hull down at summit, sir," he yelled across the inter-com. The lieutenant standing half out of the open turret, binoculars in hand, acknowledged and gave orders to the driver to cut the speed and crawl to the top. Each tank slowly took up position, only the turret with its long barrelled gun being exposed to view ahead, the main body of the vehicle hidden below the skyline. Mike knew what was coming next and he grimaced to Taffy the gunner opposite him in that confined, hot and stuffy interior.

"Loader, ready!" came the lieutenant's call. Mike seized a 75mm armour piercing shell from the magazine.

"Load!" came the order and Mike rammed the shell into the breech, the gleaming steel sliding and clanging with awesome efficiency.

"Loaded!" he yelled.

Then came the instructions to Taffy who had to home in on one of several burnt out shells of German tanks lying some four hundred yards ahead.

"Fire!" came the command and there was a thunderous report in the turret's interior, which filled with acrid fumes.

At a steady pace the target practice proceeded from the line of tanks, sometimes using high explosive shells, sometimes armour piercing. Suddenly there was a crisis in Tango Two. "Fire!" had come the order, but when Taffy pressed his firing button nothing happened. Again came the order to fire, again only silence from the big gun.

"Loader, unload!" came the next order and Mike, with much trepidation swung the breech open and saw the shell still lying there, lethal and unpredictable.

"Clear the gun!" called the lieutenant and Mike, fighting fear, had no option but to grasp the shell in both hands and clamber awkwardly out of the turret. With his heart beating a desperate tattoo, he climbed gingerly down off the tank and, following further orders, walked about fifty yards to the rear, terrified that with every step his last moment might come. Nothing but the unquestioning obedience to orders had prepared him for this crisis; he had no idea how great was the risk of being blown to bits by the maverick shell he was clutching. He put it down slowly and, with the relief of a man reprieved at the eleventh hour, beat a hasty retreat to the tank, sweating profusely.

That one incident apart, Mike and his mates were having a wonderful time on manoeuvres, playing at war in a remote area of the Ardennes. Under canvas in high summer with each day dawning fine and clear leading to unfailing hot sunshine, they were fit, bronzed and increasingly self assured with their strenuous training.

The journey out from the devastated industrial wasteland of the Ruhr where they were stationed to the high, deserted hills of the Ardennes, was unlike any other he had undertaken. The regiment travelled with its tanks by rail, loaded onto long transporter wagons during an interminable, sweating summer evening. Each tank was securely shackled by its crew who then settled down in the open, sitting or lying around their vehicles in their warm tank suits as the train moved slowly off into the fading twilight and on into the long night hours.

Mike lay comfortably on the timbers, his pack for a pillow, the cool night air on his face and above him the star-spangled vault of the dark velvet sky. The chains creaked slightly and the black mass of the tank loomed ominously as the train rolled steadily, rhythmically on over the rails through a land where only the occasional light shone out in a blackness otherwise seemingly devoid of all humanity.

From marvelling at the sheer beauty and immensity of the shining vault above him, his thoughts ran on to the mystery and meaning of it all - his minute speck of pulsating life, this planet Earth, insignificant as a single grain of sand on all the world's beaches and those countless stars above him, stretching away into infinite space. He felt at one with those men of all the ages who had looked up in wonder at those constellations that now wheeled above him and he felt instinctively that this was all creation, design and purpose, not blind chance. He was aware of himself moving through this space at the train's steady rate as the stars were rolling onwards and the Earth was rolling round to meet the day. Even his own heartbeat, that he could feel slow and steady, was part of this great cosmic motion, at one with the whole universe in a mysterious but certain way. It was an experience that impressed itself into his innermost being and remained long after he had drifted off to sleep in the cool night air.

Halting the reel of memories turning in his head, Mike pondered a moment on how the passing of a lifetime had not basically changed his reaction to that impressive night journey of long ago. He was still unwilling to follow the fashionable path of atheism, and, beset by doubts though he was, he was still willing to view the possibility that design and purpose was at the heart of everything. Nothing, he considered, in all the changing, developing insights of science, had ruled out the likelihood that beyond the Big Bang was the Creator...

He switched back to memory mode, recalling that they had returned to their out of town barracks a couple of weeks later with something of the bravado of seasoned soldiers returning after a successful campaign, scarcely conceding that none of their action had been in anger, their fatal casualties nil and, as all the old hands who had seen real action with all its attendant horrors were long ago demobbed, there was no one to rob them of their glory.

Their unforwarded mail awaited them and Mike and his mates, in a well built and decently decorated room of four beds, sprawled around and eagerly buried themselves in news from home. Mike had only a couple of personal letters. He slit the first envelope, not recognising the handwriting, and glanced at the signature. It was from Mrs Colston who had signed herself Emily. He opened the sheet of paper fully and read:-

> Dear Mike,
>
> I thought I would take a few minutes and drop you a line to keep you up to date with things here and to hope that you have settled into your new unit and that your manoeuvres go well. Judging by your first letter(that I ought to have replied to earlier, sorry!) you're going to have a good time there even though the destruction in the towns sounds truly dreadful.
>
> Well, we began harvest work a fortnight ago now and things have been going quite well. We're very busy of course and it's a pity you're not here, we could do with your help, but luckily Harry Blake can come up most evenings and Eric comes in when he's not too busy. Dennis has taken a lot of work off his dad's shoulders this year though Norman still works hard, harder than he ought, I think, though he seems to be keeping well. Mary is well too. She still hasn't decided whether to apply to go to teacher training college or not but meanwhile has taken a holiday job as a waitress in Dunstable and she helps out here when she can with her new boy friend Tony from Stanbridge.
>
> Well, I'd love to go rambling on but I mustn't, I've got to get a meat pie in the oven soon or there will be a mutiny at midday!
>
> So I'll say Cheerio for now and send best wishes from us all.
> Emily C.

Mike scarcely registered the final paragraph, his brain was reeling from those few explosive words 'with her new boy friend Tony'.

It can't be true, he tried to convince himself, there's got to be some mistake. In a second though his mind flew back to Mary's cool attitude when they last spoke together and in his heart he felt that the words were true. That trivial and unfortunate incident that he tried to gloss over in his own mind had grown for her into open rupture and now this, an obvious break.

The letter that he'd sent her soon after his arrival in Germany, with one for Dennis too, in which he had explained in detail how he'd come to neglect her on that Saturday night of his leave and making his affection for her clear, as he'd thought, with a light but meaningful reference to the barn dance, had obviously had no good effect.

The cheerful comments of his mates to items in their letters kept him from further introspection, forcing him to pay cursory attention to them. Privacy was a very scarce commodity in barrack room life.

"Hey, it's time for NAAFI break," Lofty called, glancing at his new watch. "Come on."

They all went off to the crowded canteen for their tea and doughnuts and half an hour of talk, basking in the golden memories of the Ardennes. Mike's mind was more than half elsewhere, back in the reverberations of Emily's letter, trying to understand what had gone wrong and what, if anything, he could do about it. 'Of course,' his reason told him with savage candour, 'there never was this wonderful relationship, that was the trouble. A simple kiss, a brief romantic moment at a dance, that's all that it was. The rest was all in my mind. And anyway to get anywhere I should have been more decisive at the time, more direct. I should have told Mary clearly what I thought about her when I was with her. It's all my own fault.'

The cosy picture he had fabricated of future bliss with Mary and taken as assured as his next breath, disintegrated before his mind's eye as he went over and over those few fateful words written in all innocence, he felt sure, by Emily.

He sipped his tea and bit solidly into his doughnut. "Ah well, sod it," he muttered defiantly as the chatter raged around him, "If she's been looking for a chance to throw me over there's nothing I can do about it. She can't think much of me that's for sure, if she's not prepared to wait."

It was a common enough scenario after all, he reflected. He had heard it several times already in the regiment - girl friend sees no reason why she should be put on ice for a year or more and starts to play the field. Only it hadn't occurred to him that Mary might be like those others. Well, she obviously was. 'But still, I will write to her again,' he determined, still ready to clutch at straws. 'Perhaps if I explain more clearly how I feel about her she'll give this other fellow up.'

"You're looking bloody miserable today, Mike, what's the matter?" Taffy's remark broke in on his dejection and forced a rueful grin.

"Oh, nothing," he said. "Nothing a good stiff drink wouldn't put right anyway."

"That's all right then, man. All you get in this damned place is tea laced with bromide but we'll see what we can do about it in town tonight, shall we?"

"That's fine by me," Mike said, and the conversation swung onto some new topic.

After their break they split up onto various light duties and it wasn't until mid afternoon that Mike got back to his room, alone as it happened, his mind dwelling on Mary's seeming defection and suffering the raw sense of betrayal that only the young and idealistic can feel in all its sharpness.

It was then that he saw the other letter on his pillow, the one that he hadn't yet opened, had indeed quite forgotten about. He picked it up, saw the familiar postmark and recognised his aunt's writing. He sat down heavily on his bed, slit the envelope, took out the single sheet of pink writing paper and read:-

Dear Mike,

It gives me no pleasure at all to have to write to bring you tragic news but I have to tell you that Dennis Colston was killed in a motor cycle accident yesterday afternoon, Saturday. The whole village is in a state of shock and can scarcely yet take in that such an appalling thing has happened. The effect on the family can hardly be imagined, I haven't seen or spoken to them. I know that you two were so close, almost brothers, that this dreadful news is bound to cause you great distress but I felt that you had to know. You are so far away and powerless to join us physically in our grief but I know that you will be with us in heart and mind as we, and all who knew Dennis, mourn his tragic loss.

This must suffice for the moment I'll write again later.

Your loving aunt,

Marjorie.

P.S. Dennis was apparently on his way to a cricket match in Leighton on his new motor bike with his cricket bag slung across his back when he hit an army lorry on the bend by the council houses.

Mike sat gazing straight ahead, the letter limp in his hand. It was too much. It couldn't be true. It mustn't be true. Dennis dead? That was impossible! He who was so much a part of Mike himself, so alive, so warm and human and friendly and so - so immortal as one feels oneself to be. Dennis could not be dead. With childlike anguish Mike felt the hot tears welling up.

Then it was he was aware that Lofty had entered the room. Lofty was not like his other mates. They were rough and ready fellows, good cheerful company most of the time but basically of a coarser nature than his own. Lofty and he were two of a kind.

"Are you all right?" was his question, as he glanced at Mike sitting glumly on his bed.

"No, not really," Mike admitted. "I've had bad news. Here, read it for yourself."

"Oh, all right, if you're quite sure," Lofty said. He scanned the sheet quickly as one does when reading someone else's private letter.

"Christ," said Lofty. "I'm sorry Mike, it is bad news and no mistake."

"I still can't believe it," Mike said. "It just doesn't seem possible that such a thing could happen. What's the date on it? Oh no, it was over a fortnight ago. No use trying to get leave to go to the funeral, it's too late."

"I don't reckon you'd have got it," Lofty said. "Compassionate leave is only for close relatives."

"Close?" Mike thought. "Ah yes, we were close all right."

"Look," Lofty said, "we're off for the rest of the afternoon. Why not come out for a walk? It will be something to do, better than hanging around here feeling miserable."

"Okay," Mike agreed, mechanically.

They had wandered along sunny woodland paths in countryside beyond the barracks, though Mike scarcely saw it. He had practically told Lofty the story of his life so far. He who was always so reticent in talking about himself poured out the details to his mate as they had wandered far and wide in the sunshine.

All about Dennis' offer of a partnership in the farm he'd recounted, realising as he did so that his hopes and plans in that direction must certainly have died with Dennis. Lofty whistled softly, aware even as a city boy of what it would have meant having a half share in a prosperous farm. "But I don't care about any of that," he declared vehemently, and he meant it. "It's nothing compared with having him alive," and the hurt almost choked him as lively images of his friend continued pouring through his mind.

Lofty listened. He didn't say much at first. Mike could feel his sympathy and that was enough to encourage an outpouring of all that Dennis had meant to him as a friend and all-but brother. All the happy details of their growing to manhood on the farm, all the shared experiences of work and play. As he poured out these things, put them into words for the first time, he brought to his own realisation just how important a role Dennis had played in his life, how much richer his experiences had been because of Dennis and how much he was going to be missed.

Gradually the monologue became a conversation, with Lofty asking questions and contributing experiences of his own, so that by the end of the walk the desperation had eased and Mike had regained a more or less even keel emotionally. The first shock waves of this latest tragedy had spent themselves and left him tortured and bruised inside but outwardly calm and, he hoped, little changed from usual.

He was grateful to Lofty when he thought about it afterwards, and said as much to his friend, though Lofty disclaimed all credit, saying wasn't that what a mate was for? The latter-day Mike on his sick bed lifted his mind out of the past and thought of Dennis across all the years, as he often thought of him, as a loved key figure in his own destiny. His disappearance had left a gap in his life that had never been adequately filled, though life had gone on, as it must, and had even had blessings showered on it.

But how much was it possible or practical to relate to grandson Paul? Why not, he suddenly thought, write it all down as a family history? Then it would be available for all family members and could contain so much more detail. Maybe, but for now he would concentrate on what he could actually tell the boy and that was by no means everything. There were certain episodes that were too dark and dubious for a grandson to hear...

Taffy was as good as his word that evening. He organised the four room mates and they spilled out of the 15cwt truck that served as taxi down to the town centre, where the forces club for other ranks was situated among the bomb sites. They soon found themselves in the crowded, smoke-filled lounge where the serious drinking and talking was done, usually several times a week, that helped soothe the troubles of army life far from home. Lofty must have had a word with the others about Mike's tragic news, for they were unusually solicitous in their bright and breezy way, plying him with drinks, shorts, which wasn't their usual poison, and studiously avoiding questioning him or talking of home. Anaesthesia, they considered, was the best cure for tragedies and perhaps they were right.

It was a merry evening, growing merrier as time passed and the intake of schnapps increased, dulling Mike's sharply felt double loss to a hazy golden melancholy, then drowning it altogether in alcohol. There was not a lot of entertainment laid on that evening. Sometimes they had a German pianist or singer to evoke shades of The Blue Angel, then the whole room would belt out its sentimental Dietrich favourites. But not that mid-week evening. There were only a few hard core card schools and snooker in a back room, otherwise it was just drinking and talking. Never again would Mike spend so many hours in drink and nothing talk as in the army overseas. He didn't care a lot for it but had no practical alternative in the circumstances, nothing else was available in the flattened town centre and the soldiers lived completely insulated from all contact with the cowed local population.

At last the time came to leave. Though not strictly enforced, 10.30 was the time to be in by, and it was around that time that the last truck returned to barracks, the only way of avoiding the long uphill trudge of a couple of miles.

They went out laughing and staggering from the fug and fumes into the last glimmer of summer dusk and turning the corner of the street they saw, as so often, standing opposite, half hidden in a ruined archway, a couple of women. They stopped and Taffy with a leering grin said, "Fancy one?" to Mike.

"Why not?" something whispered in the back of his brain, something till then suppressed, now let loose by alcohol. Something frustrated and depressed, something calling for solace. He nodded.

"Come on then," said Taffy coaxingly and pulled him across the street.

"Don't miss the truck," Lofty called. "It leaves in ten minutes."

"We'll be there," Taffy said, giggling.

The two young women stepped out of the shadows and, without speaking, slipped their arms into the men's arms and walked them off in opposite directions. Mike, full of drunken wonder and sudden randiness, his nostrils filled with the scent of cheap perfume, let himself be led like a child by his escort. In the darkness of an overgrown patch of waste ground only yards away she stopped and sank wordless to the ground among the weeds, pulling him down with her, and primitive nature was at once let loose.

A few hectic minutes later she quickly buttoned herself up and he stood up too, his head suddenly cleared and, like an old hand, silently paid her off with such notes as he had and all his cigarettes, whilst gazing keenly into her expressionless face as he exulted in the ecstatic aftermath of his first experience of fornication.

A voice came out of the darkness nearby. "Are you there matey?" It was Taffy. "Come on man or we'll miss that bloody truck."

Mike walked towards Taffy's voice and when he turned after a few steps his woman had gone. "Phew, a bit of all right that," Taffy said, still fumbling with his uniform as they hurried off to the pick up point.

"How was yours?" Taffy asked.

"Pretty good," Mike said, loath to elaborate.

"Great. That's the stuff," said Taffy, with the air of great experience.

"Come on, you two bloody lechers," Lofty called from beside the truck. "The driver won't wait any longer."

Reveille in his new unit was at the more civilised hour of eight o'clock and, as he lay awake next morning grappling with an almighty hangover, Mike's mind was a confused mass of reflections. Dennis, Mary, death, defection, incredulity, grief and betrayal all swirled about in a ghastly, formless mix. Gradually the anarchy steadied and his thoughts came to dwell on Mary. The notion of her lying with another man as he'd lain with that prostitute last evening was a torture made all the more lively by his new knowledge. Then for a moment the wonderful sensuous feeling came over him that it would be Mary that he would soon be making love to. Now that he knew what it was like, this supreme act of physical pleasure, more than ever he wanted to experience it with her. He began to formulate in his head the letter he was going to write to her, the one that his hopes would be pinned on, that would confirm that everything was all right, that Emily had somehow got it wrong. He was spared further introspection on that occasion by loud thumps on the door and the sergeant's hearty rousing voice.

Over the next few days Mike was acutely aware that he ought to write to Emily and Norman to offer words of sympathy, but somehow he couldn't. Yes, he could now accept intellectually that Dennis was gone, there was no escape from that bald fact, but to write about it, actually to put the words down on paper himself, that he was still very loath to do. It was the same for replying to his aunt. The bottom had dropped out of his world and it was as if either writing or talking about it would confirm and emphasize the fact, would let Dennis slip away among the dead, confine him to the past.

But as day followed day he knew that a letter to Mary just had to be written.

For his peace of mind he had to know that she hadn't deserted him, that she would be his when he returned. But how to mix that with some sort of response to Dennis' death? It was an impossible task. It would be seen to be too self-seeking, too calculating to mix the two things, though both were genuine. He hesitated still, not sure how to tackle this delicate matter.

Then suddenly a tragic accident occurred in his own squadron which shocked and stunned everyone, lulled as they had been into thinking that, with the war well over, death was no longer part of their soldiering. Tanks, getting ready for some small local activity, were being driven out of the workshops and were parking one by one in a long line beside the parade ground. Crews had already dismounted and were standing about talking as they waited for the next move to be announced. The last tank to join the line failed to stop in time and hit the one in front just hard enough to nudge it forward into the one in front of that, crushing and instantly killing the driver who was standing between the two.

Once again a young life was snuffed out, another Dennis gone, and, although the victim wasn't a close friend of Mike's, the fact that he and his mates were there, only yards away and were horrified witnesses, brought the sense of tragedy home to them, overpowering their personal concerns and leading to a very subdued air in the barracks for several days.

It was after this incident and somehow prompted by it that Mike, sitting on his bed one afternoon, made up his mind to write to Mary. He tried several drafts, screwing each one up impatiently before settling for a few simple lines, omitting, after much reflection, all mention of his own fears.

Dearest Mary,

I hardly know what to say to you but I must say something about the tragedy of Dennis' death. Words are largely superfluous and inadequate at this time but I did just want you to feel that I am with you in your suffering and loss. Dennis, as you know, was as a brother to me so I hope it is not presumptuous of me to say I feel his loss as one of his family and although far distant I assure you that my thoughts at this dark time are constantly with you.

Write to me when you can, I long to be at your side.

Mike.

He read it through and winced at its inadequacy but folded it and put it in its envelope. It was that final sentence that contained in its few casual words all his needle sharp anxiety about their relationship. It would be, he hoped, in response to them that she would declare herself sufficiently to allay his fears for their future. In the face of clear evidence to the contrary he clung to hopes of a favourable reply.

Then, aware that he couldn't very well send that letter without penning a few similar lines to Emily and Norman, he quickly dashed off the following whilst still in an uninterrupted state of deep emotional involvement.

> Dear Emily and Norman,
>
> What can I say except to wish you strength and courage to endure these dark days? You are all constantly in my thoughts and I would dearly love to be with you in your time of suffering. I feel so isolated here. There will never be anyone so like a brother to me as Dennis was and I am very proud to have known him as I did. I am sure that the memory of the good times we had together - and there were so many of them - will always remain bright and undimmed when the pain of his loss has eased.
>
> Forgive my not writing more at this time, the words come with difficulty at present, but be sure of my warmest thoughts and affection for you all.
>
> Mike.

That done and the letters despatched, he felt the burden of worry over Mary lifted somewhat and, in spite of the deep sorrow of Dennis' loss that lay just below the surface of his days, time rolled away in a very pleasant and leisurely fashion for Mike and his fellow time servers in summertime Germany. There wasn't a lot of urgent soldiering to be done so he was able, for example, to qualify for the regimental shooting team and spend many happy days competing with other regiments, travelling hither and yon about the country receiving such minimal hospitality as the army deemed fitting for national service other ranks.

He was also able to start doing something about remedying his lack of a decent education, for as a result of contact with several well informed comrades he had become aware that his wartime schooling had been seriously deficient and he was becoming more and more determined to do something about it. So when he learned that he could use the regimental education section to pursue a course of general academic studies leading to the Forces' own examination, he was firstly amazed that the army should offer such opportunities and grant ample time to use them, then lost no time in eagerly grasping them. He and Lofty were the only ones in the whole regiment to do this and they were looked upon with tolerant curiosity by their mates who, though keen on skiving - which they assumed was the object of the exercise - drew the line at anything so outlandish as education with its attendant shades of the hated schoolroom.

Mike and a small group of his mates were able to spend a few days leave in Denmark, arranged and subsidised by the army. They passed a pleasantly boring time in a rural mainland area, bemoaning the army's cunning in thwarting their yearning for the fleshpots of Copenhagen. The contrast between the devastated German towns and the intact condition and hygienic cleanliness of Denmark was impressive, as was the comparative plenty in the shops. But the high spot of that short break for Mike was the purchase in a Kolding bookshop of the unexpurgated version of Lady Chatterley's Lover, then unobtainable in Britain. All his mates were keen to buy a copy too, the first time most of them had ever bought a book. Their evenings were partly at least spent in pin-drop silence, punctuated by guffaws and earthy expressions of incredulity at the naughty bits. Then they would drink quantities of weak Danish beer and walk the neat deserted streets in a vain search for some Nordic femme fatale.

A few weeks after sending his letters of sympathy he received an answer. He recognised with a pang of disappointment that the writing was Emily's, not Mary's, and it was with a mixture of lingering hope, fear and sorrow that he opened the two folded sheets and read:-

> Dear Mike,
>
> Thank you for writing, we appreciated it. I'm afraid I don't feel at all cheerful yet, which won't surprise you, I'm sure. In fact it's as though we are just emerging from a nightmare to find on awakening that it is all too true. But life must go on, at least the outward forms, and in ourselves we are all surprisingly well and no doubt in time the worst of the pain will be healed, or so we try to tell ourselves. Everyone has been marvellous, helping Norman with the work and trying to get him to rest, but of course work is the best healer and the worst thing would be to sit around doing nothing. So we are coping. Arthur has been a tower of strength and Mary's Tony has also been very good, so that Norman hasn't had to do too much which is just as well in view of his medical situation. If you'll excuse me I won't write any more at this time, except to say that we look forward to seeing you eventually, nothing has changed that. Mary says thank you for her letter and hopes you'll let my reply go for us all this time. She is well and working hard at school. Tony has been a tower of strength to her.
>
> Emily.

Mike read the letter through several times. His worst fears were now realised. 'Tony has been a tower of strength to her.' That hurt. And she hadn't bothered to reply to him although he considered he had made it obvious both that he felt for her and that he was seeking an assurance of her feelings for him. All self delusion, all hope was now killed off. He had to admit that Mary had turned elsewhere for affection, for whatever it was she wanted from this Tony, and that he, Mike, had no course left but to accept it. He refused at once to consider writing again to her, he wouldn't plead, he wouldn't throw away all pride and dignity.

Probably because in his innermost heart he had known since Emily's first letter that Mary had finished with him, after the initial re-opening of the wound, the latest signal of her defection didn't upset and depress him as much as he had feared it would. Helped by his regimental activities and his mates' cheerful company he coped with the situation and was able to preserve his good spirits.

It was months later, in the depths of a snowy winter when regimental life was at a low ebb with much time being spent in their comfortably heated rooms and cheerful, well stocked NAAFI canteen, that another of Emily's occasional letters brought Mike up sharp with a passage that startled him in spite of its inevitability:-

> "You probably won't be surprised to hear that Mary and Tony have become engaged. Their relationship has positively blossomed over recent months and we weren't at all surprised when they told us their good news. They talk of getting married in the summer soon after Mary's 19th birthday - he'll be 21 by then. Maybe this will lift us from our gloom, I hope so. You probably don't know Tony, he works with his brothers on his father's farm in Stanbridge, it seems likely they'll live over there but all that sort of thing still has to be worked out."

He felt the stirrings of anger and jealousy as he read those words in spite of his reason having long resigned itself to the loss of Mary. But now he realised that in some dim corner of his mind the hope must have lingered that when he got home in a few months time he might still, against all the odds, be able to put things right between them. That their meeting might prove sufficient. It was that secret, illogical hope that was now dead and its dying had power to torture him.

He reflected, too, on the supreme irony that it was Emily, Mary's own mother and a mother figure to him, Mike, who completely unwittingly was the one to go on twisting the knife in his wound. Would he rather not know all this about Mary, he asked himself. Should he be frank with Emily and cut himself off from them once and for all to save himself more hurt? It was difficult to say, though he knew from deep within himself that he couldn't bring himself to excise the village and all that it stood for from his life. It was in any case his home, the place he would return to. But certainly the agony was prolonged and was being doled out in increasingly bitter parcels.

There was nothing now that he could do about Mary, he decided for the umpteenth time, calming a strong impulse to rush off a pleading letter to her with a mental picture of how it would be received - with cold contempt or amusement or, even worse, pity. Time and distance now made credible any distortion of her character which suited his mood. And another thing, he reflected ruthlessly, he hadn't the exciting financial prospects now that he'd envisaged at the peak of his optimism, when Mary was to have shared the bliss of his partnership with Dennis. Heaven alone knew what he would earn his living at now. He certainly couldn't rival Tony's solid farming potential.

Mike and Lofty gradually drew closer in friendship, this natural tendency being greatly helped by studying together. During the long, dark winter days they were often the only occupants of the regimental reading room, in one corner of which they worked under the occasional and relaxed supervision of an education sergeant. There they read a little Chaucer together and Mike was introduced to Shakespeare and to the love poems of John Donne which burst upon them with all the power of youthful discovery and all the better, probably, for being delayed beyond school days. Wordsworth too, was a discovery which for Mike in particular was so heady and unforgettable a draught, confirming everything he had ever felt about the beauties of his own rural landscape and the importance of Nature's everyday objects in the nourishing of spiritual values and in living a decent life.

As the last days drew on before return to England with demob not long delayed beyond that, they would often sit and chat in the reading room and always their future hopes and plans were aired.

"I think I'll probably go back to the same office I worked in before call up," Lofty said one day without any particular enthusiasm.

"What were you doing exactly?" Mike asked.

"I was just a junior in a small stockbroker's office in the City; you know, running errands, making tea and all that sort of thing. I was lucky to get the job really, a friend of my dad fixed it. The trouble is, after army life I'm not too sure I want an office job. It seems a bit tame, don't you think? I might even be tempted to sign on if I thought I could get a commission."

"Yes," Mike agreed, "an office job in London is going to seem pretty tame after tanks. Just think of those days in the Ardennes! Me, I don't think I could stand office work but then, I never intended to do that sort of thing anyway."

"Of course," Lofty said, "farming is your thing, isn't it? It's funny to think of you farming somehow. After all, you're a Londoner born and bred aren't you? Don't you ever feel like going back there?"

"No, not at all," Mike said, laughing. "I couldn't stand it. It takes someone like me, brought up in the slums and who knows it for what it is, to really hate it."

"You'll have to come and visit me when we're out," Lofty said. "We're not posh but it's a pleasant part of south London where I live."

"And you'll have to come down to where I live," Mike countered. "You'd love it. It's real countryside."

"Have you got a girl friend there?" Lofty asked, for Mike had still never said anything on the subject.

"No, not really," he answered, loath to be questioned. "No," he added more definitely, "I did have once, sort of, but not any more. She's a casualty of conscription. You have, haven't you?" he asked, quick to deflect further enquiries.

"Yes," Lofty said," but we're not serious yet. So," he went on, "you're going to be a lecherous farmer are you? Dairymaids in the hay and that sort of thing?"

"Ah yes, it's a great life down on the farm," Mike retorted in similar vein. "After all, it's being close to nature isn't it?"

"You certainly won't be typical of farming folk, will you?" Lofty went on. "Not many of them go in for reading Shakespeare and Wordsworth, I'm sure."

"You may be right," Mike agreed. "Though I can think of no good reason why they shouldn't. They'd be all the better for it."

"It's probably got something to do with the type of person you have to be to make a go of farming," Lofty said. "They are too close to life in the raw to bother about books."

"You can never tell," Mike replied. "Look at Robert Frost whose poems we were reading the other day. He was a farmer for years and he didn't go broke." He pictured some of the farmers he knew. There was Tom Turvey at Church End, a jolly, rotund, red faced son of the soil yet shrewd and with a mind like a razor and Ralph Archer, a pale, lean and quietly good humoured fellow, always gently teasing. There was John Costin of Eaton Bray, a sharp featured, strong minded and forthright character who with a glance and a few pithy words could sum up a cow's or a man's good and bad points. They were all very different from each other, no one type, and all good farmers. None of them had much book learning as far as he knew, and he smiled as he remembered Ralph's fondness for Billy Bunter in the 'Magnet' which he used to borrow from Mike and read avidly.

"Yes, you have to be a very practical person, I suppose," he conceded. "But then, when you're young there's no harm in being a bit of a romantic, in the classic sense, is there?" You risk getting hard bitten in most jobs in the end, it seems to me, even stockbrokers," he ended with a mischievous smile, "just hollow shells of materialism."

"Don't! Don't remind me!" Lofty protested in mock horror. "No, I suppose what I'm getting at is that farming seems to me to be one of those jobs you have to be born to."

"Maybe," Mike admitted, unwilling to give real credence to this theory. "All I know is that I've lived or worked on a farm for the last, what? nearly seven years and I've enjoyed every minute of it."

"But would you know how to run a farm?" Lofty persisted.

"No," Mike said. "Quite frankly I've still got a lot to learn. But then, to be honest there's no chance of me ever having to run my own farm."

"Have you ever thought of going in for teaching?" Lofty asked suddenly. "You'd be wasted as a farm labourer, don't you think?"

"Teaching!" Mike echoed. "Whatever put that idea into your head?"

"Oh, I don't know. I can just see you in front of a class of kids, somehow."

"I'm blowed if I can," Mike said with a laugh.

"Anyway, whatever happens, let's keep in touch. I'd like that," Lofty said, gathering up his books with a glance at the clock nudging towards rendezvous time at the cookhouse.

"Me, too," Mike said, his thoughts turning ever more directly towards home and life after the army.

Easing his thoughts off those long ago scenes, the post millennium Mike ruminated on the changed world he now inhabited. How, he wondered, had they got from there to here. How and by what steps had the widespread practice of leaving doors unlocked in perfect safety degenerated to the streets becoming unsafe after dark and was this inevitable? How was it now normal for cemeteries to be desecrated, handbags ripped from shoulders, drugs to be a world wide problem, warfare to be as rife, the environment to be as threatened, morals and discipline to be as lax? It surely isn't mere coincidence that the many downward steps in society that he had witnessed in his lifetime went hand in hand with the decline in belief in anything much beyond the individual. Therein lies the crux and all else flows from it. And all this in the face of rising opulence, wonderful medical progress, moon travel and unparallelled ease and comfort in the home, to mention only a few modern miracles. What does the future hold now that we are well on the way to the global village? Is the outlook for mankind grim or good? And can it be directed or is it locked into some unalterable path? Civilisations have risen and fallen, Rome did decline and fall and where now is our society heading?

Yet, he reflected, age must not be too condemning, that would be too easy. Even in a small, personal way one should encourage the young, try to be positive, do one's little bit to help and be optimistic. Optimism, in spite of some hard knocks, was certainly my prevailing mood when I left the army, he reflected as his recollections once more began to roll.

CHAPTER 6

Ghosts Laid to Rest

In a concert of hissing steam and screeching metal the single coach train slid to a halt at the tiny country station of Stanbridgeford. Mike lowered his window, leaned out to turn the handle, pushed the door open and stepped onto the platform, clutching his old suitcase. He was the only one to alight at that isolated spot stranded amid flat fields and, as he left the platform, with the train clanking slowly off over the level crossing, the stationmaster was already preparing to return to his garden.

A good ten minutes walk lay ahead of Mike and it was a walk he loved, which explains his whim of arriving home by train instead of the bus from Luton which goes directly through the village. Fields of wheat and oat stubble spread wide on every hand, for it was early September and the harvest was recently gathered, but there were also fields of potatoes and mangolds and long, willow-lined pastures dotted with cattle beside the Ousel Brook. The lane he was walking snaked before him across the level landscape for about a mile, until the green mass of chalk hills rose high to close the scene and below those slopes amid the dark trees he could see in the distance, lay Totternhoe, the long ribbon village of home.

Whilst walking in leisurely fashion his eyes feasted upon the well-loved scene with an affection sharpened by more than a year's absence. It felt good to be coming home at last, a day he had looked forward to so keenly for so long. Yet his mind dwelt only marginally upon visual pleasures, it was largely preoccupied with other considerations. Ever since he had left Lofty at York, where they had been demobbed earlier that day and given the suit which he now awkwardly wore, he'd been mulling over the people and events of the little world which was his and which now loomed increasingly large before him. He stopped when he came to the ungated entrance to a large stubble field where so often in the past he'd gone with Dennis to shut the hens in at sunset, and a lump came in his throat as he pictured the two of them wandering in close fellowship there and the regret in his heart became almost palpable as his eye ran along the hedgerows and out across the broad acres where they had many, many times worked together among the sheaves of ripened corn. He began to realise that he would have to face up to the loss of Dennis all over again in his own loved places.

Tearing himself away and plodding on, he thought wryly of how different his homecoming was going to be compared with that of his hopes and imaginings before Dennis took his fatal motor cycle ride. The triumph he had envisaged, the threshold from poor boy to farming partner he was to cross, the excitement and satisfaction of an agricultural career ahead and its financial and social rewards and of course, Mary to share it all with him, Mary to have and to hold and to be his and he hers in this earthly paradise for all their days!

What a fool he had been to permit himself all those dreams and still was a fool to harbour their ghostly remains! He'd got his life, he told himself firmly as he strode out, his health and a place where he belonged. The rest was up to him to make what he could of himself. It was pointless mourning the past. He had broken with that and was now entering on an entirely new chapter.

At least as far as Mary was concerned he knew what he was walking back into, for Emily's letters had continued to chronicle the development of her plans. In the spring she had written:-

> "Mary and Tony have set the date for their wedding, July 14th, which we hope will be a little before harvest when things here on the farm should be fairly quiet. The wedding itself will be a pretty quiet affair too, in view of the shadow which has hung over us all since Dennis was taken - it will be almost a year by then. Norman and I would very much have liked you to be there but we gather you won't be home until September and they felt that July would be best for them. They'll be living in a cottage on Tony's father's farm after they come back from their short honeymoon. They'll be Mr and Mrs Pierson by the way, in case you didn't know Tony's family name."

For several days after the receipt of this letter, Mike, by summoning up his total stock of simulated indifference to its contents, was by day able to deal calmly with this final severing blow. He was thankful he would still be in Germany when the wedding took place, it saved him declining an invitation, which he would certainly have had to do. But sometimes in bed, in the darkness and the small hours' vulnerability, he was unable to prevent the agony of picturing Mary in bridal white walking down the aisle with that indeterminate stranger, and many times his dreams were fantasies where Mary was his in episodes of delirious passion and where his first waking thoughts were ones of misery and despair.

The misery had eased, but as time for demob grew close he was faced with the prospect of being in near proximity to Mary and her husband until such time as he might leave the village and move right away, a course of action he thought probably best. In any case it was a situation that was best confronted and overcome as soon as possible so that he could get on with his life with that ghost of the past swept clear.

It was with that intention firmly in mind that he was walking towards the village that early evening in September, his national service over and civilian life to be faced up to and a future to be carved from somewhere.

How Marjorie responded to his knock! She threw open the door, gave him a bear hug and kisses on either cheek and had him in and filling much of the space in that little, low beamed sitting room that used to seem so big. Over tea from her best pink and gold service they chatted enthusiastically.

"Your room's all ready," she said. "It's been redecorated ready for your return. Do you want to see it?"

"Sure," he said and bounded up the stairs. He came down in an instant, full of compliments for the new decor, though he'd had no complaints about the old one.

She of course had given much thought to his position after demob and, without knowing anything about his involvement with Mary, had come to the conclusion that he was unlikely to stay on at the farm working.

"You're going to have a break before thinking about work?" she asked.

"Yes, we get a week's paid leave anyway so I thought I might as well take it. I might go up to London to see my army pal."

"Good idea," she said. "Well, well," she went on looking him over with approval, "I must say the army hasn't done you any harm at all. Filled you out a little, I'd say. Have you enjoyed it on the whole?"

"Yes, I suppose so," he conceded a little grudgingly. "We've had some fun these last few months and we were treated more like human beings than we were at Catterick. I can't help thinking though that it's been a bit of a waste of time."

"No, I don't think so," Marjorie said laughingly. "It's made a man out of you, I can see that."

"Perhaps you're right," he admitted. "Anyway, it's over now."

"So what comes next?" she asked.

"I'm not sure. I'll have to think it over seriously during the next week or two before I run out of money."

"You needn't worry too much about money," she said. "But there's no shortage of jobs round here. The newspapers are full of them. You'll want to get something worthwhile, I presume, not any old dead end job?"

"Oh yes, of course," he agreed. "But what am I qualified for? I ask myself. There's not much call for tank drivers and wireless operators in civvy street. I've lost two years when I could have been getting qualified."

"It's not too late," she insisted. "You're only twenty. You can still train for most careers."

"Yes, you're right," he admitted. "I'll have to make my mind up pretty quickly, I suppose." He was aware that he had no burning ambition for anything in particular and thought again of Lofty's suggestion that he might consider teaching. There would be no harm in finding out a bit more about it, he supposed.

"I daresay the army will have unsettled you a bit," Marjorie went on. "But you'll soon settle down, I'm sure."

"Yes, I suppose I will," he agreed, but with the private thought that he wasn't at all sure that he wanted to settle down, especially there in the village. Much might depend on the next few days. "Are you sure it'll be all right me being here?" he asked. "How about your job?"

"Of course it will be all right," she insisted, astonished at his question. "This is your home for heaven's sake. I'm looking forward to it. The job's no problem. You know I'm manageress now, don't you? I like it actually, it gives me a great deal of satisfaction. The people I work with are very nice and it is pleasant working among the carnations. But yes, have no fear, we shall have no trouble managing very well."

As he walked back down the path from that old cottage, with its rows of blackcurrant and gooseberry bushes on one side and the venerable russet apple tree on the other with its low, sweeping branches over the lawn, he felt the sudden onset of that special sense of homecoming which is dependent only on a deep love of place and not at all on its size or grandeur. He didn't have to own it all to love it, just a small stake in it was enough. The feeling of home and of belonging was intensified with every step he took along the road to the farm where he had been invited and with every aspect of the orchards by the roadside, the details of cottages and of the grassy chalk slopes rising to his left. He was a walking bundle of heightened awareness, every nerve alert, every sense reacting sharply to the so familiar and well-loved scene.

In spite of his initial misgivings about returning to the farm at all, he was now in the grip of his deepest emotions, aware only of the rightness of his being there and of the almost overpowering affection that he felt for this spot. There were no conscious thoughts then of the dispiriting East End streets where he had been raised but they were there, in his subconscious, sharpening his love of this superb rural setting.

Exquisite pleasure was his as he turned off the road to walk down the slope to the farmhouse door, with the black tarred barns and cobbled farmyard to one side. Whatever it is that makes us attach ourselves with such fierce love to one cherished spot on this earth was possessed by Mike in great measure and made its presence felt at that moment, so that he had to stop until his eyes had taken in great satisfying draughts of the scene as of life-sustaining breath.

Once inside, he was warmly welcomed by Mr and Mrs Colston, the latter insisting straightaway that he call her Emily now that they were on an adult footing, though her husband made no such insistence, which Mike found quite acceptable in an age when first name use by all and sundry hadn't even started to be fashionable. He had to recount all his recent doings and was marvelled at for his continental travelling which was quite outside their experience. As he talked he couldn't help noticing how they had both aged since he last saw them. They looked careworn and weary in spite of a determined effort at liveliness and he could only speculate that it was the loss of Dennis that had principally worked the deterioration, plus the effects and anxiety of Mr Colston's health.

Emily cooked him a delicious meal of eggs, ham and beans which he mopped up with gusto, pausing now and again to sample the atmosphere and to reflect on how different the house felt now, how quiet with no Dennis and Mary about. Emily and Norman were seated in their customary chairs watching him eat and throwing in comments from time to time, but he was surprised that very little was said about Mary's wedding and the couple's subsequent activities, he had certainly expected more and had braced himself to take it on the chin.

"So what are you going to do now, Mike?" Mr Colston enquired when he had finished eating and had a mug of tea put in front of him.

"What, for work you mean?" Mike said. "I don't rightly know, I haven't decided on anything. "Good," Mr Colston said with a smile.

Mike looked at him quizzically, half sensing what lay behind the smile.

"If you've nothing better in mind for the time being," Mr Colston went on, "I wondered if you'd care to give us a hand here. I've had a couple of casual chaps in from the village to help with harvest but they aren't much good and they're both starting factory jobs soon anyway. What do you say?"

"Okay," Mike said, acting typically on instinct when put on the spot and without a second's hesitation for thought and, helped by that 'for the time being', he ignored all his previous doubts and reservations about getting involved at the farm again. His deepest, inarticulate desire had spoken for him.

"That's fine," Mr Colston said with enthusiasm. "When can you start?"

"Is there any great hurry?" Mike asked.

"Well, no, not exactly," he replied. "But as I said these two chaps are leaving in a few days and it would be very convenient if you could start about then."

"I was thinking of having a few days off," Mike said. "Shall we say next Monday?"

"Done," said Mr Colston.

"Gosh," Emily exclaimed, "When I think of the scrawny little Cockney lad that first came here in the war and then look at you now. What a difference!"

"Ah, I daresay there is," he agreed, laughing. "Even scrawny little Cockneys grow up." Then more seriously, "It is strange how things work out, isn't it? Who would have guessed I would have landed up here from Poplar of all places?"

"Ah yes," Emily agreed with a deep sigh. "I've always thought there was a guiding hand in our lives."

In the silence that followed she sat a moment in reverie and Mike had no difficulty in sensing her trying to perceive the divine purpose in the taking of her son and at her seeking a Job-like acceptance of that which she could not comprehend and to console herself a little thereby.

Mike got up and looked more closely at the wedding photograph of Mary and

Tony on the mantelpiece and which had been referred to briefly. Mary looked radiant, he acknowledged grudgingly, but then she always did. She had looked like that when he had kissed her at the barn dance. But now in bridal white she had given herself body and soul to the dark haired, sallow skinned individual who stared smugly out, his arm casually around her waist where his had once been. He felt the blood singing in his ears.

"It's not a bad photograph, is it?" Emily commented. "Mary does look lovely."

"Ah, well," her husband said, "I just hope she's chosen wisely, that's all."

"Norman," his wife remonstrated, "what a thing to say!" Mike listened in astonishment and of course made no comment. It was quite obvious that Emily hadn't the slightest idea of his own involvement even though he had totally ignored the wedding, sending neither present nor congratulations. He had felt sure at the time that such a snub would be his best way out of any future involvement with the farm. But no, it seemed to have passed unremarked. He wondered how Mary had apparently been unable or unwilling to give any intimation to her mother that he was a sensitive issue. Or perhaps, he reflected grimly, she had simply forgotten all about that little incident of burgeoning passion that he was still tempted to make so much of. Perhaps, even, she remembered it, if at all, as mere childish flirting, something she would laugh at indulgently and even joke with him about when they met. That thought still had the power to send a chill of humiliation down his spine and he had the sudden urgent desire never to set eyes on Mary again.

He went for a stroll in the orchard later, his thoughts whirling but drawn by his love of those dark trees sloping down from the black-boarded barns to the brook at the bottom. As he walked through the cropped grass he was increasingly aware through a growing feeling of pleasure, that he was renewing his loved associations with this place - the times he had played there as a lad with his friends, Dennis in particular, and the times he had worked there picking fruit in those venerable trees. And now, after two years of absence, he was back there again, thankful to be home.

He was keenly aware of those emotions as he stopped on the open stretch of grass beside the orchard and looked around at the lower chalk slopes of the hills rising steeply across the road, flanked by giant elms, and at the cluster of barns beside the rickyard, all with their warm human associations which he was now hoping to renew. Would he be able to do so without Dennis? That was a worry and a situation which time would resolve, happily he hoped.

He didn't try to look ahead at what he had done by agreeing to work there again, he was just aware of the deep feeling of satisfaction at the decision he had taken, at knowing that his instinct had been right. He had no idea where this path might lead nor for how long it might continue. For the moment it was enough to bask in the deep love of all he could see around

Mike spent the evening at the village social club in the Memorial Hall, it being the best he could come up with to celebrate his demob. He was made welcome amongst old acquaintances, although his closest friends weren't there. Eric, so he was told, had gone away to work on an uncle's farm in the next county, more or less permanently as far as Mike could gather, and Mac was still away in the Air Force, though there seemed to be some doubt as to whether he had signed on for a career or not. He played snooker and drank cola happily enough with those members of his old schooldays tribe though he couldn't help thinking back to when he'd last been there, that unforgettable evening with Dennis after their momentous talk of partnership.

Afterwards, all his companions living at Church End in the opposite direction, Mike walked back alone along the unlit road. He was aware of a sense of inner emptiness that he churned over and over as his steps sounded solitary and soft beneath the roadside trees. Strangely enough, he realised he was missing his army pals, for there was no one in his hour of need to be really jolly and convivial with, no one to call in at the Cross Keys with as he passed, and mark with a few drinks and merry talk that re-crossing of his important frontier back to civilian life.

There was no girl friend either, he was aware, none to appease the yearning gnawing away at him as he walked in the darkness, wondering how and when and with whom he could reach out a hand and touch and hold and no longer feel alone in the world. All the older people around him were admirable, but at that moment he felt the need for close contemporaries with whom he could relax and feel at home. He would have to find someone, which was a thought that had struck him at the club as he looked around at the few girls and young women there. He didn't think he was going to be easy to please and couldn't imagine he would be easily pleasing to the opposite sex, rather reserved and seemingly stand-offish as he appeared to himself to be.

A couple of days later he went up to London for the day, having 'phoned Lofty and arranged to meet him in the afternoon in Trafalgar Square. Behind the desire to have a day out before starting work was his deep longing to go back to Poplar, to re-examine just one more time that cradle and nursery which he hadn't seen since the day he'd left in such a hurry in the blitz. He wanted to find if possible the relics of that life that used to be his with his parents and friends all that seeming eternity of years ago.

Whenever, in the army or again recently in the village, he'd thought about his East End childhood and of his parents, it was always with a small but persistent sense of guilt. He was profoundly aware that fate had dealt kindly in sending him to that lovely village, to his aunt and to the farm amongst people of whom he could become very fond and whose standard of living and general values and expectations were so superior to his own and which he had lost no time in adopting as his own. He knew that none of all that could be changed, the impression was lasting and would stay with him for the rest of his days. He had been, he knew, transformed once and for all into a lover of the soil and of everything connected with the land. Never again, he knew with a young man's iron certainty, would he willingly live in a city. And none of this had been of his own choosing. He knew himself to have been the powerless shuttlecock of fate, propelled willy nilly into that new existence that had turned out so far to have been to his immense advantage.

And yet, his thoughts continued, as he resolutely tried to face up to the guilt - making truths of his life, his parents had to be killed so that he could profit from that new life with all its benefits. Although it was obvious that he was entirely guiltless of anything to do with their actual deaths, yet his complete and definitive escape from the depressing trap of material and cultural poverty that had been his lot in Poplar, seemed to him to have been at the price of his parents' deaths.

Every time that he saw in the fiercely critical light of his mind's eye those mean streets of monotonous awfulness, the poverty stricken barrenness of his early home, the countless aspects of want and drudgery that remained as vivid to him as if it were yesterday that he were there, he felt, with the shame and distaste, a strong sense of disloyalty. It was his parents' lives that he was so critical of, their environment. What right had he to condemn his own upbringing? But no, it wasn't his parents he was critical of, he knew that. It was the life that they too were condemned to lead; but it was still a confused and guilty reaction that he felt. It was almost as if it had been a self sacrifice on their part and it was his ambivalent attitude, rarely expressed, towards this central tragedy that generated the guilt that he was to feel, though in gradually diminishing form, for all his days.

As he travelled up in the train from Luton however, his mind wasn't totally occupied with such weighty and gloomy considerations. He was looking forward with lively curiosity to exploring his boyhood haunts, many of which he could clearly remember, to seeing again his old school, several storeys high and with the playground on the roof, and who knows, encountering some old friends whose names he could easily recall.

The bus ride through the City began to bring home to him the tremendous scale of destruction that London had suffered. Though tidied up, with unsafe buildings demolished, there was not yet any major rebuilding started since the war had ended. Great scarred vistas were opened up where buildings had jostled. St. Paul's rose damaged clear above the desolation whilst everywhere, in every crypt or cellar, every patch of cleared rubble, the year's last flowers of the tall rose bay willow herb flourished where the centuries' old life of commerce had throbbed.

It was, he reflected as the bus swept along, much on a par with his experience of German cities. He recalled seeing Cologne cathedral standing black and forlorn above vast seas of devastation and was forcibly struck then with the sad truth of it all, that mankind seemed so constituted that war, though manifestly stupid and murderously irrelevant, was inevitable or even an essential part of its make up, regardless of the consequences. Would it ever stop, he wondered, even now that the atom bomb was unleashed upon the world? Looking around upon the devastated City he could only hope it would.

Even those scenes of destruction did not fully prepare him for the sight which met his eyes when he finally got off the bus in the East End and walked for several minutes towards his destination. The lively spirit of curiosity with which he had started out changed to sombre mood as his memories came up against the present realities of mass destruction all around him in which he found few points of reference to support those memories. Street after street lay flattened, with only isolated blocks standing here and there.

With the rubble cleared away, the sites more or less levelled and many containing those sturdy little prefabs that had been hurried in to house much of the surviving populace, it all looked sanitised, cleansed and deathly quiet. It was difficult even for Mike to remember what a densely crowded, chaotic, smelly, noisily heaving and teemingly alive district it had been. With a sinking heart as he traversed this scene of almost total destruction, he stood at last in his own street and walked down the carefully renewed tarmac surface till he stood where he knew his own house had been. There was just a clean gap embracing several houses. He walked into the levelled space and tried to recapture in his mind's eye the house when it was whole - the little bare walled, lino floored room where he'd slept on a black iron bedstead, the staircase laid with lino pads up to the dark, minute kitchen area on the top landing and the cheaply furnished living room where he had spent so many hours on his own playing with a few battered toys. He pictured his mother cooking, his father making him a scooter on the landing - how proud he had been of that red painted scooter!

He was risking being over sentimental, he knew, as he fought back the tears which tried to come, though he determined not to distort the true picture. He knew the rooms had been mean, in a permanently wretched state of decoration, sparsely and cheaply furnished, the whole house inconvenient, poorly serviced, dirty, the haunt of lice and bed bugs. He had heard say that Hitler had done the council's work well in demolishing so much slum property. Yet that was his mother and his father that he pictured there, his own flesh and blood, with thoughts and feelings as valid as his own. Here was the very place they had lived out their days and, whilst he was safely away, in chaos and in terror, had both been killed, here where the sun shone brightly on the rubble. No wonder that tender feelings welled up inside him for those vanished lives, as he gazed intently at the point which connected him with his earliest roots.

He turned away at last and looked along the street. One or two people were walking about, none of whom he recognised. He wondered where everyone had gone, there used to be such throngs everywhere. Mr Stokes who lived opposite, now a gap, who had a hook instead of a right hand and was an object of dread for the children, and his boy Kenny with whom Mike used to play.. His friend Dickie August who lived a little way along, another gap, and whose birthday party he remembered attending just before the blitz started, when they had bobbed hilariously for apples covered in treacle in a bowl of water. The pale faced girl in the house next to the brewery back entrance who practised the violin in the front room where a large aspidistra stood in the window. All gone now, leaving only levelled rubble.

What had become of them all, he wondered, as he strolled along the street ready to greet any of them. The chapel was gone, he noted, around whose wide steps he had played, climbing the tall railings to get inside the locked gates; the little factory next door where many of his friends' mothers had worked for a sweated pittance. Had it been a good life they had lived there, he wondered, half yearning, a life that perhaps he was the poorer in spirit if not in material for having lost?

No, it wasn't all good, he recalled with an angry start, as his mind re-opened a long closed door and he relived with a violent shock the several times when, as a small boy of eight or so at the Sunday school he had attended at that same chapel where he now stood, alone with an elder in the room he'd had to drop his trousers and lie over the man's knee to be punished for some imaginary offence by having his bare buttocks half patted, half stroked and told to tell nobody.

The surge of outrage soon passed and he dwelt next upon the very positive sense of community which he knew existed there. Mutual help and moral support freely given. Unquestioned honesty and close friendship of people who knew they were all in pretty desperate circumstances together, often wondering where the next week's rent was coming from and frequently having to dodge the collector. The men, he realised, had routinely gambled and drunk both rent and children's food to relieve the drabness and soulnessness of their situation. The pubs were heaving on Saturday nights. Yet even in that poor street he'd known that there were a few families who kept themselves to themselves, trying hard not to descend to the gutter, cherishing dreams of bettering themselves, though most folk struggled to be respectable, often taking out penny a week insurance so that they could be decently buried.

It's all gone now anyway, Mike said to himself as he walked back along the street, and the notion came to him loud and clear that he no longer belonged there, to whatever there was left to belong to. It was a life, a childhood that existed henceforward only in his head. He paused a moment at the gap marking his former home but found no new thoughts, only an intense, unalterable sadness. It was all dead and gone, that life, and as he hurried away he thought warmly of his aunt's cottage, the farm and the high chalk hills and vehemently re-affirmed that there was where his future lay. He wasn't betraying his East End upbringing. Through none of his doing, the link was broken, his life had moved on and there was no going back. He would build on those foundations, make the most of his new opportunities. Poplar was in the past, undeniably part of him but superseded, and he was immensely grateful to have had such a rich and rewarding replacement.

The rest of the day went well. He and Lofty had stood and laughed at each other in their civvy suits among the pigeons of Trafalgar Square. Mike was earnestly entreated to drop the Lofty and use Peter instead. "I hate being called Lofty," he said, "but couldn't do anything about it, you know what the army's like for nicknames."

"Okay, Peter," Mike said. "So, how's things?"

"Look, I'm gasping for a cup of tea," Peter said. So over a tea and a bun in the nearby Lyons Corner House they swapped their news.

"I've decided to go back to my old job," Peter said in a tone which had more than a hint of wistful regret. "I've thought it over and talked it over with dad and I don't think I'm likely to find anything better, not with my qualifications or, shall we say, lack of them. Actually, I've been quite lucky, they're moving me up to assistant buyer with a big jump in salary." Mike saw that his friend would quickly become a solid City man, all thoughts of an army commission and an adventurous outdoor life put firmly behind him.

"And, Mike old boy," he went on, eyes gleaming, "the next best news is that I'm back with Denise. You know the one I told you about. I've taken her out twice already."

"All right is she, this Denise?" Mike asked teasingly. "You know …"

"Great," said Peter. "A real fireball. Not quite like your German bints maybe but it's there, I can tell. It just needs a little more time. You'll have to come over and meet her sometime."

"Sure," Mike said unconvincingly. "Tell me," he went on, "have you missed army life so far?"

"Missed it!" Peter exclaimed, nearly choking in his tea. "No, not likely. I've been spoilt rotten since I've been home, I don't know about you. Breakfast in bed every morning. Of course it won't last, I start work on Monday anyway. But no, I don't miss any of that lot. I can get down to real living now. I've signed up at the local tennis club and there's badminton every Tuesday and my dad's dropped a heavy hint that I can have a new motor bike for Christmas. Why, do you miss the army?"

"No," said Mike. "Like you, I'm glad to be out. But I can't see my future so cut and dried as you can." He explained to Peter about starting work at the farm, just temporarily, he emphasized, and all about his aunt's cottage, insignificant stuff compared to Peter's high powered beginning.

"It sounds great," Peter said. "I envy you in many ways, I really do," he went on. "It's a much more natural and sane life than being stuck in an office in the City."

"That may be, "Mike agreed, "but it sounds as if you're the one who's got life organised and is going places."

"Well, there has to be some compensation for living in the Smoke, doesn't there?" Peter replied grinning. "Have you got a girl friend?" he asked.

"No," Mike shook his head firmly.

"Mm," said Peter. "You'd better do something about that, my dear chap. A girl friend would help you settle down in no time at all. And anyway you won't find street corner girls here for a few fags."

"A pity," Mike said banteringly. "I could do with one right now. Anyway, what have you got in this big city to entertain us on an autumn afternoon?"

"Till I've made my first thousand, not much, I'm afraid," Peter replied. "We can go and have a free look in the National Gallery across the Square if you like and go for a stroll in St. James' Park."

"Okay," Mike willingly agreed. "Let's keep it simple. And cheap, he almost added, with the thought of how the few pounds in his wallet had taken some hard knocks from his basic travelling so far.

So the two friends had dutifully toured many rooms of the art gallery, admiring the great paintings on view. Mike, for his part, was keen to do this, being eager to acquire more of that mysterious abstraction 'culture' that had for some time been growing more important in his eyes by reason of his conscious lack of it. The outward evidence of this culture, it seemed to him, consisted of the ability to talk knowledgeably yet casually on suitable subjects, one of which was great painting. Aware as he was of the superficiality of this attitude, he still embraced it as one accessible avenue of attack on ignorance, whilst holding himself ready to employ any other deeper and more genuine means that might become available to him. So he was ready to start by gazing keenly at the works in great galleries, hoping to find enrichment thereby and determined to remember as many of the big names as possible so that he too could lightly drop them into conversations and feel himself to be part of cultured society. This was a process that Peter had no need of, having absorbed an easy intimacy with many cultural matters from his minor public school days. He was much more relaxed about it all, knowing what he liked and what to ignore, unlike Mike who felt he had to look at everything in case he missed something vital.

After that they walked in the park for a while, strolling beside the lake and across the manicured lawns as they chatted mostly about army days, their officers and NCOs, either dragons or figures of fun at that distance, and of their late comrades that, although they were mostly good fellows, they were both quite easy at the prospect of never seeing again.

Then, after another snack in Lyons, they said farewell at Charing Cross, shook hands, said they must do this again before long and went their different and diverging ways. Mike, in the half empty compartment back to Luton, felt content with his day up in town. Although modest and low key it had satisfied his need for something different before settling down to work; he'd really enjoyed being with Peter and felt strongly that, if only they were nearer, their friendship might well continue, although he was more aware, now they were out of the army, of the considerable social and cultural gulf between them.

Then there was the morning in Poplar. That would be with him for ever but not really as a disturbance to his life in the village. He felt somehow as if he'd laid the memories of Poplar to rest. He had paid homage to them and confirmed that there was no further life in them for him. Now he was content and on his way back home to get on with his real life, with the past settled into its rightful place, save for that gnawing sense of guilt which would continue to swirl beneath the surface of his days.

CHAPTER 7

Anne on the Scene

Mike turned in his tractor seat to check the position of the three gleaming ploughshares behind him, as he completed his turn on the headland then accelerated away, whilst the silvery blades slid beneath the surface and started to turn the deep brown soil in flowing, dead straight waves. A pale November sun shone overhead, but the air was cold and Mike was well wrapped up in jumpers, woolly hat, an old overcoat and mittens for this exposed work on the cabless tractor in the middle of that open, fifteen acre field. Lapwings and gulls rose and swooped, endlessly wheeling and calling plaintively around him, his ever present companions on the newly exposed soil. For three years now he had done all the ploughing on the farm and he still felt a lively sense of pride in looking down the ruler straight furrows. Of all the jobs he had learned to do since restarting after national service, ploughing was his favourite, especially on days like this when the neighbouring chalk hills stood out firm and green above the level plain, the tall elms showed their bare and mighty frames over the nearby pasture fields and the sunlit air fairly glistened with a purity and transparency tinged with gold.

Mr Colston had taught him how to plough and to follow that up with the cultivators, the drag harrows, then the seed drilling and the rolling. He had been eager to learn, at first for his own pride in accomplishment, but once he had felt the supreme satisfaction - love is almost not too strong a word - of playing an essential part in the earth's yearly miracle of bringing forth a harvest, whether it be of oats or wheat, clover, potatoes or swedes, then he knew that farm work really was the life for him. He became aware of an almost mystic involvement in the earth's basic creative process which makes all human life possible and this made it easier to tolerate the cold and the wet, the winds and the hot summer sun, plus the bodily exhaustion at the end of the day that was the price of his deep satisfaction. He did, however, have it in mind to suggest that when the tractor needed renewal, and it was already old, they should get one with a cab!

During the long hours when the tractor went up and down the field, undeviating and monotonous, when only part of his mind needed to survey the work in case the unexpected happened, Mike often found himself with ample time to mull over the unfolding events of his life. This particular November morning Arthur was prominent in his reflections. It was just the previous Friday when that grand old farm servant had finally retired after being persuaded to postpone his going on two or three occasions for several months each. He'd got his old age pension ready to start and a good cottage rent free from Mr Colston for the rest of his days and he'd got an allotment to provide all the vegetables he and his widowed sister Ada would need.

"I'll be all right," he said, as he sipped his pint of celebratory bitter in the Cross Keys. Mike had invited him up there, wishing to mark the occasion in some way, for otherwise it had been a day of work as usual.

Mike knew that Arthur was to have a special dinner that evening cooked by his sister. "I shan't have to stay up here long, mind," he'd warned Mike, as he smacked his lips over the empty glass. "Ada's a damned good cook when she puts her mind to it and roast chicken's her favourite and mine."

Mike quickly refilled the glass. "So what time will you be getting up tomorrow morning?" he asked.

"Oho!" he exclaimed. His eyes twinkled at the thought of the possibilities. "Ah," he said, "'twon't do no good to change the habits of a lifetime too quick I reckon. Bet your life I'll wake up same time as usual. But as for gettin' up, we shall see."

It went through Mike's mind to wonder how Arthur would pass his days in retirement. He hadn't got any hobbies as far as he knew, except his gardening. Farmwork and garden work, that had been Arthur's life. He'd never married. Come to think of it, Mike knew precious little of Arthur's past and nobody he knew had ever spoken about it, certainly not Arthur himself, save for a few brief reminiscences of his time in the county regiment in the First World War. Mike promised himself he would get Arthur talking one day. He must be a mine of country knowledge and experience for one thing, his working life going back long before tractors were thought of, when most village men worked on local farms and villages were thriving, self supporting communities instead of dormitories for factory and office work in towns. Mike overcame the urge to ask him tiresome questions about his life, this wasn't the right moment. Instead he clinked glasses with him and wished him all the best in his retirement and many years in which to enjoy it. They walked back down the road together and Arthur, his tongue unaccustomedly loosened by bitter, ventured a comment. "Ah," he said, "'tain't been such a bad ole life, I s'pose. Could a done a lot worse, I'm thinkin'. Don't know but what I wouldn't do it all agen if I had my time over."

As he ploughed up and down on the tractor Mike ruminated on Arthur's words and marvelled at them. A lifetime given to the land in hard, often cruelly hard conditions and modest pay, out in all weathers, seldom a day off and with a whole battery of skills hard won and needing to be endlessly on call and yet he would still do it all over again. As one who loved working on the land himself and who was still wondering if he should make a career of it, Mike was very interested in Arthur.

There wasn't a job on the farm Arthur couldn't do and do well, he reflected. To see him scything around a headland was to see a high order of artistry in motion, scythe and man moving as one in apparently effortless ease. His stall-side manner with his ladies as he called them, in the cowshed, soothed and pacified them as, gently humming to himself, he moved about, feeding, cleaning and milking and the way he handled the bull, with courage and humane firmness, made him putty in Arthur's hands. Mike remembered, too, how Arthur had told him a little of his days ploughing with heavy horses. Now that was real ploughing, perhaps farming's highest art in the right hands, Mike thought ruefully, as the tractor exhaust blew warm in his face, not like his own mechanical efforts. He'd have given a lot to have seen Arthur ploughing with horses.

He didn't seem to be the romantic or idealistic sort, Arthur didn't. The mere thought of attributing such emotive labels to Arthur brought a smile to Mike's lips. But what was it then that he'd got out of his lifetime's work that would prompt him to say he'd do it all over again. Certainly he wasn't the philosopher deliberately opting for the simple, uncluttered life in order to think high thoughts. The life was much too tough for that. He had probably had little or no alternative to farmwork when he was young. There must have been some powerful satisfactions though, especially in the exercising of those many skills that he must know he possessed. Most probably, Mike concluded, Arthur wouldn't know precisely himself. He was just linked, umbilically almost, with the land, part of that great army - severely practical, prosaic and inarticulate yet often wonderfully gifted - whose unquestioned destiny it was to run the nation's farms in the days before mechanics finally took over.

The Mike of the new millennium came back out of what seemed to him the golden past, asserting that he was in a position to judge, having lived and farmed through so many decades. He looked back fondly and accurately to a time when government control and general interference was minimal compared to the huge volume of regulations now in force and being added to almost daily. Then a farmer was largely left to farm unimpeded by civil servants and politicians and could by his own hard work earn a decent living and sleep peacefully at night. "It's no use going into all that now," he acknowledged wearily. "They keep on saying you can't put the clock back and there's something in that, no doubt, but it often seems to me that is the only solution that would bring sanity and security to the job. As it is, I suppose we must go forward with the rest of the country, like Gadarene swine it often seems, and do what we can to remain true to farming's traditions which have served this country so well and created landscapes of unparalleled beauty and interest."

"Not that Arthur would be bothered by any of that," Mike conceded. "He would have carried on regardless, if he'd had a job at all. That's the point there, of course. If he'd had sons they certainly wouldn't be in farming today." Mike dwelt again on Arthur's simple but deep pleasure in walking down each day to work on his allotment as, continuing to plough his lonely November furrows, his mind slipped back once more to those far off days following Arthur's retirement.

"And now that Arthur's gone?" he wondered. It was then that his previous blithe, unclouded musings to himself grew more sombre. First of all Mr Colston had said that he'd do more himself - help with the milking again and look at machines to see if they were worthwhile, they were coming in on several farms around. But with Manor Farm's two hundred odd acres Mike couldn't see just the two of them managing things even if his boss did do more, flying in the face of medical advice and his wife's anxiety. Mike recalled with foreboding Mr Colston's spoken thought one day recently when they had been mentioning Arthur's imminent retirement," I might have to have a word with Tony. Perhaps he might come over and run things here."

Mike's heart had sunk at these words and did again now as he reviewed them. The first time he and Tony had ever met, he recalled, was soon after he had started work on the farm after national service. A cattle lorry had driven into the yard one morning as Mike was hosing out the cow shed, and a young fellow alongside the driver jumped out and went over to the house. When he saw Mike he called out "Ah, Service, I presume it's you. Undo the tailboard but don't let it down," then disappeared indoors.

Surprised and instantly hostile to this peremptory order from someone he had never set eyes on before, though he suspected who it was, Mike finished off the bit of hosing down he was doing, turned the tap off slowly and walked in leisurely fashion over to the lorry to ask the driver what was going on.

"Oh, that's Tony Pierson," said the little pale faced old chap at the wheel, "he's brought a few steers over to his father-in-law."

"So I was right," thought Mike, with distaste. As he was looking into the side of the lorry to see how many steers were in it, Tony came out of the house. "Have you done it?" he barked as he crossed the yard. Mike looked him up and down, his hackles rising at the imperious tone.

"Christ," said Tony, throwing himself at the tailboard and winding furiously, muttering half to himself. "Bloody townie workers."

"You arrogant bastard," Mike snapped back, clenching his fists. Then he saw Mr Colston come into the yard. "Ah, Mike," he called "I don't think you've met my son-in-law before, have you?" As he did the introductions the two young men stood glowering at each other, no attempt being made to shake hands.

Mike wasn't particularly disturbed at this hostile incident once the initial anger had passed. He reflected that he was unlikely to have been well disposed towards this Tony Pierson fellow anyway. He had wondered many times before that how he was going to deal with their inevitable meetings, whether he should try to be friendly and behave as if he had no feelings for Mary. It would have been worse, probably, if he had actually liked Tony. He might then have been forced to recognise that she had been quite justified in her choice. But now he was content to have got off on the wrong foot. He knew where he was now, out and out unfriendly, and it made things easier in his own mind.

For some weeks after that he still hadn't met Mary and, when he did, it was only briefly. He and Arthur had been a bit late after milking one evening, attending to a newly born calf and the mother who had to have the vet to her after a difficult birth. They were coming out of the yard on their way home when Mary and Tony drove in and parked their little red two seater sports car by the fence. Mike stopped and so did Arthur.

"Hello, Mike," Mary called, getting out and running over to them and shaking hands. Mike was staggered by this lovely, radiant woman standing before him, grasping his hand. There was no question of not recognising her, of course, but he was totally unprepared for the way she had matured and developed since she was seventeen when he had last seen her. This later Mary was a dazzling vision to his eyes, a vision of vibrant loveliness. "It's great to see you after all this time," she said. "How are you?"

"Oh, not so bad," Mike said with his usual self deprecating smile. "And how are you?"

"Pretty good, pretty good," she said, glancing over her shoulder to where Tony stood impatiently fidgeting with the car door.

"Well, well," she said, eyeing Mike up and down with approval, "you're certainly looking fine. Must dash now, we're late already, but we'll have to have a chat soon. Lovely to have seen you." With that she tripped off back to Tony, who made determinedly for the house while she followed, waving once more before going inside.

"Fine woman, that," Arthur growled, as they tramped off down the road.

"Yes, she is," Mike agreed. His head was buzzing with the sudden stimulus of the encounter, which he had so much been dreading but which, after all, proved more pleasurable than painful. How she could be so friendly towards him he didn't at all understand. "Was it genuine?" he wondered. He had been expecting at the very least some reserve towards himself and perhaps downright hostility, for, after all, she had thrown him over, hadn't she?

He was thinking about it all again as that November morning slowly warmed under the cloudless sunshine and the furrows continued to roll smoothly over, revealing the clean, deep loam which the birds settled on in clouds, eagerly filling their crops with abundant insect life.

He had seen Mary many times in the three years that had passed since that first brief encounter and always it was like the first time, just a quick meeting and passing with the odd few words exchanged, sometimes with Tony standing sullenly by, sometimes by herself but always as she was on her way to somewhere else in a hurry.

"Yes, she is a fine woman," he said to himself after each encounter, echoing

Arthur's words. Her brown wavy hair was more luxuriant now, her features had fined down to an exquisite leaner look, softened by a complexion of a pale rose colour and by her frank blue eyes that met his gaze unflinchingly. Her neck and shoulders were superb beneath whatever blouse or dress she chose to wear and her breasts were fine and firm in her maturity. All this Mike observed and appreciated without it disturbing him unduly, though he always felt more alive and stimulated by their meetings, however short.

He realised that the comparative contentment with his lot that he felt these days was mainly due to Anne. He pictured her fondly as he drove up and down the field. She would be exercising a horse on a beautiful morning like this, most probably, riding up and over the shoulder of the chalk hills above Church End and out along the Green Lanes on springy turf between high rolling fields where winter wheat was greening the chalky soil. Or she'd be out in the cobbled yard, grooming her charges, Sultan her favourite, a handsome chestnut gelding, or Polly the grey, brushing and combing them and plaiting their manes so carefully and lovingly, talking to them the while, their hooves echoing crisply in the enclosed yard as they fidgeted and changed their position.

They had a pretty good relationship going, Anne and he, he reflected. Never intense, never demanding and exclusive, they were real friends, with the added bonus of sex. He had been lucky to find her, he considered, and recalled again the dance in Dunstable Town Hall where they had first met. He'd gone there one evening with a couple of team mates after the Saturday soccer match a few months after his demob. They had been to Town Hall dances a few times before and the usual procedure was to prop the bar up for most of the time, getting their satisfactions from critically surveying the talent on offer as the dancers swirled and twirled their way around the fine sprung parquet floor. The truth was that they were all a little in fear of the opposite sex and aware of their technical shortcomings in the dances and needed a certain level of Dutch courage before they were willing to venture out.

On this particular occasion after a bout of egging each other into action he had recklessly gone out into an 'excuse me' waltz and worked his way through several unremarkable partners before being cut in on by this fair wavy haired, fresh complexioned girl with clear blue eyes.

"Hullo," she said, with a friendly smile, as they linked up and swept sedately on. He nodded and mumbled a reply. "Do you come here often?" she asked with a giggle.

"No, but I might in future," he quipped back, suddenly coming to life.

"Oh, yes," she drawled. "That'll be after taking some dancing lessons of course."

He winced and laughed and looked more closely at this girl who pleased him with her repartee.

She went on chattering away without the least reserve and they had finished out the dance, during which he learnt some salient points about her - her name and what she did for a living. "My work's all play," she said, and told him that she actually lived in Totternhoe, having recently come there from Kensworth at the age of twenty one to take up a job of caring for a string of horses for a farming family of riding parents and children to whom she gave riding lessons. She impressed him sufficiently to make him pluck up the courage necessary to ask her to dance again later, whilst his mates lolled against the wall with a pint in their hands grinning facetiously at him.

This time he had felt compelled to do his share of the talking. He found she was easy to talk to, not like so many girls he'd tried, who either exuded extreme boredom and indifference at his attempts at conversation or were as stiff as rakes and only half as friendly. He had straightway felt a warmth and friendliness from her to which he could respond, so that by the end of the dance they had both divulged enough about themselves to satisfy initial curiosity. He had shown her back to her seat, said hello to her friend Mandy and, as the lights dimmed and the band purred softly into the last waltz, asked her how she was getting home. "On the bus," she said. "The half past ten." Then with a glance at the clock "Oh, my God, that's in five minutes time. We'd better go, Mandy."

"I'll come with you, if you like," he offered, surprising himself.

She glanced at him with a teasing smile. "Oh, really?" she said. Then turning to her friend, "Okay by you, Mandy?"

Mandy nodded resignedly and the two girls got up and made their way around the outside of the dancers, followed by Mike who raised his hand slightly, thumb up, to his still grinning team mates at the bar.

Mandy left them when the bus stopped at Church End but Anne went on another stop. Then Mike walked with her to Middle End Farm where she worked and out through a side gate from the yard into a meadow where her mobile home stood in the hedge corner, hidden by barns. "You'd never guess this was here from the road," he said in surprise. "The times I've been by and never suspected anyone was here. Is it comfortable?"

"Yes, very," she said. "But I shan't show you now. Perhaps some other time."

"Okay," he said, smiling slyly. Then they'd shaken hands and he'd gone off, intrigued and with interest definitely aroused in this friendly, lively girl brimming with outdoor health and vitality.

"That's how it started," he reflected, as he ploughed on through that November morning, "but how is it going to end after so long and so lively a relationship?" He preferred not to carry that line of thought to any definite conclusion before he was forced to.

Anyway, from that beginning their friendship had followed a natural, unhurried progression when further meetings, both fortuitous and planned, had confirmed that they were indeed easy in each other's company, had plenty to talk about and obviously felt a mutual attraction both intellectual and physical. The inevitable frontier was crossed when he'd found himself one night a few weeks later, after another Saturday dance, in Anne's mobile home where, after a cup of coffee and a little light conversation, they had gone quite naturally to bed and fairly made the saucepans rattle on the little gas cooker.

Since then their relationship had persisted on the same basis. Always their meetings were at her place and after dark, save on the few occasions when they had arranged to meet at some isolated spot on the horse exercise trail and sampled the superb delights of love in the long grass, with her horse tethered among bushes for concealment. Now there was for him none of the previous hurried and sordidly commercial love making. With Anne he learned to relax and take his time and was rewarded by both giving and receiving sensuous pleasure of the most exquisite order.

Anne's employers knew very well what was going on, if only from being alerted by the barking of their watchful collie as Mike crossed the darkened yard. Indeed, they were soon introduced to Mike and proved very friendly. But they were young and had liberal ideas. The reigning code of conduct in the village was still very much opposed to such behaviour openly flaunted, so the couple were forced to be circumspect. The surprise is perhaps, at that time of growing permissiveness in society, that they did decide to be circumspect and have resort to subterfuge when necessary. But Mike had too much affection and respect for his friends and neighbours to wish to disturb the status quo or to ruffle feathers.

Right from the start there was an unspoken understanding between them that theirs was a light reined, open ended affair with no assumptions made, no promises given or expected. He felt instinctively that this was the way she was and went along with it without much trouble. They had occasionally touched upon their future as they lay together, relaxing after their considerable exertions. "I take my AI next week," she said one day. "I have to go down to St. Albans for it."

"Your AI?" he'd queried, idling his finger down through the cleavage of her breasts.

"Yes, assistant instructor. It's an important qualification for anyone wanting to get on in the horse world."

"Oh, I see," he'd said. "And you want to get on in the horse world?"

"Of course," she'd said roundly. "I'm not just doing this job to pass the time, you know. And I don't want to stay around here teaching kids to ride all my life."

"What do you want to do then?"

"I don't know precisely," she'd replied. "That's to say there are a lot of different openings if you're qualified. I could manage a pony trekking centre perhaps or run my own riding school. I'll probably go on and get my 'I' in any case."

"Your 'I'?" he'd queried.

"Instructor," she'd said, laughing at his ignorance, "the top of the tree."

"So you're a lady who's aiming at the top," he'd said, reflecting on what that might imply about their relationship.

"Well, I hope so," she'd said. "Ever since I was a little girl I've lived horses and I'm still pretty keen. How about you and career aims?"

"Me? Oh, I don't know," he'd replied. "I guess I feel pretty content with what I'm doing at the moment, although I appreciate that there's not much money in it. As to the future I don't really know what's going to happen. I refuse to look too far ahead."

"You might be wrong there," she'd warned. "I believe in looking ahead and having something to aim at."

"Yes, I agree about that in general," he'd admitted. "It's just that I'm really enjoying the present and don't want to spoil it by continually worrying over the future."

"Oh, I'm so glad you're enjoying the present," she'd said with a mischievous twinkle in her eye which he'd caught and with a laugh threw himself upon her once more in tumultuous passion.

So he hadn't walked out with Anne in the usual way. He hadn't brought her to his aunt's cottage either, though his aunt wasn't by any means strait laced and often used to ask him to bring his friends home, by which she mentally included girl friends. She looked forward to the time when he had a steady girl, one that he would, she hoped, settle down with and marry and maybe, as she told herself, 'take over this cottage when I'm gone.' She did wonder though, whenever she thought of Mike marrying, whether one of today's young housewives would be willing to settle in an old fashioned little place like hers. His bride would probably demand one of the new estate houses like those that were starting to go up at Church End. "Ticky tacky little boxes," she called such places, you could see dozens of them on the outskirts of Dunstable. Conceding nothing to local building styles or use of materials, they stuck out, in settled old villages particularly, like a rash of alien fungus in a beautiful garden. But, she had to admit, they had bright, well equipped kitchens with all the latest gadgets and bathrooms and indoor toilets and they were easy to clean. Whereas her little cottage had no bathroom, the toilet was a bucket and board in a draughty little shed at the back of the garden and the kitchen was so small you could hardly swing around, let alone swing a cat.

She thought back to the generations of farm labourers and their hard pressed wives who must have raised their numerous families in her cottage. She had to admit it must have been pretty grim. No, she couldn't in all conscience wish those primitive, cramped conditions on Mike and any new young bride he might wish to house and especially to bring children up in, though she herself was perfectly comfortable in her warm and snug little haven full of character that she had come to love dearly.

Then the thought came to her that perhaps the kitchen could be enlarged, pushed out at the back. She'd heard one of the girls at work talking of doing something similar to her parents' cottage at Eaton Bray and everyone had marvelled at such a revolutionary idea. But this had set her thinking of what she could do to her own place. So she took new hope that perhaps after all, if she could make some alterations, if she could afford it, then maybe Mike and any future wife might be willing to go on living there, a thought that brought her great pleasure. It would also be nice to have something worth leaving him one day. She was thankful that Tommy had had the wisdom to buy the cottage soon after they came to it. Five hundred pounds had seemed a lot of money at the time compared with five shillings a week rent but now at least the property was hers to do with as she liked. "I'll definitely look into the possibility of having the kitchen enlarged," she declared. "Even if Mike's future wife won't agree to settle here, it'll be much nicer for me. I'll have to get the name of a good builder."

Mike was very happy living with his aunt. She became even more of a friend as time went by. He knew he had no acceptable alternative anyway. His pay wasn't enough for him to buy or rent a house yet, and in any alternative he would have had no more independence and certainly no more comfort and care than he already received, rent free, at his aunt's. For she wouldn't take anything from him. "No, not yet," she always said. "Not until you're earning a decent wage." By which she meant until he'd got a proper job, not mere farm labouring.

He came and went much as he wished and didn't normally keep very late hours in view of his early rising for milking. Marjorie, on principle, hardly questioned him on where he went, knowing that prying would be intolerable for an independent young man such as she knew him to be. He, for his part, was usually pretty communicative and free in his conversation with her but not on the subject of Anne. That was his privilege to keep quiet upon, he firmly believed and would never talk about her even with his pals who occasionally saw them together, for nothing remains entirely secret for long in a village. Not that Marjorie was without her instincts in the matter. She began to guess from what she called 'vibrations' - pheremonal-like indicators, as with bees, which she sensed from him, that there was a woman somewhere in his life and was quietly content that all, in good time, would be revealed.

Mike's desultory musings were banished that November morning as the stubble was gradually reduced to the last narrow strip. He turned carefully on the headland to match up the furrows in an invisible join, then ran on down to the end and finished the job off almost with a flourish, to leave as neat a piece of ploughing as he'd so far done. Having unhitched the plough, he ran back to the farm on the tractor for lunch for it was time, in fact a little late, as he'd stayed to finish the piece off. He had long ago come to the very sensible arrangement of having his midday meal at the farm during the week, for Emily cooked for her husband anyway whilst Marjorie was away at work all day and took sandwiches.

Mike was looking forward to his meal as only those can whose appetite has been fine honed by a morning's work in the field in cold weather. He parked the tractor in front of the house and went round the back to take off his boots. Emily was in the kitchen in clouds of steam, dishing up the vegetables, and Mike was relieved to see he hadn't kept them waiting and his first words were to that effect.

Emily's face was serious as she turned to him. "I'm afraid Norman's knocked himself up again," she said. "He's quite bad this time. I had to have the doctor over, he's only just gone. Norman's sitting in his chair, though the doctor wanted him in bed. He's so stubborn at times! But I'm worried, I must admit."

She finished dishing up and Mike helped her carry the dishes through to the front kitchen. He'd offered no comment beyond registering concern. Norman was there, sitting in the high-backed old farmhouse chair, his eyes closed, his face deathly pale, his breathing scarcely detectable. Mike's first impression was that he could have been dead, he'd never seen him look so old and so ill. His gnarled hands were clenched white, gripping the wooden arms of the chair.

Mike and Emily sat down and started eating, talking but little and that quietly so as not to disturb Norman. However, after a few minutes he opened his eyes, looked around and smiled wanly on seeing Mike. "Would you like a drop of whisky, Norman?" Emily asked anxiously. "The doctor said it would be good for you."

He nodded weakly and she jumped up and rummaged in the big top cupboard where the medicinal items were kept, and soon placed a small tumbler with a modest splash of the dark gold liquid in front of him. "Can you manage?" she queried.

He opened his eyes again, reached out a tremulous hand and took the glass, placed it to his lips and sipped a little down. Emily returned to her place whilst Mike continued to satisfy the high point of his hunger, as they watched Norman slowly empty his glass and relax once again. Mike's mind was in a whirl. He realised that some new desperate and grave point had been reached in Norman's illness. It was frightening to see him like that. "But what," he asked himself, "is going to happen to the farm?" With Arthur finished, now there was only Norman and himself to carry things on and it was quite beyond the powers of one man to deal with everything that had to be done. He felt a great sense of crisis as he gazed at Norman, the one man on whom everything depended, dozing feebly in his chair.

They cleared their plates and returned to the back kitchen to fetch in the sweet. "How did it all come about this time?" Mike asked, when they were alone.

Emily shook her head sadly. "He was forking out some straw bundles in the rickyard apparently, trying to help you I suppose, when he came over all dizzy and had chest pains. He managed to get back across the yard somehow and I heard a noise and found him half collapsed in the doorway out there. I've never been so scared in all my life as when I saw him there. I thought for all the world he was done for."

"What did the doctor say?" Mike asked.

"Oh, you know old Hammond. He can be quite hard at times. 'You won't thank me for saying I told you so,' he said, 'but it's true, nevertheless. Either you give up work or it'll kill you. It's as simple as that.' "

When they got back to the table they were surprised to see Norman sitting up and looking around, more alert, a little colour returned to his previously parchment-white cheeks.

"Oh, good. You're feeling better by the look of you," Emily said.

He nodded and murmured softly, "Yes, a drop of whisky works wonders." He looked across at Mike. "I'm afraid there's nothing else for it, Mike," he said in a low voice, "you'll have to ask Arthur to come up and help with the milking. Tell him how I am, he'll not let us down. It'll only be for a few days, tell him."

After a few moments silence he went on, "Emily my dear, I've made up my mind. I'm giving up completely. The game's not worth the candle. Hammond is right. I wouldn't be much good to you dead, would I? Get on the 'phone to Tony and ask him and Mary to come over this evening and we'll talk about it again."

Emily nodded solemnly. "It'll be for the best, my dear, I'm sure of it," she said.

Nothing more was said at the table as Norman continued his climb back to normality, but Mike realised that drastic decisions were soon to be made in the running of the farm and wondered, with apprehension, how they would affect him. The prospect of working for Tony was not only unappealing, it was downright depressing. "I'll not do it," was his immediate inward affirmation. Once the friendly, relaxed and helpful presence of Norman, who treated him almost as his own son, was gone from the scene, Mike doubted he would be able to stand it. Better to start straightaway looking for somewhere or something different. "He'll sack me for a start, that's pretty certain," his inner voice said, and for the thousandth time thought regretfully of poor lost Dennis and of how things might have evolved otherwise had he lived.

CHAPTER 8

The End of the Affair

It was about midday on a warm and sunny Saturday near the end of May when Mike closed the barn door on the calf he'd been feeding, picked up his jumper from the fence where he'd tossed it and walked over to the farmhouse. The door was ajar, so he entered, then turned into the front kitchen to pick up his wage packet which Norman still put out on the dresser for him as he'd always done. "Hullo then, Mike," Norman said looking up from his newspaper. "Are you doing anything interesting this afternoon?"

"Playing cricket for Eaton Bray again," Mike said. "It's at home today, against Ivinghoe I think. How are you?"

"Oh, fine, thanks," Norman replied. "Cricket eh? I might pop over to see the game later." "Good," Mike said. "I'll probably see you there, then," and he picked up his packet and pushed it unopened into his pocket.

As he walked down the road homewards, Mike could see through the roadside orchard the new bungalow which had been steadily going up in the meadow beyond over the last few months and was now nearing completion. Mike knew that Emily and Norman were expecting to move in within the next few weeks, a prospect that was greatly exercising their minds, both in regret at leaving the farmhouse but perhaps more so in optimistic anticipation of the new life that this implied.

Mike was amazed really when he looked back on that day, eighteen months previously, when Norman had his last attack, at how well he had recovered. Of course, he'd been very sensible since then. He had taken things really easy and let go absolutely all physical work as well as all worries about the farm as far as humanly possible. It was nothing less than astonishing to Mike to see to what point he had been able to drop everything, his whole lifetime's work given up swiftly and completely in the face of the grim alternative. And now they would be moving out of the old house soon for their retirement into that spacious, well built bungalow where Emily would have, apart from no stairs to climb, modern housekeeping gadgets to make her life easier too.

Spacious and well built the bungalow may be, but Mike wondered about the revolution in living that Norman would have to undergo. How would he take to leaving that comfortable old house lived in by generations before him, its high ceilinged rooms furnished in traditional farmhouse fashion, full of character, settled and redolent of a prosperous farming life down the ages. All that to be given up to live in a bright, convenient and rather brash bungalow which would be the delight of any young, thrusting executive with a taste for a place in the country.

But that was the plan. Tony and Mary were to move into the old farmhouse. Tony had been brought in to run the farm straightaway after Norman's illness and had commuted from Stanbridge every day but that, although involving only three or four minutes in the car, wasn't an arrangement that could go on indefinitely. A farmer needs to be living on the spot to run things effectively.

Mike hadn't really been surprised at the speed with which Tony was able to drop his work at home and involve himself with Manor Farm. He had probably been expecting his father-in-law's health to deteriorate one day soon and was ready and eager for the opportunity thus presented. His three brothers could no doubt manage things adequately between them on their father's farm.

Marjorie wasn't at the cottage when Mike arrived. She worked on Saturday afternoons now and again when they had a rush order on, so he tucked into the plate of sandwiches she had left him and poured a glass of milk from the small fridge - a recent and much appreciated gesture to modernity - and changed for cricket. As he did so his mind was still on Manor Farm and the great upheavals there had been and the greater ones there would probably be in the near future.

He had to admit that he had been very worried when it was confirmed that Tony was being brought in to run things. Mike had been informed of this decision by Norman as soon as it was taken. He and Arthur had just finished the morning milking - for Arthur of course had immediately agreed to help - and he'd rolled the two big churns up to the road to be collected by the milk lorry. Norman came out to the porch to speak to him. "You'll understand, Mike," he said, "that I've just had to do something now that I've got to ease right up."

Mike nodded, but said nothing.

"So," Norman went on, "Tony's coming over to run things, starting tomorrow. I don't know how you'll feel about that," he said, with the suspicion of a smile on his lips, "but I'd like you to know that I very much hope you'll feel able to stay on and if it's any encouragement Tony said the same thing - he'll be glad of all the help you can give him."

Mike took this in without noticeable reaction. It was much as he had expected and he knew that for the time being he'd go along with it, so as not to add to

Norman's worries. As to the future, well, he'd see. "That's fine by me," was all he said.

"Thank you Mike. I knew we could depend on you," Norman said, as he turned and went indoors.

Mike adjusted the pillow at his back and wriggled to a new and comfortable position in bed as he peered back in his mind through the decades that had passed since those decisive days along the road leading to his present position. He surveyed from this still unclouded perspective a whole range of 'what ifs' that had lain along his path. He had taken none of those other paths, tempted though he might have been at the time, and yet he had not been at all aware of following any specific life plan, just dealing with circumstances as they arose. And yet, now, as he looked back he couldn't have wished for a better outcome. Perhaps that was just the mind's habit of becoming satisfied with the familiarity of any reasonable solution to life's potentials and ambitions. Perhaps if he'd taken some other completely different route he'd have been a millionaire by now or he may have attained to some other hugely satisfying status. As it was, he could tell himself with absolute sincerity that he was in the best of all possible worlds for him. He fairly purred with contentment, in spite of his 'flu, as he thought of Mary downstairs and all the family and the worrying, unstable yet ultimately hugely satisfying farming kingdom spread around him.

Still in retrospective mood he resumed the self exposition of his personal history at that stormy period of working with Tony.

Mike had reflected as he walked home to breakfast that he was sure of Norman's sincerity and good intentions but, as for being informed that it was Tony's wish to have him stay on, he took that with a large pinch of salt, assuming that Tony had kept his preferences to himself for the time being in the face of Norman's insistence on Mike staying on.

After his disastrous start with Tony, Mike guessed he wouldn't last long under the new regime. Theirs was an instinctive antipathy such as most of us feel from time to time and there was nothing radical to be done to improve it. The best thing was probably to put distance between them. Mary didn't seem to be at the root of it either, he thought, upon mature consideration. They would have been deeply inimical in any set of circumstances.

The surprising thing, therefore, was that he was still working at the farm a year and a half after Tony's coming and that there had been no big blow up, only the briefest of clashes from time to time. This was chiefly due to Tony, he was aware. He was sufficiently in control of himself not to seek confrontation with Mike. This wasn't particularly surprising, for Tony needed him, for a while anyway, to keep things running smoothly. Mike was used to the farm's ways and he had sufficient experience to be trusted to do a decent job of everything needing the tractor, for example, whether it was cutting corn, drilling or ploughing. And for those hectic months when everything was new to Tony and when Norman wasn't available, Mike's experience and solid reliability were worth their weight in gold. Not that

Tony ever said as much or even thought as much, in Mike's opinion, but at least he had the good sense not to antagonise the one person who could see him though his initial days at the farm.

Mike was at first strongly tempted to leave anyway, realising that there would never be any pleasure in working for Tony. But he decided to delay this move indefinitely, being loath to make things difficult for Emily and Norman, and he also knew that his sentimental attachment to the place was strong beyond normal reasoning. The provocation would have to be extreme to cause him to leave of his own volition - he would have to be fired. So, with the uneasy peace holding between them and still convinced that Tony was merely biding his time and that the final blow would come, he had been content so far to let things go on.

He had thought the writing was on the wall when Tony had casually mentioned one morning that he'd got two young fellows starting on the farm in a few days. Mike had paused in his sweeping and looked Tony straight in the eye, awaiting what he thought would be the inevitable follow on. But all Tony followed with was "There's enough work for all of us, for the time being anyway."

Mike's impulse was to say, "And how does this new arrangement affect my future here?" but he held back, not wishing to give Tony the easy opportunity of a final judgement. "If he wants me to go, he'll have to tell me straight out," he thought to himself as he resumed his task, the conversation over.

That had been six weeks ago. The newcomers had duly started and still he hadn't been given notice to quit. "Tony's probably feeling confident enough now not to worry about incurring Norman's displeasure if he sacks me," he thought. But as the weeks passed he began to wonder if that was the intention after all. There was enough work to keep them all going, that was for sure. Nick and Terry from Church End proved to be very pleasant young fellows and had quickly fitted in and worked with a will and were quick to learn.

"But what of the future?" Mike thought, as he combed his hair carefully in front of the mirror before cycling off to cricket. "With the Colstons gone to their bungalow soon and with Tony ensconced in the farmhouse and feeling that at last he's the boss, what are the chances of getting the sack then?" Quite high, he felt sure. "But it's no use worrying about that now," he argued. "It may never happen and if it does I'll face it at the time. I can look for another job if I have to, plenty do. Come to think of it," he mused, "I might just write off to see if I stand any chance of getting a place in a teachers' training college somewhere. It's getting a bit late perhaps, but I could at least see what the position is." The notion of teaching that Peter had lodged in his brain years ago had somehow refused to go away. "Yes," he concluded, as he watched himself in the mirror, "if I have to leave the farm I might try for teaching. I don't know that I fancy labouring on another farm and there's nothing else that's realistic that appeals at the moment. Teaching's a useful enough job," he reflected. "Somebody's got to teach the rising generation and I might just conceivably enjoy it."

So thinking he cycled off to Eaton Bray, only to meet Mary walking up the road carrying a basket of vegetables. He stopped and so did she. "You walking?" he asked in banter.

"Oh yes," she said with a smile. "I still can, just. Actually, Tony's gone to the races today in the car and I wanted to get these vegetables to mum."

"Oh," Mike said, puzzled. "Tony's supposed to be doing the milking this afternoon. That's what we arranged, anyway."

"According to Tony, Nick and Terry are doing it," she said.

"How's Tony liking it, running Manor Farm?" Mike asked, aware that he was taking a risk asking a personal question about Tony when he didn't know how frank, if at all, Mary was prepared to be about her husband.

"Oh, I think he's more or less resigned to it now," Mary replied. "Of course, he wasn't at all keen at first, you know."

"Wasn't he!" Mike exclaimed, astonished.

"No, not at all," Mary said. "Well, it's not so surprising, I suppose. He had a nice little set up on his dad's farm you see. With four brothers running the place, he didn't have the sole responsibility and he had more free time. It's harder work here and for a similar income, as far as we can see."

"Oh, I see," Mike said, meaning that he could understand her words though he couldn't understand Tony's attitude, when he personally would have thought that the chance of having sole ownership of a good farm was something to jump at, even if it wasn't quite as rich as the much larger one at Stanbridge. However, he decided it might not be tactful to pursue the subject.

"I see your parents' bungalow is nearly finished," he said, looking across in that direction.

"Yes," she said. "I do hope they'll be happy in it. It's a tragedy that dad has had to give up the work he loves but… " she shrugged her shoulders, "C'est la vie, as they say."

"And you're looking forward to moving into the old house?" he prompted.

"Oh, yes," she answered enthusiastically. "I've always loved that house. It was one of my chief regrets when I got married that I was giving it up. But now … I like it here much more than Stanbridge anyway. Well, I would I suppose, being born here. And how are you getting on, Mike?" she asked. "I know that you and Tony don't - er - what shall we say, don't exactly see eye to eye, do you?"

"No, that's true," he agreed, frankly.

"It's such a pity," she went on. "It would be nice if we could all be friends. But anyway," and she rested her hand briefly on his forearm," nothing has changed between us as far as I'm concerned. Well, I must get on now," she said, snapping back to the usual busy and breezy Mary and avoiding eye contact for once.

"Yes, so must I or I'll be late for the game," he said as he cycled off, pondering her words and content to have had at last a little close and meaningful conversation with her and to be reassured that the Mary of his boyhood days had in truth developed not only into a superb physical maturity but had also become a thoughtful, warm and considerate personality.

"Yes, it would be nice if we could all be friends," he reflected, as he crossed the little stone bridge over the stream at the foot of the slope, disturbing the heron fishing there, which flew off on ponderous wings. Yet the blunt truth, he knew, was that there existed invariably a huge gulf between what were the hard realities of people's characters in life's real encounters and the ideal ones attained only by our hopes and imaginings. No amount of wishful thinking could mask the reality that Tony and he were sworn enemies, not potential friends.

Mike enjoyed his cricket. In his mid twenties now, he was still hungry for success in those modest inter-village clashes and he put all he'd got into the ten overs he was called upon to deliver at his fast to medium pace that afternoon. The one wicket that he'd captured gave him immense satisfaction, especially as it was clean bowled. It had unleashed great rejoicing among his team mates for his victim had been amassing runs at an alarming rate. That was his second great satisfaction with cricket, the genuine camaraderie, mutual support, praise and commiseration that were inseparable from that band of brothers. He knew them all well by now. Some he'd known since schooldays and this helped reinforce that feeling of belonging which he so felt in need of.

In the leisure moments of semi-alert fielding which that level of cricket allows away from the wicket, he surveyed the ground and its surroundings with quiet conscious satisfaction. He loved the large, close-mown expanse of grass and the rough beyond, the young trees spaced around the boundary and hedgerows enclosing. The villagey feel of it gave him great pleasure, with the red painted corrugated iron roof of the smithy across the lane where as a lad he'd often brought the horses for shoeing, some old carpenters' sheds and a row of dark red brick cottages at one side. It wasn't classic village green scenery perhaps but it was truly homely and quite untarted up. He had given up soccer at the end of last season. He just wasn't good enough at it for him to derive satisfaction from his performance and the hurly burly of it no longer appealed, what with the mud and the injuries and the often appalling weather they had to endure. It was a game increasingly like war, with true sportsmanship increasingly lacking. There were plenty of youngsters coming up behind, so he'd hung up his boots without regret. But cricket was a deeper, maturer, more civilised and altogether pleasanter experience at which he knew he had some real if modest ability, and he hoped to go on playing for several seasons yet.

After the tea interval, which was always a jolly occasion with much banter and wisecracking, and whilst waiting to bat, he'd gone across to chat to Norman and Emily, who were seated in deck chairs among old cronies. The strong local accent was a delight and puzzle to his ears, as the gossip bounced back and forth across this circle of intimates. As he listened he felt a sense of enduring value in the act of country folk coming together amid the archetypal Englishness of the village cricket scene and he was content to be part of it. "What does it matter," he thought, "if I choose to spend my days in this little rural backwater? There's as much scope here for as happy and fulfilling a life as I'm capable of. And I know that I'm following my true bent, one that is really me and not forcing myself into some artificial way of life in a city perhaps, far from living contact with the land and those who know and love it as these people do."

His reflections ceased, as he became aware of a little wizened old farmer in a brown trilby hat sitting opposite who was pushing on with a tale. "Oh, ah!" he exclaimed gleefully, rubbing his knuckles together, "th'ol' vicar upped and married 'er an' 'im nigh on sixty an' a bachelor all 'is days. Course there was some as di'n't approve. Said as 'ed got no right to marry a wench scarcely dry behind the ears. But lordy, he di'n't give a damn." There was a great shout from the field and all heads turned. Another wicket had fallen. "Ready, Mike?" called the captain from in front of the pavilion. As he turned away from the little group, Mike caught the trailing words of the story, "an' they all said they'd never seen such a gleam in 'is eye as 'e preached his sermons with 'er sittin' in the front pew - - - ." Emily was smiling indulgently as guffaws of laughter wafted to Mike while he tightened his pad straps.

Mike went to evening service at chapel next day. It had become ingrained in him to do so for as long as he had been in the village and seemed, when he thought about it, to be as much a part of his life as the cricket, the lure of the chalk hills, the fields in which he worked, the changing of the seasons and all the many facets which made up life in the village.

Mike paused again in the mental re-run of his life. "How this country has changed; how the whole world has changed! Not village cricket, though. That seems to be prospering as it did in my young days. No rule changes, whites still required, tea still taken, third umpires a controversial innovation and only on television. All very reassuring. But going to chapel? The scene nowadays is barely recognisable. Along with the welcome rise in prosperity has come the undoubted downturn in this country's moral health. The village chapel sold and converted to a dwelling while the parish church is part of a group of churches cared for, thinly, by a non-resident priest, the vicarage sold off. Street crime? Tough on crime policies? Don't make me laugh! Why, I've witnessed the demise of religion as an active force in this country, seen it as it slipped inexorably away. We've become a land of atheists as even the archbishop of Canterbury admitted, and I've seen it happen and aren't we just reaping the fruits! Ah well, che sera, sera. Let's see how neighbourliness and a community spirit thrive on moral emptiness. What a brave new world we are entering upon!"

His aunt always came with him to chapel and they always saw the Colstons there and most of their neighbours in that society which changed but little over those years - the Kings from the thatched cottage alongside, the Holtons who kept the butcher's shop, the Saunders next door to the farm and the many others who made up that encouragingly large congregation. After the service they would stay and chat together on light and fine summer evenings in that unconscious contentment with a life lived close to nature which seemed destined to go on forever unchanged.

Later, after they had walked down the hill in friendly groups and dispersed at last and he'd changed out of his suit, Mike cycled back up the village to visit Anne who wasn't of chapel going inclination. As he walked his bike up the hill his mind was very much on Anne. In spite of how they had started out and long continued - no promises asked or given for the future - it wasn't going to last much longer like that, Mike felt sure.

He was coming to the stage when he wanted them to make a firm commitment to each other. He was beginning to weary of their more or less clandestine meetings and wanted an understanding that marriage was an eventual goal. He wondered how he was going to convince Anne to agree with him, though he was fairly confident and didn't pause to consider what his course of action might be if she didn't agree. It was still daylight, so they walked the fields where they were unlikely to be seen, whilst she chatted about the day's events and the riding lessons she had given.

"They're so good, those two children," she was saying, "and so fearless. I put up some jumps in the field this afternoon for the first time this year and they went at them like experienced jumpers. Lisa, the little one, she's only seven, fell off at one jump when the pony stopped dead." Anne put her fingers to her mouth to register her horror, then giggled. "Right over the top she went and hit the ground with a terrible crunch. It scared me to death, I can tell you. But she didn't shed a tear, just leaped straight back on and took the jump again. That's the sort of courage you must have to be a good show jumper, and I reckon she's got it. And the boy, Mark, he's only nine, but I'm sure he'll make a first class rider one day. He already says he wants to be a jockey and he might if he stays small and light. But you should have seen him take those jumps, he was glued to the saddle!"

"It must be the expert tuition they're receiving," Mike said lightly.

"Oh, yes, of course," she agreed laughing. "No, but seriously, they're just naturally brilliant. Of course their dad is a good rider and Bernadette's not bad, which helps. I'm hoping the two kids will do well in the gymkhana at Toddington next week."

"Do they do jumping for that?" Mike asked.

"No, not the gymkhana," Anne said. "It's mostly games. All sorts of relays with hoops and balls and things, and weaving in and out of canes and suchlike. It's good fun."

"You really enjoy what you're doing, don't you?" he said.

"Of course I do," she replied. "Don't you?"

"Yes, I do," he said. "But you sound so enthusiastic."

"Well, yes, I am enthusiastic, I suppose. You've got to be with kids, haven't you? I never even think about it. I know I enjoy everything I do with horses tremendously. It's just good fun really. I had a lovely canter on Sultan this morning along the Green Lanes with Mandy on Snowball. I could have gone on forever. It's a pity you don't ride, you know. I'm sure you could borrow one of the horses."

"Thanks, but no thanks," he said, shaking his head firmly. "I don't fancy it, I'm afraid. You have to start young to be happy on a horse, I reckon. Unless it's one of those poor dead beat creatures they use for novice pony trekking, and then all you get is saddle sore."

"That reminds me," she said brightly. "I haven't told you that I've got an interview on Tuesday for a job running a big riding school in the New Forest."

"Oh," he said flatly, taken aback. "I didn't know you had applied for a job."

"Well," she continued, "I reckon it's time to move on if I'm going to get anywhere in the riding world; I've been here long enough. You won't mind much, will you?" she asked archly. He looked at her long and hard, undecided for a moment whether to let his natural instinct have its head, to get angry and risk a row, but above all to be completely honest with her and tell her of his hopes to marry. He took a deep breath and controlled that impulse. "No, not if that's what you really want," he said coolly. If the idea of marriage had never entered her considerations, at least not effectively, it was no good him persisting with it or even broaching the subject at this stage.

"It is," she said, looking him candidly in the eye. "I may not get the job, of course."

"There will be plenty more to apply for, no doubt," he said, feeling the bitterness rising, in spite of himself.

She was silent for a moment. "Well, you know what we've always said," she murmured.

"Yes, I know," he admitted. "It's a bit of a surprise I suppose, that's all."

"I'm sure you'll soon get over it," she said blithely.

"Oh, will I?" he rejoined bitterly.

"Yes, I'm sure you'll forget all about me in a few weeks when I'm gone," she said, with a smile.

"Don't be silly," he insisted. "I'll never forget, that's certain. You're the one who'll do the forgetting. I'm very fond of you, you know. But still," he went on before she could react, "let's not dwell on it. It's been very nice to know you, as they say, so there's no regrets."

"Okay," she said, with what he perceived as a relieved laugh. She took his arm and they made their way back in the twilight towards her caravan. There were so many things he knew he wanted to say to her which he'd rehearsed over and over, but realised that most of it was too late or irrelevant and nothing appropriate seemed to come. As so often he chose silence amid the confusion of thoughts. He stopped outside the door.

"Are you coming in?" she asked.

"No, I don't think so," he said, feeling his heart give a sudden leap of emotion. "This had better be it, I think. The grand farewell." He smiled as her eyes opened wide at his untypical touch of theatre, and then there was a moment's silence. "Well," he said, "I'll be off."

He laid his hands on her shoulders, looked deeply into her inscrutable blue eyes, then kissed her long and passionately, before breaking away and walking quickly off. He raised his hand without turning his head as she called out "Good luck," and called back, "Good luck to you, too." He hated to contemplate the ending of anything that was dear to him. The acceptance of the end of a relationship brought one up against thoughts of the eventual finality of life and of one's powerlessness where it really matters. But, through all his darkly whirling thoughts as he cycled back down to Lower End, was the one reassuring conviction he could hold on to. "No, it would not have worked as a marriage, that's obvious. She's a career girl and her ambition must have its run, so this parting is probably for the best."

For the next few hours he clung to that to mask the very real pain and wounded pride of being abandoned. When he awoke after a surprisingly calm and quiet night's sleep, most of the pain had gone and he was well on the way to convincing himself that the break up with Anne was inevitable and that he'd been deceiving himself if he'd got more emotionally involved than was warranted. "I just didn't love her enough to fight for her," was how he soon came to look at it, and he used that judgement partially to drown his admiration for and fear of Anne's courageous drive for self fulfilment at all costs.

"She just hasn't yet met the one to make her abandon everything for love," he admitted ruefully to himself. After a few days more he wasn't sure that he shouldn't be grateful to her for preventing them from making a dreadful mistake.

Mike looked back, at seventy, over that episode which, thanks to a mercifully clear memory, he could still vividly recall with all its attendant mental images. He hadn't set eyes on Anne from that day to this and often wondered what became of her, whether she fulfilled her ambitions and who, if anyone, she fell in love with and married. It was, he knew, an episode in his life that had remained fresh and green because he had been so deeply involved, so deeply stirred.

CHAPTER 9

An Opportunity Spurned

On a warm and sunny Saturday morning at the end of June, Mike walked back to the farm after breakfast to help Emily and Norman move into their bungalow. Everything had gone more or less to plan. The plumber had only been a couple of weeks later than his intended date, the other tradesmen had soon recovered the lost ground and as soon as the plaster was dry a local firm of interior decorators had moved in to put the final vital touches and to install the new furnishings chosen expressly for the bungalow.

All that remained to be done was the moving of a few small choice items of furniture from the farmhouse, such as a favourite dressing table of Emily's, Norman's roll top desk in which he kept papers connected with the farm going back decades and a pair of cherished bedroom chairs, besides some choice crockery and glass, all of which would come to Mary in due course. Mike had arranged with Emily to run these few items down to the bungalow on the trailer, whilst they themselves would simply walk the short distance down the road to start their new life.

Mike brought the tractor and trailer round to the house and backed into the yard, stopping before the front door. As he did so, Mary and Tony drew up outside in the road in their little sports car and Mary got out whilst Tony drove off. She came down the path as Mike climbed down from the tractor. "It's good of you, Mike, to help mum and dad move," she said warmly.

"It's no bother," he said. "It's the least I could do, really."

"Yes, well, I had hoped Tony would help too, but he particularly wants to be at the races today." She laughed awkwardly. "And there's not much to do, is there?"

"No," Mike said cheerfully, "only a few bits and pieces."

"Let's go in, shall we?" Mary said, and pushed the door open. She went upstairs where her parents were collecting together some last minute items, whilst Mike waited downstairs. Inside, the house looked much as usual, very little was being taken, it was all awaiting Mary and Tony's occupation which was to follow immediately.

Mike looked around that front kitchen which he knew and loved so well. This was the one place in all the world where he had felt most at home, outmatching even his aunt's cottage as the interior dearest to his heart - the solid oak dining table and farmhouse chairs on which he'd sat for so many happy meals with Mary and Dennis as he'd slowly evolved from city urchin to country boy. The lovely old dresser stacked with willow pattern crockery, the massive fireplace round which he had sat warmly on so many winter evenings, the bundle of walking sticks in the corner with a couple of twelve bore shot guns amongst them, the big old wall clock slowly ticking the hours away, all so familiar, so lived in, so venerable and dependable and so full of his youthful memories.

An air of sadness hung about the room today, he felt. An unaccustomed quietness too, different from how he chose to remember it, lively with young voices and a cheerful, wise maturity. The old house was as if waiting breathlessly to see what its fate would be at the hands of the next inmates, the Piersons. Mike snapped back out of sentimentality as he heard steps on the stairs and in a moment Emily came in, followed by Mary.

"Good morning, Mike," she said brightly. "Well, it's come at last, the great day and now that it's here I only want to get it over and done with. Is Tony about?" she asked, turning to Mary.

"No, I'm afraid not," she replied apologetically. "He's, er - well, he's gone off to the races as I told Mike. Apparently he's going to win a fortune today. He'll be back by mid-afternoon," she added, hopefully.

"Fortune my eye!" Emily muttered in disgust. "Anyway," she went on, as if casting off an unpleasant subject, "it's good of you to help, Mike. The only heavy thing is Norman's desk."

"And I'll help Mike with that," Mary put in quickly.

"Oh, good," Emily said. "I'd rather Norman didn't have to lift anything heavy."

Norman came downstairs just then and the four of them stood in the room looking around for a brief moment, lost in thought at the quiet revolution that they were enacting, aware that they were now facing the precise moment of irrevocable change.

Norman broke the reverie with, "Ah well, there's only one way to look now and that's forward. So let's get on with it, shall we?"

"You're right," Emily said. "We've got our memories always with us, but for now we must make the most of the present and the future."

With that they all set to, collecting up and moving things onto the trailer outside. There was no sense of urgency, they had all day if need be for the little work there was to do. Norman's desk had been emptied, so Mike and Mary were able to deal with it easily and with a big heave the two of them lifted it off the ground nearly to shoulder height, then pushed it onto the trailer.

"Phew, that's that," Mike said. "Are you all right, Mary?"

She was studying her left hand. "I think I've got a splinter," she said.

"Let me see," he said, and came round, took her hand and examined her thumb closely.

"No, it's all right, really," she said, an unaccustomed flush upon her cheeks. "I'll get a needle from indoors."

"Okay, if you're sure," he said and released her hand, then, catching her embarrassment, he turned away, picturing the last time he had held her hand, years before.

When everything had been loaded on, Emily and Norman came outside with the two shopping bags of things they insisted on carrying by hand, and stood in the yard looking their last on the old house as its inmates.

As he watched them, Mike speculated on their feelings at that very emotive moment. A working farmhouse is not like any other kind of house, he reflected. It is more the heart of a kingdom over whose broad acres the farmer reigns, spending his years in struggles with the powerful forces ranged against him - climate, pests, diseases, market forces, red tape. Sooner or later, if he is lucky and hardworking, he might know success, he also might come to love his domain with a maybe unvoiced but tenacious love, the like of which only those deeply rooted in the soil can know. What must it cost in heartache to give it up?

Norman and Emily said nothing, but through their clasped hands Mike could feel the emotional charge as they gave each other support at this vulnerable time. True, their own daughter was moving in, so the house and farm were staying in the family, but it was nevertheless a definite change of direction and a decided break in their lives, a whole new shift of emphasis.

Norman turned the key in the ancient lock and handed it to Mary. "There you are, my dear, look after the old place well, won't you?" he said.

"Of course she will," Emily said briskly. "And we shan't be a hundred miles away, shall we?" Mike set off slowly with his precious load, whilst the other three walked on down. Then they all reversed the loading process in leisurely fashion, Mike having first been shown all over the shining new home, the last word in modernity. He privately knew which house he valued most, but concentrated on being full of praise and optimism, for, in spite of their cheerfulness and forward-looking attitude, he couldn't help wondering if there would be a period of anti-climax settling in, once the actual bustle of moving was over and they were left alone with their thoughts.

"Well, let's see if this bungalow makes a nice cup of tea, shall we?" Emily said, when everything had been unloaded and positioned. They sat down around the table in the kitchen whose windows had open views across the meadows where Norman had grazed his cows all his life, and sipped their welcome tea, which all agreed was well up to farmhouse standards. "I daresay we can toast in tea, can't we?" Mike asked on impulse. "I don't see why not, do you? So here's to you,

Emily and Norman, may you enjoy good health and many happy years in this new little nest you've built."

"I'll say 'hear, hear' to that," Mary said. So they raised their tea mugs and drank deeply.

"Thank you," Emily said. "Actually, we're going to start enjoying ourselves more or less right away, aren't we, Norman? Next Saturday we're off on a fortnight's coach tour of the Scottish Highlands, as a sort of celebration and to get our new life style off on the right foot."

"Well done!" Mary exclaimed. "Gosh, you kept that a close secret, didn't you?"

"No, not really," Norman said. "I only booked it yesterday. We were talking about this move, your mother and I on Thursday, when suddenly she said that we hadn't been on holiday since before the war, not a proper holiday, anyway. So we decided to put that right and Scotland it is to be. So we've got just a week to get settled in here first."

"I envy you," Mike said. "I've always wanted to go to Scotland, especially the Highlands. I'm sure you'll have a lovely time."

"We've got this brand new idea, brand new to us anyway," Emily said, "that now that we're going to have plenty of time we ought to start seeing a bit more of this country than we've seen so far. When I think about it we've only been to Frinton and Ilfracombe and Cliftonville. That's about the sum total of it. There's an awful lot more to see, so we'll probably be popping off for weeks here and there, we've got a lot of catching up to do."

"And then there's abroad," Mike put in.

"Oh, I don't know about that," Norman said, "unless it's somewhere where they speak English. I can't be bothered with all the foreign jabber at my age."

"And when we're home," Emily continued, "we'll probably be going out a fair bit. We've decided to join the bowls club in Leighton and we're even thinking of playing a bit of golf. We might as well, we've got a whole new life to lead and we're not ready yet to sit at home all day doing nothing."

"Good for you," Mary said. "People need to live a little and enjoy themselves, I say. You've worked hard enough all your lives, heaven knows."

"Exactly," Emily agreed, firmly. "Life shouldn't be all work, should it? There needs to be time for pleasure and that surely includes the retirement years."

"I've enjoyed my working life," Norman said quietly, addressing himself to Mike. "I've been very lucky, I think, to have had a job that has given me such real satisfaction as working on the land. My old dad went on till he was well into his seventies, though he did have heart trouble. He used to come outside and help us on fine days. He'd pick up a pitchfork and get busy and you could see it helped keep him alive. I can't do that, so it seems, not at the moment anyhow. I've had to cut myself off completely, make a clean break, though I do hope to keep a friendly eye on what's going on. But it's obvious I've got to make a new life. I've seen only too well what happens to those farmers who retire after busy lives and don't know what to do with themselves and how they just fall off the perch before long, more or less out of boredom."

"There's no risk of that with you, I'm sure," Mike said. "You don't seem to be exactly short of ideas for your retirement, do you?"

"When it comes down to it, it'll be second best of, course," Norman went on. "I have to admit that my best times have been on the farm, working. I was always happiest out of doors. It's been a simple life but a healthy one, I believe, in spite of my recent troubles and I certainly wouldn't have chosen to do any differently. But, as I say, when you can't go on doing that you've got to do the best you can."

"And we're going to work hard at it, never you doubt," Emily added bravely.

Mike realised as he made his way back to the farm, mulling over what had been said, how important Emily was going to be in supporting and prompting Norman, chivvying him along to fill his days with interest and purpose and he had no doubt she would put all she'd got into it.

A couple of mornings later Mike received a letter with a south coast town's postmark. It was one he had been expecting in reply to his enquiry about the possibility of a place at its seaside teachers' training college. Marjorie gave him a quizzical glance as he looked up at her after scanning the letter.

"They've asked me to go for an interview," he said.

"Who has?" she asked. It was the first she had heard about his intentions which, as usual, he had kept to himself until he had produced results. He briefly explained his actions.

"Why, that's splendid!" she exclaimed. "But what has brought this on at this particular time?"

"I'm afraid it's because I feel sure I shan't be working for Tony Pierson for much longer, now that he's moved into the farmhouse. Oh, yes," he explained, noting his aunt's raised eyebrows, "he and I aren't likely to hit it off for long with Norman out of the way. And I don't somehow feel like taking another farming job, even if I could get one. I wish I did, but I can't imagine being happy anywhere else and I wouldn't be so willing to put up with the low pay. So that's what prompted me to consider teaching," he concluded. He didn't add, though he might have done, that his finishing with Anne and the restlessness that had induced might have had a part to play in his application.

"It's a shame," was Marjorie's comment, "that it's a personality clash that's making you do this, but to be frank, Mike, I'm so pleased that you have at last decided to go in for something worthwhile. It's a step in the right direction, I'm sure." Whilst keeping pretty rigidly to her principle of not overtly interfering in his life, she had long been anxious and disappointed that he seemed so unambitious and from time to time was unable to prevent herself making some allusion to her hopes for his future. It seemed such a waste of talent to her mind.

"Listen to this," he said, and read out part of the letter. "At this college we especially welcome mature students who have experience of the wider world. We think they have a valuable contribution to make to education. From the information you have so far provided I am happy to invite you for an interview."

"Wonderful!" she exclaimed. "Oh, I'm so happy for you." She came round the table and gave him a resounding kiss on the cheek.

A week later he arrived at the railway station of that modest coastal resort in the early afternoon and walked along the promenade on his way to the interview. He was early, so he stopped at a beachside cafe for a cooling drink and shade from the hot sun. As he sat overlooking the glassy sea, watching the swimmers and paddlers along its edge and the scores of sunbathers lolling about on the sands, he luxuriated in the feeling of being on the loose, of an unaccustomed break in his routine, a feeling he did not often experience. He had the thought that it was worthwhile coming for an interview to such a place for the pleasure of a day out, even if he didn't get accepted.

He tried to put himself in an interview frame of mind, guessing at some of the questions he might be asked and formulating replies. But his concentration was being sapped by the sun, the sea and the pleasurable activities going on just yards away from him. "It wouldn't be at all bad to be in college here for a couple of years," he speculated. "Better than the middle of London or some other city." He had never spent a holiday by the sea and the sight of the spacious promenade with its pier, elegant hotels, its theatre and cinemas, its many cafes and restaurants and the busy press of traffic and people promised an exciting and interest packed location.

"Lots of distraction from studying, though," he supposed without undue concern. "Of course I might not get in," he acknowledged, thinking of his lack of academic distinction. At least, if it all ended in failure, no one beside Marjorie, who was sworn to secrecy, knew what he was up to. He had just told Tony he wanted a day off now for personal reasons, before they became busy with haytime and harvest, and had received a grudging assent for only reply. He still told himself that what he was doing was only an insurance against getting the sack from the farm, it was merely another option should he need it. He didn't really want to give up working on the farm, he still insisted to himself. But now that he was actually involved in another choice and sitting in that beachside cafe, he felt carried away by the novelty, the excitement of a seaside town and the challenge of getting accepted by this college to which he was making his way. Was the world still his oyster, he wondered, as he liked to think it was?

An hour or so later, after a rapid tour of the college's chief buildings in the company of the bursar, which gave him the impression of a small, sympathetic place of learning in fairly comfortable old world surroundings, he had been asked to take a seat in a small waiting room off the principal's study. There were two other candidates there already, a dark haired, smartly dressed young woman and an older, jovial Welshman who had just time to tell them he was an ex-miner from Penrhiwceiber in the fastnesses of the Valleys, who painted and wrote poetry, before he was called in. Mike and the girl exchanged sympathetic glances.

"Have you come far today?" was Mike's unoriginal but safe opening gambit. Talking to this attractive fellow sufferer was likely to be a good antidote to sweating out the suspense in silent anxiety, he reckoned.

"No," she replied in a friendly and faintly West Midlands accent, "I've just flown in from Salisbury, that's all."

In response to his raised eyebrows and incredulous 'Rhodesia?' she laughed and said, "No, Old Sarum." She went on to explain that she was in the W.A.A.F. and a friendly pilot had given her a lift down to a local aerodrome. Mike looked at her more closely. She was bright eyed and seemed completely at her ease, this girl who apparently flew about the country much as other people catch buses.

"And are you getting an air lift back?" he asked.

"I don't know yet," she answered. "I've got to 'phone the airfield at Tangmere to find out. The R.A.F. doesn't exactly run a taxi service unfortunately, not for mere physical training instructors like me anyway."

He reflected a moment that with an ex-miner, a service girl and himself, a farm hand, all up for interview at once, the principal probably meant what he said about looking for students with experience beyond the classroom walls.

"Was this your first choice of college?" she asked.

"It's been my only choice so far," he told her.

"I tried to get into Whitecroft in London," she explained, "but I was too late applying. That was all women, whereas this of course is mixed. I think I'll like it better here by the sea," she said, with a mischievous grin.

"Mm," he uttered thoughtfully.

By the time Mike had been asked where he was from, and watched her eyes in vain for the expected flicker of surprise when he said he worked on a farm, the ex-miner came out, still smiling broadly, and he was called in.

A man in late middle age greeted him by shaking hands warmly. He had a thick silvery-white mane of hair brushed straight back and blue twinkling eyes set in a tanned and weather beaten face. His bottle green corduroy jacket, light check trousers and plain woollen tie lent him an air of the philosopher poet somehow, Mike thought, reinforced by the young man's recent awareness of the principal's Oxford degree. After the shortest preamble he gave Mike a book and asked him to stand in the large bay window and read aloud. Thus was he introduced to Dickens' 'Old Curiosity Shop' but he didn't get more than half a page into it that day before the principal interrupted him with, "That's fine, thank you. You spoke up very well. It is very important for a teacher to have a good, clear speaking voice, as you can imagine. Take a seat, won't you?"

They sat and chatted informally and Mike, feeling quite at ease with his interviewer's friendly, relaxed manner, was easily led into describing his present life and work, his interests and preoccupations, and something of his transformation from London to village life.

"You may well feel drawn to teaching in a village school by the sound of it," the principal remarked.

"Yes, that is a distinct possibility," Mike agreed, although he had never really thought about it before.

"I can recommend it," the principal said. "We send students to many village schools for teaching practice, so we know them well. There's a wonderful, almost family atmosphere in most of them. It is quite different from city or town teaching."

After a few more minutes of general conversation the principal stood up, shook Mike's hand and said, "Goodbye young man. You'll be hearing from us in a short while."

Mike gave a thumbs up and an encouraging smile to the young woman as he passed through the waiting room. He stood a few moments in the sunshine on the gravel drive and looked around at the various College blocks, originally a large private school, the bursar had said, built mostly of mellow old Sussex bricks and with large Georgian windows. With many magnificent trees lining the drive, it looked a very pleasant spot to spend time in, an elegant, cultured atmosphere in which to prepare for the dimly conceived hurly burly of a teaching life. He wondered, as he walked back into town, whether his destiny lay that way or not. "That girl looked as though she might be worth getting to know," he thought. "And the ex-miner." At that moment he felt very much at one of life's important cross roads, conscious that there was a definite choice of direction to be made. The important thing, he vaguely realised, was to know himself, to be aware not only of what he could do best but also what was in keeping with his own character and deepest desires. Such serious thoughts having had their play to no definite resolution, didn't spoil his enjoyment of the return train journey through the high chalk downs and the prosperous Wealden farming country of southern England.

One of the curious anomalies of farming is that at a time when the population at large is enjoying the long, fine days of summer, going on holiday or having days out at the beach or in the country, having leisure time filled with pleasurable activity or indolence according to character, the tillers of the soil are at their busiest, have least time for relaxation and are least likely to take a holiday.

That summer was as busy as ever for Mike, with haytime leading with only a short interval into harvest work, and he had little time for personal enjoyment off the farm, but even so it seemed to him that the summer season of field work had got noticeably shorter, by a week perhaps, compared with his earlier years at the farm, which could only have been because of the effects of new methods.

The last gesture to modernisation that Norman made before his total abandonment of personal involvement in farming, was the erection in the rickyard of two large Dutch barns. This was prompted by Arthur's retirement, when all his vast experience of rick construction and thatching was no longer available and only Norman himself could have possibly continued the tradition. So now, for the first time, all that was needed to store the harvest was the ability to lay the sheaves in straight lines between the iron girders which divided the barn into bays, building up and up and trying to maintain the perpendicular up to the curved, corrugated iron roof. This was a job that could be reasonably done by more or less anybody after some practice. Mike himself did a spell of it and coped fairly well. It marked another little step, of many being taken then, on the road to abandoning the farmworkers' ancient skills in favour of the new agro-industrial technology carried out by operatives. So now, instead of the rickyard after harvest looking like a small, huddled hamlet of thatched straw cottages, it held henceforth just the two high, rectangular, girder-framed blocks of corn. "They'll still be useful for storing the straw when combines have taken over harvest work, as they undoubtedly will," was how Norman justified that dubious expense.

The other great modernising revolution on the farm for the second season now was the advent of the tractor-drawn trailer for fetching in the harvest, instead of the old horse-drawn carts. All through the busiest weeks of haytime and harvest the four working horses now spent their days peacefully grazing in the orchard and the carts stood unused in the open fronted shed, their shafts pointing suppliant arms skywards whilst the tractor and trailer sped swiftly between field and farm on pneumatic tyres, bringing back each time a far bigger load of sheaves than even big Captain could pull.

Mike found himself in two minds about the profound changes in farming he was living through and being intensely aware of. Horses, for one thing, were so traditionally a part of farm life it seemed callous, soulless to give them up. They brought colour, life and personality to whatever task they tackled. There was no comparison between taking the lively, high spirited Dolly down the road with a cart and taking the merely mechanical tractor. One was always engaged with a horse, aware and sensitive to the character of a living, sentient creature with needs, reactions, likes and dislikes such as we ourselves have. And once arrived, how Dolly responded to a bit of nose stroking and patting on the neck!

Progress was progress, however. Few farmers, young or not so young, could resist the appeal of new, exciting developments in their craft, especially where savings in both time and money seemed inevitable and the prospect of rising profits after so many lean years, alluring. With scarcely a thought among the hard, unromantic majority for the time-honoured methods, the sweeping innovations were welcomed with open arms, for in an era of supersonic air travel, who would seek to justify the retention of horse and cart speed on the farm? And all this at a time when wartime rationing still lingered and farmers were constantly urged and encouraged by the government to increase their food production by every means possible.

On all the farms around, Mike saw change taking place at breakneck speed. Combine harvesters were becoming more and more common, doing away almost overnight with most of the labour required in field or rickyard. Horses were disappearing at a very fast rate, being sold off the farms. The fields were beginning to empty of workers for the first time, as a deliberate policy, in farming history, a process that has been continuing ever since and scarcely anywhere lamented. Instead of weeks with gangs of men working together with all the human contacts that welded that society together and made those days so memorable, there was increasingly the silence of the lone, cab-bound worker confined to his thoughts within the incessant roar of some powerful machine.

Mike used to argue these things with his contemporaries at the village social club from time to time. None of them worked on a farm now, though some of their fathers still did and they had all been needed at busy times in the past. They had all gone to factory work in Dunstable, which itself was rapidly changing from the small market town he had come to know in the war with its little family shops, to super stores of national chains and to industrial estates with talk of London overspill and vast expansion to come.

He found himself in a minority of one when he said at the club one night he regretted the loss of the old ways on the farm, a statement which he realised sounded a bit odd coming from a young man. But still, that was what he really thought and in that familiar company he felt reckless enough to come out with it.

"You must be joking," said Jim, a thoughtful young chap. "I reckon if machines make work easier, so much the better. They're much more efficient too, which can only be a good thing, surely?"

"A bit of hard work never harmed anyone," Mike slipped in provocatively.

"Look," said Tommy, a keen horseman. "I used to have bloody blisters as big as saucers on my hands after I'd been forking sheaves all evening. I can feel 'em now. There's no damned sense in hard work just for the sake of it. Christ, no!"

"You could have worn gloves," Mike countered relentlessly.

"Hard work is not the point," put in Perce. "If you deliberately refuse to be up to date you're not doing the best for your line of work, whatever it is. And you can't hold the clock back, not for long. Change has got to come, like it or not. And why should you try to hold it back, anyway?" "Well, as far as farming goes," Mike said," I suppose I think that the old ways are more enjoyable, taken over all, and probably better for the countryside and the people in it. And is every change necessarily progress? And it does seem a shame to me, really, to lose all the interesting times of working together with all the fun you can have, just for the sake of having machines do everything. They're so impersonal."

"Well, work with machines might seem less interesting to you," said Jim, " but what you call interesting might seem to a lot of people like drudgery. Not only that, but it was poorly paid drudgery too. Some of those old farmers were not only slave drivers but they were skinflints too, they paid rock bottom wages."

"According to you," Tommy said with a laugh, "we might as well be back with bloody scythes and sickles cutting the corn and tying it by hand. That's when everyone was working together with a vengeance, by Christ."

"Yes, and they were worn out and good for nothing by the time they were fifty," Perce added.

"Oh, I know all that," Mike said, seeing he was forced to admit that there had always been change in farming. "I don't say there shouldn't be change. It's obvious that there should. But change is coming so fast these days. It's all change. And it's a different sort of change to what there's always been, much more drastic and done without thought of the consequences.."

"So much the bloody better," said Tommy.

"Go on, admit it, you're just a romantic," said Perce. "But you should face up to reality and the reality is that machines have been invented to make life easier and to be more efficient and they can't be disinvented."

"Oh, yes," Mike said with feeling, "and will people be any happier, do you think, when machines do everything for them? When they are just slaves to machinery. There may be a higher price than you think to be paid for all this so called progress."

"But of course people will be happier," said Jim. "Instead of being worn out at the end of the day they'll have energy to do really interesting things, all sorts of hobbies for instance."

"Look," Mike said, desperately searching for the telling phrase to overcome the mountain of adverse opinion, "when every farm has its combine and machine milking and there are no more working horses and no threshing machines coming round to the farms, how many men are going to be needed to work on the farms?"

"So what," Tommy shrugged, "if there's not so many bloody jobs. It's a price worth paying in my opinion if machines make life easier. There are plenty of jobs in town."

"Okay, fair enough," Mike agreed. "Though you might give a thought to what might happen in factories too, eventually. But anyway, it's going to be a mighty different sort of countryside isn't it, if hardly anybody works in it? What's it going to do for village life? All this worshipping at the altar of efficiency, efficiency, efficiency, it's not healthy. There are other things to consider."

"You worry too much, Mike old chap," said Perce. "It'll be all right, you'll see. Change is always like that. People get worried at first but it turns out all right in the end. There's always been change in villages after all."

"That may be so," Mike said, "but I'm not so sure it will be all right this time."

"Anyway," said Tommy, "now that we've sorted that out, who's taking me on round the bloody board?" He picked up the darts, ready for a game.

Mike's personal history re-run paused again in mid-reel as he savoured that decades-old airing of attitudes to farming. Progress, if that is the appropriate term, had gone remorselessly on since then as it always will, and he certainly didn't feel he could say at seventy that the future of farming was now settled and assured for years to come. The reverse, in fact, was the case. He still hankered, in his secret heart, for the past as he had known it, he knew he did and always would. He was an anachronism, he had to admit, though he didn't regard that term as in any way derogatory, though he had to admit that the younger generation probably wouldn't ever understand such an attitude or think it was any more than wishful thinking. But he had lived those happy, settled and stable times in farming when every week didn't bring some revolution or other and farmers weren't swamped under a tide of regulations from Whitehall or from Brussels. They, the young, had to deal with the harsh realities of today and they had his sympathy. What they desperately needed, and deserved, he knew, was a government, or at least a relevant minister, who showed some understanding and sympathy with the farming scene and was prepared to fight for fair treatment. Why should that be too much to ask, as it apparently was? With a mental shrug of his shoulders Mike peered back again into his past …

Tony told Mike one morning after milking to spend the day cutting logs in the sheepyard. "There are several fallen branches in the orchard," he said, in his usual cold and unfriendly tone, not even looking at Mike as he spoke. "You can cope, I suppose?"

"Yes, I can cope," Mike replied quietly, recognising the onset of a new era, or perhaps the resumption of the old one. "You want them all cut up do you?"

"Of course," Tony said, impatiently. "I'll have all those bloody trees down before long," he went on. "There's no call for the plums now. They're more trouble than they're worth."

Mike's eyes narrowed as he listened to this, this sacrilege to his ears. But it was pointless saying anything, and Tony turned abruptly anyway and went off. Mike brought the tractor round to the sheepyard later and soon had the belt onto the circular saw and the engine running smoothly. Then he took the handsaw and set about trimming up the fallen branches ready for pulling back to the sheepyard and cutting into logs. "What a shame to cut all this down," he thought to himself, as he looked around at all the mature plum trees which had for generations provided abundant good fruit. "And what will he do with the ground, replant it with fruit? I doubt it, he's not the sort to bother with it". He thought back to the many happy days he and the farm team had spent in those trees and all the fun it had been. "The trouble is, he's probably right. There probably is a declining market for this sort of thing. And yet -" It didn't somehow seem a good enough excuse for getting rid of the trees. It seemed as though he enjoyed having an opportunity for grubbing them out. He had no heart.

Mary came across the yard during the afternoon as the saw was snarling and buzzing and the sawdust flying. She waved and came and watched for a minute or two as he eased a branch into the whirling teeth with a high pitched scream. "She wouldn't like it if she knew of Tony's intentions with these trees, I'm pretty certain," he thought as she smiled, then went off on her search for eggs. He watched her go and the thought came to him that perhaps, in the light of what he'd heard recently, there were other things she might not like if she knew. Gossip it might be, but was there fire somewhere in the smoke?

About a fortnight after his College interview Mike received a letter from the principal, inviting him to take up a place starting in September. The moment of decision had come. In the days since the interview he had turned the question over and over in his mind, unsure of what to do for the best. He had felt vaguely uneasy about the course of action he was embarking upon. Marjorie, of course, had been enthusiastic all along and never doubted that he would be offered a place and would accept it. But once back in the village, at a distance from the College and the attractive impression it had made, Mike was in two minds. There was still no indication that Tony would sack him, though he continued to think it was only a matter of time. But even with that, did he really want to take up teaching? He was quick now to distinguish between the good time he could probably have as a student for two years in that seaside college and the thirty five years or so of hard, unremitting classroom toil that would follow. He had no experience of the latter save his own schooldays, which didn't really help a lot, but he could imagine that year after year of close contact with immature minds might have a stultifying effect upon his own mind, along the lines of the poor housemasters in Kipling's 'Stalky & Co.' which he'd recently read in his quest for relevant material.

When the actual offer of a place arrived, he sat down quietly the same evening and set himself to come to a decision now that he absolutely must. He was aware that his emotional response was to turn the offer down, he shied away from the idea of such a drastic change, but he wished to be able to justify that reaction, if possible on a logical basis. People, some people anyway, would say he would be stupid to refuse, that he was being offered a good career, not terribly well paid perhaps, so he had heard, but sufficiently well to be able to live decently, all in all a worthwhile and socially useful career. But, he argued, he loved the village, the farm, the whole area where he lived. He still cherished the hope of getting his living there where his heart was. As he focused intently on his innermost feelings, the strength of those feelings grew and filled his mind, eclipsing all other considerations. The warning voice that spoke of his imminent sacking and the uncertainty for the future was stilled by idealism and the predominance of emotion over logic. "But surely," he argued, "if my emotions about the land are so strong, the logical thing to do is to accept that fact and follow those emotions. They are me and I should surely not deny what is essentially my deepest need in the name of some supposed external logic."

"What I'll actually be saying," he told himself, half aloud as he sought for clarity, "if I turn this offer down, is that when I'm sacked as I surely will be, make no mistake, when I'm sacked I'll get a job on another farm. That's what I'm saying if my feelings are so strong for the land. And is that what I'm prepared to do? Yes, when it comes to it I am, if I can find the right one. Unless," he reflected under sudden inspiration, "unless I go in for something closely related to farming, like - er - like the animal feed industry for example, or corn merchants, perhaps. Yes, there may be alternatives there, I can at least look into the possibilities." Having recycled this thought through his brain several times and approved of it, he had no hesitation in writing a short note to the college principal, regretfully declining his offer of a place and apologising for wasting his time. He felt genuinely sorry about this, he'd liked the man and the place very much, but he reflected that he probably needed that abortive sortie for him to see clearly what was fundamentally important in his life and to act on it. He felt light hearted with the letter gone, quite certain that he had taken the right decision.

Marjorie, although clearly disappointed, kept most of her feelings to herself as she could see that her nephew's mind was quite made up. "I just hope he doesn't come to regret it," she thought. "He may not get another chance like that." She consoled herself with the thought that at least the air was now cleared and Mike must live with his decision, it was his life after all. He straightaway looked in the copies of some of Norman's old farming magazines he'd been given from time to time. These were the source of much information on the farming world and he always read them with great interest and derived much benefit, especially from articles written by practising farmers. Now however, he was particularly interested in the advertisements of those companies whose business it was to supply farms with everything they needed, from binder twine to combine harvesters.

The cattle feed firms in particular, he saw, had addresses in Liverpool, Bristol, Glasgow or London, big cities far from farms, and his immediate reaction was to shy away from approaching them. Thinking about it and looking at the situations vacant columns, he realised that such firms probably needed men to go round an allocated area of the country drumming up sales to local merchants who sold retail to the farmers. He knew there were such salesmen, for several called regularly at Manor Farm though he hadn't had dealings with them. He wondered whether he was cut out to be a salesman. The idea didn't appeal much. He doubted whether he would be any good at the smooth patter, the glib expertise, the easy approach to strangers that such people need. Would his experience of farming be of benefit to him in any of this, he wondered. "It's no use being defeatist about it," he thought. "I'll never know if I can succeed unless I try. After all, a living is not going to fall ready made into my lap. I've got to make an effort. But then again," he admitted a moment later, "it's a waste of time trying for something that is the antithesis of your character. It won't succeed and you certainly won't be happy doing it."

In the end he decided to wait a little longer before making any application, to ponder on what sort of niche in the agricultural world he might try for and be suitable for, or even to see if there was a local farm with a vacancy that he might consider working for. Perhaps he would have a word with Norman one day soon to see what his advice might be.

One Saturday in the middle of harvest work Mike came back to the farm early after breakfast to look the tractor over before starting work. He noticed Tony's sports car standing in the yard by the farmhouse door which stood open. Then, as he started tinkering with the carburettor, he heard raised voices from the house and in a moment Tony came out and got quickly into the car. Mary followed him, very agitated, as Mike saw in a quick glance up. As the car started up she called out "Tony, Tony," in an anguished voice, but with a roar it sped off up the slope and away. Mary stood there a moment, evidently in some distress, then, wiping her eyes, she turned to go back indoors and, as she did so, caught sight of Mike in the corner by the barns. She turned her head away immediately and rushed inside, slamming the door behind her. Mike, feeling guilty about intruding on private troubles even unintentionally, went on with his work, trying to concentrate on the fuel pipe problem, but at least half his mind was speculating about what he had just seen and heard. Something was up, that was certain. What could it be, he wondered? Just a little ruffling of the surface as was inescapable from time to time, or was it a sign of deeper trouble in the seven year old marriage? He hadn't seen much of Mary over the last few weeks, in fact ever since the couple had moved into the farmhouse, but in the few glimpses of her that he'd had she had not looked her usual cheerful self but was as if pre-occupied and rather solemn. He hadn't dwelt on it, thinking she was merely busy settling in.

It was, of course, only to be expected that her time and attention would be much taken up with the new domestic arrangements, but he was a little disappointed that he hadn't so far had an opportunity to ask her what she thought about living once more in her childhood home and to share with her his own strong feelings about the place. But now this latest display of discord! It seemed to confirm other disturbing signs and odd things he'd heard. He didn't know what to think, but for the moment tried to push the whole business to the back of his mind as being no concern of his. "But it's funny that Tony has driven off like that," he thought. "How about the morning's harvest work?"

Some time later Harry Blake came into the yard, saying he'd just been asked by Tony to put in a morning's work as he, Tony, had to go off on important business. So work went ahead as intended and Nick and Terry shrugged their shoulders when they turned up and laughed at the news of the boss's absence, though Mike kept quiet about the scene he'd witnessed.

It was after the cricket match at Tilsworth that afternoon, as he was cycling back alone, most of the others having motor bikes or small cars, that Mike saw a lone uniformed figure ahead of him just beyond Stanbridgeford station. As he drew nearer he suddenly realised that the outline was familiar and a few more yards confirmed this. He slid to a halt as he came alongside the walker and burst out, "Well, blow me if it isn't Mac!"

There was instant recognition on both their faces which were wreathed in smiles as they shook hands and looked each other over with great enthusiasm.

"What are you doing here?" Mike demanded. "Are you on leave?"

"No, not on leave, I'm out, finished."

"Good Lord!" Mike exclaimed. "Well, it's smashing to see you again. How long has it been? Eight or nine years I should think."

"Yes, It must be all of that," Mac agreed.

Mike pushed his bike as they made their way to Lower End, swapping information as to their activities.

"The last time I was home here," Mac said, "was at the time Dennis was killed. I went to the funeral." They both reflected a moment on that key to their shared adolescence.

"You're looking well enough, anyway," Mike went on, surveying his friend who stood a tanned six feet, strong looking and darkly handsome.

"So are you," Mac responded. "I've been in Gib ever since that last leave, except for the last few months up at Kinloss."

"And now you've really finished with the R.A.F., have you? Did they kick you out or did you quit?"

"I've come out voluntarily now my ten years are up. I didn't fancy signing on for any more. I made it to corporal, as you can see," Mac said showing his sleeve. "But from there on promotion is very slow, almost a case of dead men's shoes. Plus the fact that my wife to be didn't fancy being a service wife."

"Wife to be, eh!" Mike exclaimed.

"Yes," Mac said proudly." My little Jeannie, a Scots lass from Inverness."

"And when is this to be?"

"Oh, not for another eight months or so. It's going to be a spring wedding."

By the time Mike had brought his friend up to date with many village matters, they had reached his aunt's cottage.

"There's been a few changes made, I daresay," Mac said, looking around, but the old place seems much the same as far as I can see."

"You'll see the Colston's new bungalow on the way to your house," Mike said. "That's the only new building in Lower End so far."

"What are you doing this evening?" Mac asked, as he was about to go.

"Not a lot," Mike replied, with the unspoken thought that most of his Saturday nights used to be spent with Anne and that since then he had done more reading.

"Come and have a drink then," Mac said. "Up at the Cross Keys, perhaps. I'll call for you at eight."

"Okay," Mike agreed and they parted, Mac to go on to his mother's house towards Eaton Bray and Mike indoors, each reflecting on the other, both pleased that after a gap of ten years their friendship was ready to carry on as if those years had never been.

Up at the Cross Keys later, in the crowded, convivial Saturday night atmosphere, the two friends propped themselves up at the end of the bar and dug themselves deeper into companionship and confidences.

"And what of the future, now you're out?" Mike asked, sipping his pint.

"A job, you mean? Well, I've been on to Vauxhall's already and I've got an interview next Wednesday. I was in the technician branch you see, engine maintenance and all, that so I reckon I won't have any difficulty in landing a job."

"So you'll be settling down here when you're married?"

"That's right. Jeannie will come down here, she's keen to come. I've got to find somewhere for us to live, of course. We could stay with mum, I suppose, but it's not the best solution, is it?"

Mike agreed that it was best looked on as a last resort.

"And there's one thing I want to ask you," Mac went on. "I know it's a hell of a long way to Inverness and I won't mind if you say no, but I wanted to ask you to be best man at my wedding."

"Well, thanks," Mike said, surprised and pleased. "Right, there's no hesitation, I'll do it. Provided I can get time off from work," he concluded, with the unspoken proviso of "wherever work happens to be by then."

"That's smashing," Mac said. "Here, drink up and let me refill your glass and we'll drink to it."

As Mac was attending to the drinks, Mike felt a hand on his shoulder and looked round to find Perce Tompkins standing beside him. "Hullo, Mike," he said, "have you finished harvest yet?"

"No, not quite," Mike said. "We've got another field of wheat to pick up on Monday if it stays dry."

"Oh, I see," Perce said. "Only I saw your governor at the races today, so I thought perhaps you'd finished."

"No," Mike said, with a forced laugh. "I guessed that's where he might have gone when he told Harry Blake he'd got something important to attend to." The image of Mary standing in some distress, calling to her husband came painfully to mind.

"Oh, it was important business all right," Perce said, "judging by the smart piece hanging on his arm. I'll bet his wife doesn't know about that."

"No, I'll bet she doesn't," Mike agreed mechanically.

"Actually, I've seen your governor and this woman about together before," Perce went on. "Once I remember, it was in the Railway Hotel at Towcester, near the course. Bold as brass they were, coming down from some upstairs room, looking very pleased with themselves. He's a bloody lecher, that one, if you ask me."

"Did you lose your shirt today?" Mike asked quickly, trying both to feign indifference and to deflect Perce from getting too keen on his subject.

"No," he said. "I actually made a few quid today, had the winner of the 2.30. That's why we're celebrating," and he nodded over to the corner where Tommy was in animated talk with a couple of girls, all dolled up.

Mac came back with the drinks and he and Perce exchanged a few friendly words before Perce went off to order another round and Mac sat down.

They lifted their glasses and drank to Mike's being best man then to Jeannie and to their mutual good luck and good health. But a terrible black cloud was on Mike's mind now. Perce's words resounded in his head. Poor Mary, she was being two timed, it was obvious. His vague suspicions were now confirmed. "That rotten sod, Tony," he muttered to himself and involuntarily ground his teeth and clenched his knuckles white in anger and frustration.

CHAPTER 10

The Storm Breaks

No matter how busy the season, rare was the Sunday when Mike didn't make time for his walk over the Knolls. These high, open chalk hills were his habit and delight ever since he came back to the village after national service and way back before that to his years of playing there as a boy. This delight in altitude and wildness was doubled by the unending interest of looking down upon the well loved, man-created scene that spread far out below the miles of chalk escarpment.

He took the rutted track upward in the early afternoon following his evening at the Cross Keys with Mac. He was alone; his aunt, who sometimes accompanied him, declined on this occasion on account of her back which was increasingly arthritic. He never tired of the thrill he felt as he climbed the grassy slopes whilst the view quickly widened and extended out over the nearer orchards, heavy now with plums, and the elm fringed meadows beyond the roofs of cottages into the myriad fields and farms that receded to the blue wooded hills of the far distance.

His mind, which had been busy with other matters, let them drop away as the splendour of the scene invaded his senses. He stopped a moment to sit on top of one of the pitted slopes to admire and drink in the rural beauty that lay below, aware that no words could possibly express the feelings that stirred within him. He felt a oneness with all the summer loveliness he could see, there was something in his soul and in the scene which merged as a river empties into the sea, filling him with great joy and peace.

He particularly loved this view in full summer when the fields held ranks of golden shocks, marching dozens abreast to the horizon. He gazed closely down at the nearer fields of Manor Farm where he himself had worked to cut and stand the corn and which were now almost emptied, leaving the bare stubble where he pictured the creeping coveys of partridges and the odd brilliant plumed pheasant taking their fill. His sense of harmony with the scene was not now as a mere observer but was strengthened by his work within it. Those golden fields, he had ploughed them in the autumn, sown them, rolled them, spent hours upon them so that he knew them intimately, and in return they gave him the wonderful satisfaction of sharing in their fruitfulness.

As he got up and walked on, climbing the steepening track which led to the topmost point, he rejoiced again that this lovely place was his home. He marvelled anew at the accident of fate - or providence - that had brought him, an East End boy and surely undeserving, to the village and kept him there so that now, even should he for some employment reason have to move away, he would forever hold this earthly paradise in his heart as home.

With his back now to the wider scene as he walked through grass studded with pale blue scabious, tiny clumps of sky blue harebells and tough purple knapweed, his thoughts turned again to Mary. He'd thought of little else during a disturbed night. Did she know she was being deceived, he wondered. Perhaps she suspected. In any case, he told himself, it was no business of his. Yet that was false. It was his business because, well, he couldn't help it being his business. All he knew was that he hated to see her unhappy and he knew she was unhappy at present. And he hated to think that she was being shabbily treated, lied to probably, the victim of deceit and infidelity.

He knew he could never say anything to her of what he had heard. That would only risk making her more wretched. So he was going to be in the position of a powerless and unwilling observer of a sordid and miserable situation. That thought plunged him into a gloom which filled his mind in spite of the beauty unfolding as he neared the top of the hill, where a vast panorama of fertile plain and green enfolding hills spread out around him and a cooling breeze modified the summer heat.

What more could a man want, he wondered, than what Tony already possessed. He mulled over Perce's words which were as burned into his brain. There was no room for mistake in them. Tony was definitely having an affair. The distress, too, that he had seen on Mary's face as Tony drove away yesterday and the tears he could swear were there, they were convincing enough evidence now that all was far from well.

Mike sat on the bench at the top of the beautiful Knolls and churned these things over and over in his mind and scarcely saw the mighty green canopy of beech groves below him whose tops were like a heaving sea around the steep slopes, nor the Sunday gliders silently wheeling in the thermals out over the long arm of Downs running above the broad vale.

At the same time in the back kitchen of the farmhouse, Mary and her mother were beginning the washing up. They were a few weeks into the routine they were creating of Emily and Norman coming to have Sunday lunch with their daughter and son-in-law. Norman was snoozing on the large chesterfield in the dining room whilst Tony, in an armchair, was listlessly going through the Sunday papers.

"Now Mary," Emily said, making sure the door was firmly closed, "there's something the matter, isn't there? I can feel it like a wall between you two."

"Yes, I'm afraid there is," Mary said after a brief hesitation. "I'm sorry it shows. I don't want to inflict our troubles on you, you've got enough on your hands with dad."

"Is it serious?" Emily asked.

"I don't know," she answered. "Yes, I suppose it is. I've tried to talk things over with Tony but he won't. He just says it is all imagination. But of course I know it isn't."

"Yes, but what do you mean?" her mother asked. "Is he just less loving or what?"

"Let's face it mum," Mary said with a wry smile," he never was very loving. Looking back, I can see it was mostly me making the running."

"That's true," Emily said. "Mind you, that's the way it is in the majority of cases, I'm thinking. But you would have him at all costs. Not that I blame you my dear, he was an attractive catch."

"It's the loving that's missing more or less completely now," Mary went on. "Though I think I could stand that, strangely enough. It's the cutting me out of his life in all sorts of ways that I can't stand. I am worried, mum, I've got to admit it. We never do anything together now, never go out, nothing."

"Mm," said Emily. "It sounds pretty bad, worse than I feared. You'll just have to be frank with him and tell him of your anxieties."

"I've tried many a time over recent weeks but he won't listen. He just flies into a rage and storms out."

Emily pondered on this for some moments. "So do you think there's another woman involved?" she said.

"I don't know. There could be, I suppose. Yes, it's most likely, I have to agree. It all started since he became very keen on Towcester Races and I don't think it's a mere coincidence that he hardly ever takes me along. He always dreams up excuses to go alone."

"Have it out with him then. Tell him to his face what you suspect," Emily said forthrightly. "It seems to me he needs a good straight talking to, your husband. You've a right to know exactly where you are."

"I was hoping it wouldn't come to that. We might both say things that won't easily be forgotten or forgiven."

"My dear girl," her mother said heatedly, "it's no use you going on as you are, you'll break in the end."

"I thought that, too," Mary said. "But somehow I don't think I will. I've had my bad moments lately, I'll admit, but I somehow feel strong enough to cope. I must have a streak of family toughness in me, I think."

"That's just as well, by the sound of it," Emily said, adding grimly, "And perhaps it's just as well you haven't got any children."

"Yes, that's what I say. It's probably a blessing in disguise, for I must say I've often wished for some. Yet they do say children can help hold a rocky marriage together, don't they?"

"Perhaps things might improve," Emily said hopefully. "Many marriages go through bad patches like yours but manage to come out of them, sometimes even stronger."

"I know," Mary said wistfully. "I've always wanted a really strong marriage, a full partnership. And I believed I'd got it for a while. But now …?" She shook her head sadly and gazed thoughtfully out of the window.

"Perhaps it's just as well, too," Emily said, "that your father hasn't yet been able to deal with all the legal papers transferring the farm to Tony."

"You won't worry dad with any of this, will you?" Mary begged earnestly.

"No, of course not," she replied.

"It's good to have talked it over with you, mum," Mary said. "I feel better for it."

"That's what mothers are for, aren't they?" Emily said with a smile and gave her daughter a loving hug. "And don't forget that I'm here and ready to listen anytime. You don't need to bottle everything up inside yourself."

Mary stayed behind in the kitchen to clean the saucepans and oven tins, whilst her mother went to join the other two in the dining room. It was true, she felt sure, that she was strong enough to see her predicament out to whatever conclusion it might reach. To that end she found herself once again passing her married life in review, seeking reasons for the present trouble and wondering if there were grounds for optimism.

How she had loved Tony in those early days! He was handsome, decisive, thoroughly manly she thought him and an excellent horseman. Everything, in fact, that her adolescent dreams could have desired. And of course he was a farmer from a long farming background. That, with those other attributes, clinched the matter for Mary. The match would be ideal, she had thought. The family would be delighted, she knew, to have the farm in sound, experienced hands. All thoughts of rivals for her hand, of which there was no shortage, were forgotten. Even the strong upsurge of feeling for Mike, she recalled, had sputtered out with his absence and the overwhelming presence of Tony.

She searched her memory for early signs that hers was not indeed a marriage made in heaven. She paused in her cleaning, hands immersed in water, her eyes lost in the distance of the window view as she dragged long buried truths to her reluctant consciousness. The memory of her first honeymoon night was still painful. It had been a fiasco and a deeply wounding disappointment to her because so keenly looked forward to. She had admitted as much to herself at the time, then buried the hurt, hoping and expecting better things in time. But that intimate, physical aspect of their lives only marginally improved and never gave her the satisfaction which she had assumed would be hers by right. So right from the start, she admitted to herself now, Tony had let her down. And they never seemed to be able to talk about it. Whenever she tried, hesitatingly, to steer some words that way, he would dismiss them with that same decisiveness she had once admired.

And what of him, she wondered. If she was bitterly disappointed in their sex life, how did he take it? He still mechanically went through the motions until recently, she acknowledged, though less frequently as time passed. But the knowledge that she was passive and unsatisfied must have been deeply wounding to him. Like her, when he married he had been, by his own admission, inexperienced at making love. They had seen this as no disadvantage to their relationship, rather the reverse. They had both, she felt sure, looked forward with trusting confidence to immediate and effortless perfection. The let down must have been as catastrophic for him as for her, surely.

As she looked back over the years of her marriage she saw with a sudden, painful shaft of insight the gradual, inexorable erosion of their finer feelings for each other. Disappointment had had its corrosive effects on them both but for Tony, perhaps, the effects had been, if anything, worse, so that now he had not only changed drastically from the man she had married but had, she feared, taken the decision to abandon her and try his luck elsewhere. But was there any solution other than the present dreadful mess leading to their break up? "We must try," she determined. "I must try. I'm not going to let my marriage collapse without a struggle. Our life together isn't yet so poisoned, surely, that there is no hope. But something must be done quickly before the point of no return is reached. I'll talk to Tony," she decided. "I'll get him to come away on holiday. We'll have another try, a second honeymoon. We must do something."

Excited and determined to try desperate measures to remedy an increasingly desperate situation, she resolved to tackle Tony at the earliest opportunity and went back to join the others, impatient for the moment when they would be alone to put her plan in motion. She sat reading for some time in a desultory, uncommitted fashion, her mind dwelling more on her plans for dealing with her own marriage crisis than on the intricacies of the novel she had chosen.

"Ah, there's Mike come up to do the milking, I suppose," said Norman, who had just woken up, as he watched him bringing the cows into the yard from the orchard.

"Terry's on with him," Tony said, "and I'll go out and do the cooling in a few minutes."

"How are you getting on with young Mike?" Norman asked. "I ask because I used to find him most willing."

"Well, willing maybe," Tony said, smirking. "I suppose you can't expect a city bred chap to have much idea of farm work. I don't know why he bothers really, he'd be better off in some office or other."

"Oh," said Norman, genuinely concerned. "Don't you find him up to the work then?"

"We never had much to complain about in his work, did we Norman?" Emily put in heatedly.

"No, I can't say as we did," Norman said calmly. "He was learning all the while, of course, so I suppose he wasn't as quick over some things as another chap might be. But, as I say, wc found him most willing and genuinely interested."

"Ah, I reckon you've got to be born into farming to have any real idea," Tony said complacently. "I don't exactly blame him but I don't think he'll ever make much of a go of it."

"Yes, in general I'd agree that it's best to be born into farming," Norman said. "But I've known several men from other walks of life come into farming and make a very good job of it."

"You depended on him very much when you first came here," Emily said bluntly. She wasn't going to take such patronising of Mike without remonstrance.

"That's true," Tony agreed, realising that if he persisted he would antagonise his in-laws. He saw also that it might be good tactics to postpone for the time being his firm intention of getting rid of Mike off the farm. He couldn't really stand the chap, never had liked him but it was obvious that he had powerful allies in Mary's parents.

"Well," said Norman, standing up and stretching, "we'd better be going my dear and leave these folks to get on with their affairs."

After she had seen her parents off, Mary came back indoors and found Tony still lounging in his armchair.

"Tony," she said, fixing a brave smile on her face as she decided that the moment had come, "how about you and I going away for a short holiday?"

He frowned. "A holiday? I hardly think I can go away at the moment, we're pretty busy."

"Tony." Her voice had a slightly firmer edge this time. Then she managed another smile and said almost casually, "It would only be for a short break. I think it would be good for both of us and harvest is just about in, isn't it?"

He looked at her suspiciously, as if wary of her wiles. "I really don't see the need," he said irritably.

"Well, I do," she shot back, a trifle too heatedly, she regretted at once. "Look, my dear," she went on cajolingly, "won't you do it just to please me. A few days away, that's all. I don't ask for much these days." She heard the bitter note in her voice and checked it at once. "I wouldn't suggest it if I didn't think it was important," she continued, as calmly as she could.

"I really don't know what you're on about," Tony said, standing up and eyeing her aggressively. "But I'm afraid a holiday is out of the question, right out of the question."

"But Tony," she protested wildly, "what I'm on about is trying to save our marriage. Surely you can see that." With her voice rising in agitation, she went on, "We can't go on like this for much longer. I can't stand it, I don't know what I've done or what you want, but this is no way to run a marriage." Then more calmly she added, "That's why I want us to go away for a holiday. Can't you see that? It might put us back as we were in the early days." She looked at him in supplication as she lapsed into silence.

"Another neurotic outburst!" he spat out at her, his face white with rage, his knuckles clenched. Then checking himself, he assumed a deadly calm before going on. "You might as well accept that no holiday can put things right between us. It's too late for that, far too late. In fact..."He stopped himself in mid-sentence. "I've got work to do," he said decisively and strode from the room.

Mary stood there a moment staring after him, her heart thumping, her skin exuding a cold clamminess. Then with a sob she rushed from the room, clattered upstairs and fell on her bed in a flood of tears.

Mike liked the atmosphere of Sunday afternoon milking. With no other work done during the day he hadn't got his old working clothes on, but wore his long brown milking coat over the clean shirt and flannels he'd been walking in. Several cows had been sold lately, so the herd temporarily numbered only a dozen, an easy milking task which he and Terry would soon get through without undue hurry.

With most of the neighbouring farms having already installed milking machines or planning to do so, Mike assumed it wouldn't be long before this latest technology came to Manor Farm too, so he was conscious of working out the last months, probably, of the old hand milking era. He wouldn't be destined, he told himself, to sit on his three legged stool for much longer, a stool whose seat was highly polished by generations of milkers.

Milking was a peaceful occupation and he liked it. That is, if he hadn't got a restless, fidgety cow, as they sometimes had, who put her foot in the bucket, wouldn't stand still and generally made life difficult for the milker. Otherwise, as on that Sunday afternoon, he sat there, his greasy old cap pressed well into the cow's flanks, his hands pulling and squeezing rhythmically at the teats and the milk hissing and frothing into the bucket between his knees.

The air inside the cowshed was heavy with the smell of hay and sweet cattle cake on the cows' breath. Sunbeams shone through the doorway, lighting up the whitewashed wooden walls which higher up were dim with the dust and cobwebs of years. The only sounds besides the frothing of milk were a cow's occasional cough and the jingle of a chain at the manger, whilst the two milkers slowly proceeded along the line of contentedly munching beasts.

Tony came in with a terse greeting and collected the full buckets to take back to the cooler. Mike glanced at him and speculated again on how things might be between him and Mary. It was strange wasn't it, he mused, how Tony seemed to have all that a man could reasonably desire, certainly more than most could ever think of aspiring to, a lovely wife, ownership of a good farm, a beautiful house and a comfortable life style. And yet, he was beginning to suspect, there was no true happiness in it. All the most recent signs were that there was discontent and rottenness at the core of that seemingly ideal marriage.

And yet, he reflected, Tom and Eileen, that couple in the tiny cottage next to his aunt, with hardly a penny to their name, how different marriage was for them. He, hard working in the quarry to stay afloat and raise their three kids decently, she, wearing jumble sale clothes quite often, they were as happy as the day is long. Always jolly and with a friendly word for everyone, they were to be seen hand in hand walking about, the epitome of married contentment. What a contrast between the two couples! So what a lottery life is, he continued musing. And what a lottery marriage is! How can you guarantee success, he wondered. Ah, if only one could know that! There is, in the end, only instinct to guide us and that isn't infallible. Everything might seem ideal, as with Tony and Mary. All material things may be in favour of success, education, family background, interests and self interest may all be compatible, but there is always the unsuspected and often unknowable-in-advance human frailty to snatch misery from the jaws of bliss.

"Steer clear of marriage altogether?" he queried to himself. "No, not for me. There is something too powerful in the happy combination of a man and a woman to be denied. They are much more than the sum of two individuals, they are an incredibly strong unit for the most complete happiness and self fulfilment granted to human beings." This he believed unreservedly. "You just have to go on searching, without trying too hard, till you feel the genuine deep attraction which leads to love, and then take the plunge, resolved to do one's damnedest to make it work."

"Which is why," he reflected, as he got up from Daisy's side, "I'll probably never get married if I just stand on the side, afraid to dip my toe in the water."

Mike on his sick bed ran those pictures through his mind, still feeling the strength of those events which had so transformed their lives those many years ago. At some later stage, when they had entered calmer waters, he had begun to hear from Mary, and to understand, something of her experiences, her reactions, and this formed part of his whole ongoing story which over the years had taken its proper sequence in time.. . Mary had sat up on her bed, her eyes dry now and reddened. She glanced in the dressing table mirror and abstractedly took a hair brush to smooth her dark waves back into some semblance of order, thinking all the while of her failed endeavour but more particularly of Tony's brutal condemnation of their marriage. "No holiday can put things right between us. It's too late for that, far too late." Perhaps even more than the hurt of the words themselves was the tone of voice in which they were delivered, that tone of calm finality which smacked of the cold, sober truth.

She felt calm in herself now, the paroxysm of tearful emotion was spent. She sat there on the edge of the bed glancing at herself in the mirror and knew that her marriage was over. In all its essentials their living, loving relationship was at an end. This she now perceived with that certainty of knowledge from the heart which does not mistake these things.

She could and would go on with life as usual, she knew, as she turned her head first this way then that to contemplate the person to whom this dreadful calamity had occurred. She told herself that she would do nothing to change the status quo. She felt strong again now, strong enough to go on living with this man who so completely rejected her. She felt dead in her heart towards him, he was henceforth only a stranger who would be sharing the house with her. She no longer needed him. He had killed off all sense, not only of love but also of friendship, and left only cold duty which, she resolved, was her path for the future for as long as the formal marriage should last. She was surprised that her thoughts were so lucid and precise in spite of the emotional turmoil she had just endured.

Upon a thought she went into the next bedroom and made up the bed there. From then on she would not dream of sharing his bed, the mere thought of it was deeply repugnant to her. As she emptied her wardrobe and transferred its contents she felt as though she was dismantling her life without any idea of whether and in what way it could be rebuilt. It was a frightening prospect. Everything she had hoped and lived for was being demolished. She was heading for an emptiness, a casting adrift of her life and yet she could do no other. Her passionate nature insisted that without love in a marriage all is lost. "The empty shell of marriage is not for me," she told herself, torn between anger, with its accompanying desire to sweep away the lifeless ruin, and the equally strong resolve of never doing anything to weaken the sanctity of marriage which was deeply rooted within her.

There was a good congregation at chapel that evening. The circuit minister was taking the service, which was always a red letter occasion, raising the interest and attendance, markedly above that of the worthy but mostly less polished and less inspirational lay preachers. The sermon was powerfully delivered, so much so that Mike was easily able to recall it years afterwards. It was based on the Old Testament text, 'Whatsoever thy hand findeth to do, do it with all thy might.'

He took the text to heart as was intended and applied it to his own circumstances. As he sat next to his aunt, with the village folk all around in that simple yet dignified little building with its heavy varnished oak pews and plain painted walls, he thought of what his hand might undertake in the years ahead. He glanced around that congregation, which consisted almost entirely of farm and quarry workers accompanied by their homely wives, all of whom he knew and respected and some he liked a lot. He would ask for nothing more than a simple, peaceful life in that place, close to nature and to the soil. He was strongly aware in the heightened atmosphere of that silent listening congregation, of the long, calm and uneventful life of the village, of the precious rural, yeoman tradition which he felt was present among these people and which permeated every aspect of their lives and was so appealing. He responded to this by again determining to carry on a simple, sane and healthy outdoor working life, savouring the slow turning of the seasons and the steady rhythm of farm and village life, underpinned by the tried and tested tenets of the old religion of a pastoral and farming people. He would ask for nothing more than to continue this humble but priceless tradition.

Outside the chapel afterwards he was chatting to village friends, including Emily and Norman who were accompanied by Mary who had resumed her chapel going habit, though Tony never came along. They wandered slowly down the road and Mike walked with Mary as far as the farm. He felt in good spirits and chatted at length about Mac's homecoming and she seemed lively too, telling him about the pony she hoped to buy from a friend of Joan at Edlesborough. When they parted and he rejoined his aunt, he felt the usual warm glow of pleasure from having been close to her for a while. Perhaps, he reflected as he walked away, things aren't so bad for her after all, better than he'd feared at any rate. Perhaps Perce had got it all wrong somehow. Rumour was never reliable.

"As you wish, my dear," Tony drawled with heavy sarcasm, when he discovered later that evening that Mary intended separate bedrooms.

"Well, after what you said this afternoon, what do you expect?" Mary said, not seeking a row but quite ready to stand up for herself.

"Do you have any other little surprises in store for me?" Tony continued in the same detached, affected tone.

"No, that's all," she replied bluntly. "You're the one with the surprises, aren't you, after all?"

"So we're to carry on as usual, are we, save for this one trifling embargo?" he enquired in that insufferable, supercilious tone of his. "I'd just like to know, that's all."

Mary felt a blind hatred rise within her at his mockery, but she fought back the urge to scream and scratch and instead she said as calmly as possible, "Look, I'm prepared to be civilised about this. I don't know what your intentions are, only that they seem to exclude me. All I'm saying is that for the moment I'm not going to give you the satisfaction of putting myself in the wrong by leaving you. With the one proviso that we sleep apart, I'll do my best to carry on as usual."

"Oh, will you!" he shouted, his eyes blazing with sudden anger, his body taut and threatening. Then, just as quickly reverting to his apparent languid state, he screwed his face into a travesty of a smile and said, "That's all right then, so long as I get my meals on time and my other creature comforts attended to, you won't find me complaining, my sweet."

She turned abruptly and left the room, finding his presence intolerable and also because in spite of her firmness, her eyes were filled with tears which she would not let him see.

CHAPTER 11

Cast Adrift

Harvest time gave way to fruit picking as September ushered in the early signs of autumn with its shortening days, its drenching dews upon the meadow grass and its swallows thickly lining the roadside cables as they prepared themselves for travel. Then in the innumerable plum and apple orchards long implanted upon those fertile soils, the splay footed ladders were out, the cheerful pickers were up aloft among the leafy boughs, and piles of woven skips stood in the long grass to be steadily filled each day of mellow sunshine with luscious fruit.

The fact that Tony took little part in the fruit picking confirmed Mike's fears about the orchards on the farm. Tony would organise the starting of the picking each day, then leave the three men to get on with it, using the time to visit markets and merchants, so he said, around the county. With the boss away the others worked steadily and light-heartedly, joking and laughing throughout the day, much as Mike had done years before with Dennis and Mary. He tried not to think about Tony's threat to the trees, it seemed too unreasonable to be realistic.

No sooner had this most happy and carefree of farm jobs been done as autumn deepened, than the threshing machines started upon their circuits. As a boy Mike had loved these visits to the farm of the giant steam engines, towing the huge contraptions that did the work of separating corn, chaff and straw and which, for a day or two each time, transformed the rickyard into something approaching an adventure playground. Then, his time had passed mainly in watching the animated scene and talking with the many friends who were drawn magnetically from all over the village. This was punctuated with short, frenzied periods of rat and mouse chasing as a rick was finished and the rodent population, having lived long in security and plenty, had to run the gauntlet of men, boys and dogs to escape.

Mike thought of those earlier, simple and exciting times as he walked into the rickyard and saw the same venerable engine standing there, all gleaming black and shining brass, its firebox open and glowing red as old Dan Pargetter shovelled more coal in. Dan had been touring the local farms for far longer than Mike could remember and had many hilarious tales to tell of his dealings with his more idiosyncratic clients. But these days, as the fifties declined, much of his talk was of the clients he was losing, as one after another they turned over to combining. Not that he was too concerned for himself for his retirement was not far off, but he was, in his bluff way, concerned that a way of life was disappearing and that his two boys would most likely have to find another living.

As they stood beside the new Dutch barns exchanging a few words, Mike was keenly aware that yet another piece of the richness and variety of village and farm life was under serious threat and likely before long to pass away and when that happened small boys wouldn't know anything about the sort of times he'd experienced amid the liveliness and excitement of a day's threshing. Why, it was as good as a day at the fairground!

Nick and Terry arrived. They knew all about threshing and were under no romantic illusions about it. It was going to be a hard and dusty day's work, they knew, but they were well equal to it. They weren't work shy, so they too looked upon it as a stimulating experience, matching their strength and skill. Tony came along next and said he would build the straw rick. "Service, you can be on the oat rick," he said - he seldom called Mike by his Christian name. "Nick on the straw rick with me and Terry taking up the chaff and oat sacks into the loft."

So the work got going. Dan started the great fly wheel off amid much hissing and clouds of steam and all the belts and wheels started turning with machinery clanking and banging inside the ancient thresher's frame. Dan's youngest boy was on the thresher cutting bands as Mike forked him the sheaves and soon the well tried system was running smoothly, whilst old Dan kept an eye on the engine, stoked it with coal and with a pad of cotton waste and an oil can made sure that the thousands of moving parts kept moving.

No small boys came to watch that morning, they merely passed by, wide eyed, on their way to school. At mid morning work stopped for a welcome break, when Mary brought out a tray of mugs of hot, sweet tea soon after Arthur put in an appearance. He wandered in and was warmly greeted by Mike and by Dan who had known him since they were boys. Norman too came across the yard to join them, it wasn't only boys who were attracted to threshing. They all stood about in a group, mugs in hand, discussing the progress so far.

Arthur was his usual cheerful though taciturn self. He seemed to be enjoying his retirement, so he said anyway, at least in the gardening months, for he asked nothing better than to be active upon his allotment, where garrulous neighbours received remarkably little encouragement to waste his time in idle gossip. Mike watched his eye roving around the yard and up and down the Dutch barns as he sipped his tea meditatively, lingering over the details of the familiar scene where he had passed his lifetime working. Did he realise, Mike wondered, that the oat rick they were threshing now was the last one he had built, or would ever build? He would certainly make some totally unsentimental remark if he were reminded of that fact. It was also, Mike realised, the last of the old time ricks to be built on the farm. All future work would be under the Dutch barns. "It's progress, I suppose," he thought.

Mary didn't stay long, she left the mugs for collection later. She looked her usual cheerful self as far as he could tell, as his eyes wandered from her to Tony, wondering whether they were wearing masks, and as she walked away Mike's gaze followed her, drawn by her trim figure in a flowery cotton dress revealing attractive legs and shapely ankles. Norman soon followed and Arthur drifted off as work began again, banishing all further extraneous thoughts from Mike's mind, as he was soon sweating to maintain a steady stream of sheaves to feed the thresher. Luckily, he knew that the important thing in this job was to achieve a steady rhythm and to let the fork do as much of the work as possible, only moving each sheaf the necessary minimum height and distance and never straining to dislodge the sheaves from where he was standing but taking each free one from its place without resistance. Worked thus it was possible to go on without too much fatigue, but done wrongly one would be utterly exhausted in an hour.

As the work progressed it became increasingly obvious that another person was needed on the rick with Mike. You just couldn't pitch the sheaves in one go across that space and up to young Pargetter on the thresher. Terry could easily have been asked to leave the sacks for a while to help out but Tony said and did nothing, though he couldn't not have known of Mike's difficulty. Mike fumed inwardly as he struggled, but bided his time, telling himself that he would confront Tony as soon as they stopped again.

So, as they packed up at midday, a sweating and exhausted Mike walked over to Tony as he made for the house. "Why didn't you put Terry on the rick with me?" he asked, as coolly as he could, blocking Tony's passage to the gate.

"What, couldn't you cope?" was the sarcastic reply.

Mike stared at him in utter disdain. "Would you like to try it?" he rasped.

They stood toe to toe almost and Mike felt his knuckles clenching and a rising desire to strike. He would not back down nor turn aside as he faced up to the scowling, white faced Tony for what seemed an eternity, before the latter turned away with a sneering, "We'll see."

"You'd better," Mike snapped back, then walked away to calm his hammering pulse.

In the afternoon as they were about to start and with Norman standing by the fence, Tony told Terry that he'd better leave his sacks to congregate and go and help Mike. So young Pargetter got his steady supply of sheaves and Mike smiled grimly to himself at his successful persuasion, but bore in mind the notion that he probably wasn't going to be working for Tony for much longer.

The rick was finished early enough in the afternoon for the milking to be got on with only a little later than usual. So while the returning children watched with rapt attention outside the fence, old Dan and his sons hitched the great thresher and the smaller chaff cutter behind the engine, which then huffed and puffed its way out of the gate onto the road and away towards Stanbridge and its next farm appointment. That evening Mike relaxed in his easy chair, his body glowing with healthy fatigue, his wrists and arms telling him gently of their exertions but promising to be ready for whatever might reasonably come their way on the morrow.

Mac called in at about eight o'clock. Marjorie answered his knock and welcomed him in. "Sit down over there," she said, indicating the empty chair beside the fire. "Would you like a cup of coffee?"

"Go on," Mike said, "and I'll have one too."

So, while Marjorie busied herself in the kitchen, the two friends settled down comfortably. "How's life at work?" Mike asked, not having seen Mac since hearing he'd been successful at his interview.

"Oh, I'm surviving," Mac said. "The money's good at least."

"It sounds like the sort of place I could do with working at," Mike said.

"You wouldn't enjoy it," Mac said. "It's hellish really, a modern version of hell. At least it is in the body shop where I am. It's vast and cheerless, all noise and welding sparks flying and blokes swarming over car frames and assembly lines that never stop. I can't say it's pleasant."

"That's the grim reality of modern industry, I suppose," Mike commented.

"In the R.A.F.," Mac went on, "we were taught to do a whole range of jobs on aircraft, but here of course the work's broken down into little bits and you just go on repeating your particular bit. There are chaps near me who have done nothing but screwing on wing mirrors for months on end. It would drive me crackers, I reckon."

"So you don't screw on wing mirrors?"

"Christ, no," Mac declared. "I'm on the fine tuning squad which is skilled work. But even so, I'm not staying there for long if I can help it. I've got my eye on opening my own garage. But right now I'm saving hard for the deposit on a house."

"Have you got one in mind?" Mike asked.

"Yes, there's a nice little estate going up off the Luton Road. I'm thinking of putting my name down for one there. I reckon Jeannie would like it."

"You don't mind moving out of the village, then?"

"There's nothing here that's modern that I could afford," Mac said. "Jeannie's keen on having a modern place. It'll be much more convenient for getting to work, too. I'm also looking for a little car at the moment, an Austin Seven would do me nicely."

"Sounds great," Mike said, thinking that Mac's pay must be very good if it was going to be able to finance his ambitious plans. "How is Jeannie?"

"Oh, fine. I'm going up to see her at Christmas, in the car if I've got one by then. Hitching a lift otherwise, most likely."

Marjorie brought the coffee and they went on talking until she asked if they would like the news on television.

"I'd noticed you'd got one," Mac said, glancing at the set with its doors wide open on a little table in the far corner.

"We've only just got it," Marjorie said proudly. "Everyone seems to be getting them now, so I thought we'd better keep up with the times and anyway, it's time ordinary people had a few of life's luxuries."

"I'm all for it myself," Mac agreed. "I'm certainly convinced the time will soon come when most people will own a car. We're all on permanent overtime at Vauxhall's."

"Yes, you're right, I expect," Mike said. "It could be that we are entering a new Golden Age. Let's hope it increases the sum of human happiness."

"Can you doubt it?" Mac asked.

"Well, I don't know that happiness has much to do with modern gadgets and machines," he replied. I suspect that human nature won't change much for the better in spite of increasing affluence, more likely it will get worse."

"Now, don't be so pessimistic Mike," Marjorie said briskly. "Tell us young man," she went on, turning to Mac, "how did you like being abroad? I've been telling Mike he ought to travel more. Get to see something of life beyond the farm and Dunstable."

"Gibraltar is a special case, I'm afraid," Mac said. "Quite frankly, I found it too confined. We weren't allowed into Spain, you see, so we'd only got the tiny area of the Rock to live in, though we could go over to Tangier on leave. The weather is pretty good, of course, that's what I liked best about it."

"Has it given you a taste for travel?" Marjorie asked.

"Yes, I think it has," he said. "I think we'll be going to Paris for our honeymoon, though Jeannie doesn't know that yet. I've always fancied Paris, because it's so romantic, I suppose. I've even started learning French at night school."

"Now, that's the way to do it," Mike agreed enthusiastically. "Not just aimless wandering abroad but understanding enough of the language and the culture of a country to make travelling really mean something."

"Mm, that takes much more time and effort," Marjorie commented.

"You've got to face the fact that all most people want is sunshine and beaches," Mac put in.

"I know," Mike said. "Well, let them have them. I've got nothing against the sun but personally I'd rather use my time differently from just lying about on a beach getting red like a boiled lobster, which is what would happen to me, I'm sure."

My advice is," Marjorie said with conviction, "travel as much as you can whilst you're young, both home and abroad. It'll give you a well stocked mind when you're old. You know, I'm continually amazed at the sheer ignorance and parochialism of the girls at the nursery. All they can talk about is some pretty dress that someone was wearing at the village dance or about somebody's new boyfriend. It's so trivial."

"It's always been the same, hasn't it?" Mike asked. "Since when have council house and cottage people like us had the money to travel? It's changing though. With all the factory wages being earned, they'll all be going on package tours before long. They've started already, haven't they? For myself I think I'd rather get to know this country a lot better before I start rushing abroad. When I think of how little I've seen of just England even!"

"I'd agree with that," Mac said. "I certainly had my eyes opened when I went up to Kinloss. Jeannie and I went over to the west coast and Skye, and I really fell in love with all that part of Scotland, it's magnificent."

"Yes," Mike agreed," and all the better, I'm sure, though I haven't seen it yet, for being our own, all part of the same background, history and even language - if you can penetrate the Scots accent."

Marjorie switched on the television and, when it had warmed up, they gazed with keen attention at the novelty of pictures invading the room from all corners of the country and some even from overseas.

Later, as he lay in bed, Mike was thinking over their conversation. He realised that the age of mass tourism was clearly coming and had a theory that it was, at least in part, an escape from the unsatisfactory nature of much of today's urban life and as such was no bad thing. The fact that he didn't feel impelled to rush out to the Continental honeypots reflected, in part, his contentment with his surroundings. Most people were not able to be content with their environment, it was too developed, too industrialised, spoilt, devoid of peace and beauty.

He thought of the Knolls and the pleasure he derived from harebells on the turf, the first heavenly green of beech trees on the steep hillsides, a sea of bluebells in Blackgrove Woods, the lapwings on the ploughing of a winter's day, the heron he'd just seen in the brook, so many fascinating images that filled his life, day in, day out. They were small things maybe, but he hoped he would always love the small things, they were the source of true contentment. His head thus filled with pleasant thoughts, he dropped easily off to sleep.

The next morning, Saturday, started off for Mary as most mornings had for the last two months or so since she had moved into the separate bedroom. She heard Tony go downstairs, followed by the telltale sounds of milking about to start. The cows came in from the orchard with a soft slithering and tapping of their feet upon the cobbles. Mike's boots crunched upon the gravel as he crossed to the cowshed, soon followed by Nick and Terry on their bicycles. Then there was the clash of buckets and rolling of churns, all soon obliterated when the pump motor started up as the milk cooling began.

Mary lay abed awhile, her head filled with the customary unhappiness she had lived with for a long time now. Her spirits had descended to a sort of plateau of dejection, a state of weary pessimism, not sinking lower into clinical depression and breakdown, but not ridding herself of misery either. She had now abandoned any lingering hopes she had of a reconciliation with Tony, though for weeks part of her had clung obstinately to that desire as the only possible solution to her wretchedness. Mary didn't in her heart surrender her marriage without a struggle, but as she lay thinking that morning she was aware that all such hopes had withered and died. She was waiting for something to happen, she knew. She had wondered so often how long things could go on as they were. The atmosphere of only partly repressed hostility that she felt emanating from Tony whenever they were alone together was surely so corrosive that total collapse of all relationship seemed inevitable. She wasn't looking forward to that collapse, she just expected it to happen, regardless of anything she could do in the matter. Whatever happened, she was determined to hang on and not be forced out of her home. Not that she detected in Tony any attempt to dislodge her but she had a strong sense of property, not so much for its financial value but more basically as her legitimate shelter and refuge, coupled with a horror of being made homeless, of having nowhere to call her own.

"Why has this happened to me?" she asked herself for the hundredth time. "Am I at least partly to blame for the mess I'm in?" She paused a long minute to consider the possibility. "No, I honestly don't think so, except in so far as our sex life was a failure and I'm half of that sex life. If I'm to blame at all I don't think I could have done anything else or been any different. I'm the way I am and he's the way he is and it doesn't seem as if we were destined to combine happily. You can't just by will power make a marriage work. Though enthusiasm will take you a fair way, the physical chemistry will tell eventually."

As her friend Joan had pointed out with a gleam in her eye when they had last met, "The sexual side has got to be right, my dear, and then all the other aspects have a fair chance of fitting in, providing they're reasonably compatible. The tragedy is that one often only learns this when it's too late."

"It's all right for Joan," she had thought, "but what can I do about it now?"

"How about divorce?" Joan had said, to Mary's surprise.

"No," she had replied, "not if I can help it. It is after all a confession of failure. In the end it may be unavoidable but for the moment I'm much too confused in my mind. I can't see the future with any clarity."

She had her breakfast alone, as usual now, Tony being not yet in from milking. She had originally hoped and expected to be one of the farm's team of workers and had been quite prepared to get up to do the milking or see to the cooling, as well as help with any number of jobs throughout the day. This, she had thought, would be her pleasure and privilege, considering her background and being still without children. But such hopes had been largely stillborn in the sourness of her marriage and she contented herself now with caring for the numerous poultry and tending the pony and four carthorses still living in retirement in the orchard.

The days had begun to drag and this, Mary knew, was potentially disastrous. She needed distraction in her unhappiness, needed to be busy in order not to dwell overmuch on the empty core of her life. Fortunately she found great comfort in visiting Joan in nearby Edlesborough where she lived with her farmer husband. They usually went out riding together across the fields, where they could discuss things without fear of interruption. Joan was sensible and gave good advice and would not gossip even, save in very general terms, to her husband.

So Mary felt reasonably confident and self-possessed as she ate her breakfast, thinking of the day ahead and of seeing Joan in the afternoon. This would probably be their last outing for a while, for Joan was three months pregnant and had been told it was high time she gave up riding.

She busied herself in getting Tony's breakfast, knowing by the sounds of the cows being let out that he would soon be in. As the fat in the frying pan spat and crackled round the egg, she dwelt again on how long the impasse in which she found herself could go on. Would she be relieved if he walked out, she wondered. Emotionally, she couldn't see herself being much affected, he meant nothing to her. It was only the ending of the old habits, the housekeeping, the meal preparation and the washing and ironing for him that might leave her life seemingly emptied. But on the other hand, she reflected, she had begun to move from her former determination not to change the status quo of being a good, dutiful wife, providing for ever for this man who seemed to grow firmer in his dislike of her. She wasn't so sure now that she had the resolve to condemn herself to that life sentence.

But then again, as she had argued with Joan, there was that 'for better or for worse' clause in the marriage service. At the first sign of 'worse' was she ready to ditch the whole thing? Mary took her church wedding seriously. It hadn't been for her an occasion merely to look lovely in white and to process down the aisle of the charming old church, the envy and admiration of all eyes. She had entered into a solemn and binding contract. Though motivated more perhaps by instinct and upbringing than by theology, she knew in her heart that such was the right and proper way for mankind. Her vows were not to be lightly broken, of that she was determined. Let others do as they like, she was quietly unshakeable in her conviction of the sanctity of marriage and in avoiding the chaos of 'anything goes.'

Joan's inclination when they first discussed the matter had been to advise her friend to think of herself more. "You've got a duty to yourself, Mary," she'd said. "You'll only be young once. You can't condemn yourself to a mere existence with Tony, surely. It's just not right these days."

"But right doesn't depend on 'these days' or 'those days', does it?" Mary had asked. "Surely right is right, regardless of the times."

Thus faced with Mary's firm views, Joan had to tone down her remarks, so as not to sharpen still further the conflict in Mary's mind and avoid edging her friend towards a breakdown.

The whole matter was made hugely more complicated and difficult, Mary acknowledged, when she posed the question of what would happen to the farm in any break up. They were both tied to the farm. It wasn't like a job you could just walk away from. It was them, the heart of their life. She couldn't run the place herself, so how could he walk out? She couldn't contemplate walking out, this was her home, her birthright. The farm was a huge brick wall across all thoughts of a different future, one she couldn't even begin to scale.

But now, faced for a long depressing period with Tony's implacable hostility and his frequently repeated declaration that their marriage was beyond hope of saving, she was confused over her stance and even leapfrogged over the enormous obstacles to dream sometimes of making a new life for herself. "I'm still young and not altogether unattractive, I suppose," she said to herself, glancing in the mirror over the fireplace. "What sort of life can I expect if we go on for long like this?"

She was bitter at the thought of the other woman in Tony's life, for she was sure by now that there was one. They hadn't had a blazing row over it yet, when she might force him to admit his infidelity. Not only was she scared to arouse Tony's anger, she felt she didn't need his admission. It had to be like that, she told herself, in view of their non existent sex life and his frequent absences from home, growing rapidly more frequent in recent weeks. He had to be trying elsewhere. "In a way I wish him luck," she conceded. "But why should I be left on the shelf? We would be better off if we ended our marriage now, surely. After all we have no children. Then we could both start to rebuild our lives." She now began to see clearly that, with their marriage being definitely dead and with no apparent hope of resurrection, she had as much right as Tony to a full life. "If only there wasn't that brick wall of the farm in the way," she thought.

She had ventured such an opinion the last time she had ridden out with Joan and received the vehement approval of her friend, who was relieved that Mary was beginning to think positively. "There's absolutely no doubt about it in my opinion," she said, as they walked their horses beside the hedgerows, "You have the same right to happiness as he has. Why should you suffer for his selfish actions whilst he goes blithely on as if nothing's happened, getting every material consideration? That's intolerable, in my view."

Mary felt her awakening sense of self assertion strengthened.

"There's another point you may well have to consider before long, Mary," Joan continued. "Do you consult a solicitor? It sounds from what you've told me that things are getting rapidly to that stage. I know one hesitates before taking that sort of step, but the time might well soon come when you have to do so to protect your own interests, as well as to get things on a proper, straightforward footing. It's doubly important, of course, when you think about the farm complications."

This was an aspect Mary hadn't even dimly considered so far, but she had to concede the force of Joan's advice, although the prospect of having her personal affairs made the subject of interviews with solicitors made her recoil in distaste.

Mary's thoughts that Saturday morning were interrupted as Tony came in from the cooling and without a word sat down at the table. "Can I talk to him?" she suddenly wondered, as she set the hot plate before him. Something unpredictable inside her made her decide that this was the right moment.

She sat down opposite him and poured tea for them both. She felt suddenly calm and in control. "Tony," she said, passing his cup, "how long are you going on like this?"

He glanced sharply at her. "Like what?" he snapped irritably.

"I suppose you're waiting for the right moment to walk out of this place for good," she went on, aware suddenly of her heart thumping.

"Well," he began, smiling and sitting back in his chair, "since you ask… "

"You can take that supercilious smile off your face for a start," she interrupted him sharply, conscious that things already risked getting out of hand.

She paused a moment to regain her poise. "I want you to be serious," she went on more calmly, "and listen to me for a moment, please."

He went on eating, looking away from her.

"I don't think we can go on for much longer like this," she said quietly. Quite unrehearsed and from the depths of her being the next words slipped effortlessly out. "If you're going to go, I'd like you to go quickly. Then at least I would know where I am."

He looked up at her, surprised at her frankness, narrowed his eyes and replied as calmly as her, "And how do you think you would manage here if I go?"

She recoiled as if slapped in the face, then, "I would manage," she replied quickly, fiercely, not really knowing what she was saying but determined on carrying things through to a conclusion.

"Oh, you'd manage, would you?" he threw back at her sarcastically. "That's all that has been holding me back, I can tell you."

She swallowed hard at that, hurt and frighteningly aware of the huge mountain of responsibility toppling over on her but still hell bent on maintaining her headlong rush into the abyss. "I'll manage, I tell you," she declared vehemently.

He said nothing for a few moments, just looked at her long and hard. "You're right, of course," he said quietly at last. "We can't and shouldn't go on like this." He paused again. "I'm sorry it's turned out like this, Mary," he went on with uncharacteristic warmth, "but it'll probably be best for you in the end if we split up now."

"Yes, yes," she said eagerly, then felt a sudden constricting of the throat and smarting of the eyes amid a panic flooding over her that the parting of the ways forever with Tony was at hand. The previously unthinkable was happening. She turned away, looked back at him once more, then fled out of the kitchen, out of the house, anywhere just to be alone amid the confusion roaring in her head.

She walked and walked, only marginally conscious of her direction, instinctively aware that being alone in the open countryside keeping up a steady rhythm of movement, was what she needed at that time to regain her serenity.

At first she couldn't see even the beginning of a solution to her predicament and was in complete despair at her own recklessness. "What have I done?" she kept repeating over and over again. But, as she walked, the swirling emotions in her head slowly began to clear, leaving her to face more clearly the enormous practical problems entailed in depriving herself of a husband to run the farm which was her overwhelming concern. As she walked on and on and with the passing of time became calmer, she suddenly saw the obvious, simple course to take. "If he does go I'll run the farm myself," she declared out loud to the hedgerow. "I'll have nothing to lose by trying. I can work and I've got three men working for me. I'll learn to do it. I will do it. I will survive, I'm not going under." To herself she went on, "I'm not going to worry dad either. That's for certain. It might take me a while to succeed and it might be hard going, but I'm damned well going to give it a good try."

The calming effect of a decision well taken was like a tonic to her jangled nerves and her stride became stronger and more confident. It was about mid morning when she returned home, wondering what she would find. A glance in the garage told her all she hoped yet dreaded. The car was gone. Indoors there was a single sheet of notepaper on the kitchen table with the words, 'I've gone. Sorry. T.'

She breathed deeply and looked around her, fearful yet quietly confident now that she really was on her own.

CHAPTER 12

Invitation to Supper

Mike reviewed again in his mind the events of the past winter and marvelled at Mary's transformation since the time when Tony left. Of course they all knew now - all the village knew for he had been seen repeatedly - that he was living with a wealthy heiress and racehorse owner from near Bedford. Mike recalled the shock he'd felt when he'd first heard the news of Tony's defection. Mary had come out to him as he was preparing for that Saturday afternoon's milking, which he and Tony were supposed to be doing. She stood in the cowshed doorway as he was distributing cattle cake to his waiting 'ladies'. He looked up at her, a little surprised for she didn't often come out to the milking.

"Hullo, Mike," she said.

As he smiled to see her, she went on quickly, "I'm afraid Tony won't be doing the milking today," and something in her voice wiped the smile from his face. "In fact," she went on, her voice faltering a little and lowering, "I don't think he'll be around any more."

There was a moment's deathly hush as he received this bombshell. "I'm very sorry to hear that," he said in formal reaction, as he searched her face for how she really felt about what she was saying.

She shrugged her shoulders. "You probably realised that all wasn't well," she said. "At least I know where I am now." After pausing a moment she went on. "Look Mike, we're old friends, I can talk to you in confidence, I know. I don't know exactly what's going to happen yet but one thing I do know, I intend to carry on here if I possibly can. Give me a day or so to pull myself together, it's been a big shock, I can tell you. Then I'll pitch in with the rest of you. Can I leave you to tell the other two? I don't want to talk about it any more yet awhile."

Mike nodded his assent. "You can depend on me," he said.

"I know I can," she said. "Thanks."

She turned and wandered slowly back over the yard whilst he watched her go, a brave but vulnerable figure, back into that large, empty house to wrestle with her broken life.

When Mary's parents came to Sunday lunch as usual on the day after Tony left, they knew nothing. She hadn't gone rushing to them with her tale of woe. Her main preoccupation was her father's need to avoid all anxiety and agitation as far as possible, so she decided to be quite normal, greeting them on the doorstep with a cheerful word as usual. "Good morning, my dear," Emily said, kissing her on the cheek.

"Morning, dad," Mary called to Norman, who was looking over the fence into the yard as he always did to run his eye over the place, checking that all was well. "How's things going, then?" he asked, as he and Emily came into the front kitchen and he laid a bunch of his greenhouse chrysanthemums on the table for Mary.

"Everything's fine," she replied. "Oh, aren't they lovely," gathering up the flowers and admiring them. "I'll just pop them into a vase, then make a cup of tea."

She came back in a few minutes with the tea tray and they went through into the dining room, which already had a cheery blaze burning in the hearth. Mary knew that her parents were sensible, well balanced people who looked with equanimity on life and were not given to volatile and neurotic reactions to events. They had the steady, calculated, no nonsense approach which a lifetime spent close to nature and the soil encourages. This excluded neither enthusiasm nor cynicism when those reactions were justified, but they needed to be sure before they committed themselves and they were not likely to be mistaken or duped.

Knowing this, Mary decided to be plain spoken with them to convince them of her determination and above all to be brief. In a pause in the conversation she quietly began. "You know Tony and I haven't been getting on well lately, don't you?" She paused. Her mother nodded straightaway. "Well," Mary continued, "it won't come altogether as a surprise then that he's gone, cleared off."

Norman's eyes opened wide in astonishment, but he didn't interrupt his daughter. "I'm quite all right," she said, smiling reassuringly. "Lunch is in the oven, I slept like a log last night and I know just what I'm going to do."

"My dear girl," Emily broke in, "I'm so sorry, but I can't say I'm really surprised after what you told me a while back."

Norman's eyes searched Mary's face for proof that she really was all right. "I must say I sometimes used to wonder myself," he said.

"Anyway," Mary continued, fully in control and warming to her task, "you know I'm not your daughter for nothing. I'm going to run the farm myself." She paused again to let them catch up. "Yes," she said, "I'm convinced I can do it, with Mike and Nick and Terry. It will give me something to do, won't it, keep my mind busy, which is just what I want."

"Good Lord!" Norman exclaimed. "You've got guts girl. Good for you!"

"You'll be better off without him," was Emily's comment. "I know I've tried my best to like him and to get on with him, though it wasn't easy. No," she continued, her mind quite made up in support of her daughter, "you couldn't go on for long as you were, I'm sure of that. And why shouldn't you run things yourself? You've got a good team, you're young and strong."

So there was no shock horror expressed by her parents, only outright support as they weathered the news of Tony's departure without the least trouble, and, although Mary's fortunes occupied much of their thinking in the days to come, it did nothing to affect either of them adversely.

On a sunny afternoon in early April when the warmth of returning spring was in the air and nature's response was visible in the greening of wayside hedges and the rioting of dandelions and daisies in the meadows, Mike was rolling the big field of spring oats near Stanbridgeford station. March winds had dried the clayey soil which crumbled to a fine tilth as the rollers passed over it, pressing down the tender yet tough young oat shoots, firming them in and setting them on the road to rapid growth.

It felt good to be there working, a tiny figure in that vast landscape of open cultivated fields, bounded by distant hedges and the farther lines of chalk hills, with the Knolls prominent in cloud-flecked sunshine. As he worked across the field, endlessly up and down the broad expanse, turning on the headland by the Ousel brook and running up to the broad track which led through all the fields, Mike could let his mind roam free, cocooned within the tractor's steady roar. Since Tony left, developments had been little short of astounding. Mary had appeared for that first Monday morning's milking, dressed in working clothes which she had taken care with to be shapely and feminine and, with a cheery word to the three workers who were in a quietly excited state, wondering what to expect, took on Tony's job with the minimum of fuss. She came into the cowshed just before they finished and, with no preamble, had a very business-like discussion of the day's work, frankly asking their advice about what needed doing and insisting on playing her part whenever she was able to. When she had gone, the three men stood a moment, weighing up their reactions so far. "Good luck to her," Terry said. "I never did like that slimy toad of a husband of hers."

"True," Nick uttered gravely. "But it ain't no easy thing what she's taken on. Not easy at all."

"I don't know of any lady farmers, I must admit," Terry said. "But I s'pose there's always the first time."

"She'll be a damned sight pleasanter to work for than Tony, I'm thinking," Nick added. "And easier on the eye, which can't be a bad thing either."

"We'll just have to see how it goes," Mike said. "I hope for her sake it works out."

With that they went off for breakfast with growing optimism about the new regime and ready to back up their new lady boss.

Norman put in an appearance for a short while in the early days, just to give stability to the new situation and to be available for his experience, which was in fact crucial in those first weeks until Mary felt able to organise the work and issue orders. Norman said it did him good to be close to things again, unlike with Tony who had begun to resent his advice. He felt so much better, since he no longer risked knocking himself up with physical effort, that giving advice when asked, being a technical consultant as he jokingly put it, was a real pleasure. He and Emily had naturally been concerned for their daughter in the early days, in spite of their underlying confidence in her. He had a few broken nights worrying, though knowing he shouldn't, but the basic strength of Mary's position - a good farm on land in good heart that had been well run for generations and with adequate willing help available - was clear to him. Soon, as they witnessed her inner strength and determination to succeed, they learned to relax and own that she had indeed the makings of a good farmer.

The most striking effect of all this on Mike, the one that had leapt first to his mind, was that the cloud of summary dismissal that he was convinced he lived continually under with Tony, was lifted. He no longer need fear the sack, at least not on the grounds of personal dislike, and that was a great relief. As for his personal feelings, although he couldn't help feeling something of a smug satisfaction at witnessing the foundering of the relationship which had been the death of his own hopes, he nevertheless quickly took the line of anaesthetising himself in all thoughts of Mary. "It's nothing to do with me," became his watchword, his self protective instinct which warned him against attempting to go over that ground twice.

He recalled one Saturday afternoon just before Christmas when he and Mac had gone out shooting along the hedgerows. They had borrowed Norman's pair of four tens which he said he was glad to see being used again after lying idle for months. Those guns were a bit of his old life that he had insisted on bringing to the new bungalow where they looked rather incongruous on the wall of the smart suburban hallway. Norman made great play of taking them down and examining them carefully before handing them over, treating the young men to reminiscences of his own shooting days. "Ah, it does me good to know someone still goes out over the fields with a gun," he said, wistfully. "Not that I couldn't still do it of course, but I don't know, it's something you grow out of when you're older, I guess. Like so many things, you need to be young to enjoy it. Anyway, off you go and enjoy yourselves. And if you should get a rabbit too many you know where it'll be welcome."

Mike returned to the new millennium from those distant reminiscences as he pondered once more on how the world had changed since his young days. Shooting, fishing, hunting, for instance. Enthusiasts and diehards had all been there with him on their protest march. Determined they certainly were and some were even confident of success. But the facts were against them, Mike reluctantly conceded to himself. You only had to consider the vast cities that sprawl over this country, their populations, by and large, ignorant of and indifferent to the life of the countryside, susceptible though to the easy 'fluffy bunny' sentimentality which governs today; and their representatives in parliament deeply dyed in this 'new realism'. Animal rights, admirable within reasonable limits, have got out of the jar and now overwhelm the human rights of country people to engage in their traditional and peaceful activities. It looks as though sad times lie ahead for country life, emasculated, enfeebled and rigorously controlled, it seems condemned to creeping suburbanisation, thriving only in the remotest areas.

On facing once more this unpalatable likelihood, Mike's thoughts returned to the days of relative freedom when rural life was strong and vibrant. He recalled how supremely content he felt as they walked the meadows. This was the simple sort of country activity he revelled in and much more so when he had company such as Mac to share it with. It was a day of lowering, slate-blue cloud but still, with the meadow grass a faded green, bleached white almost near the hedge whose bare framework of bush and occasional tree stood stark in the steely afternoon light.

They hadn't talked a lot as they patrolled the hedges and clumps of elms, but what talk there was had been of the new regime at the farm. Mike filled Mac in with all the interesting details.

"I don't think I'm going to stay on there much longer," he remembered saying at one point as, on a sudden decision, he resolved to be frank concerning his own involvement.

"Yes," he went on in response to Mac's look of surprise, "you see, Mary's always been, well, sort of special to me, I suppose you might say. Right back before I went in the army. Only nothing came of it, obviously." He paused, searching for the right note to strike so as not to make his account seem either trivial or over dramatic. "I don't think I'd be happy to see her get into a new relationship," he concluded, with typical understatement.

Mac digested this a moment. "Does she know?" he asked.

"What? That I might leave? No, I don't suppose so, I've said nothing."

"I didn't mean that exactly," Mac said. "I mean…"

"Oh, "Mike interrupted. "You mean my reasons for going? She hasn't got the slightest idea, I'm sure. Not now. And in any case there isn't really anything to know."

"Mm," Mac pondered. "Well, perhaps she ought to be told?" he offered.

"I don't somehow think it would do any good," Mike said. "To be honest I had my moment a long while ago now and I was turned down. Perhaps it was at least partly my own fault, I don't know. But I don't feel like going through all that again."

"So what would you do if you left the farm," Mac asked, with a flash of mischief in his eye, "join the French Foreign Legion?"

Mike chuckled, "That's quite an idea, I'll give it some thought."

"Well," Mac said, after a moment when solemnity had been regained, "far be it from me to offer advice where it's not asked for, but are you quite sure it's not worth a try?" You're the only one who can know that, of course."

"I'm not aware of any encouraging signs," he said, but even so Mac's words had an impact on him, raising in his own mind the question of his courage and resolve.

Nothing more was said on the subject, and the afternoon continued enjoyably and profitably with a good bag of rabbits and pigeons. Mike came away with a certain sense of relief that he had at last confided in his friend.

After the first numbing shock of Tony's leaving and in spite of the brave facade she had presented to the world, Mary had for several weeks taxed her inner resources severely, having sleepless nights with fears of a nervous breakdown. Her nerve was tested even more severely when, a few days after he had gone, she came across a letter in Tony's overalls that she was clearing out. She froze as she saw it and one quick glance was sufficient to confirm all that she had long suspected. "Louisa," she breathed, as her eyes raced to the unknown signature. "The bitch," she muttered angrily, then pushed the overalls over the letter to hide it. She sat down to calm herself, aware of her racing heart and swirling emotions, then gingerly drew the single page out again and, after calmly reading it through, folded it once, twice and again and again, till it lay tiny in her clenched fist whilst she gazed thoughtfully through the window. "It makes no difference," she told herself after a moment, "only now I know for sure what he had been up to and with whom." Completely controlled now, she put the letter carefully in her desk, vaguely aware that it might prove to be valuable evidence at some future date, then went on with her task of clearing out all traces of Tony from the house with more relish than before.

She was undoubtedly helped in weathering her tribulations by her physical exertions on the farm. As she involved herself more and more in the day to day running of things, so the colour returned to her cheeks, a natural sheen to her hair. She rediscovered her appetite, her eyes sparkled with returning vitality and, as spring edged winter out of its stronghold on the land, so she began to realise that she was enjoying life again, treating each new day as an adventure.

It was at this time that Mary, from the house one Sunday morning, saw Mike tinkering with the tractor in the yard. The plugs had oiled up yet again and he wanted to have them functioning well for Monday's work, so he stayed awhile after cleaning out the cowshed. Mary stood still a moment, looking at him through the fence. Some sudden fascination held her as he bent over the tractor, hair awry, the sleeves of his old check shirt rolled up. She began to think. Mike had been there so long now, what with his boyhood years and now his working years, always there on the farm, always ready to help. She was suddenly filled with a strong sense of his reliability, his dependability, his steady good nature and also, more recently, of his lively and interested mind. He must love this place, she thought. He really was a gem.

As she turned to tidying the room, her mind went hesitantly back over the years to the time when she knew he had been very fond of her and she of him. She dwelt smilingly on the memory of the intense discussions she'd had at the time with

Joan, she all centred on Mike and Joan on Dennis. "But I was only a girl then," she reminded herself. It was a chaotic, confused time in her memory, one resurrected now with an almost guilty reluctance because of all the trauma of her brother's death at that same time which was inextricably intermingled with and eventually overshadowed her memories of Mike at that period. Tony had appeared on the scene and she hadn't rejected him when he started to make himself agreeable and helpful.

She remembered some things so clearly across the years. The moment she was told of Dennis's fatal accident was as a dagger thrust into her heart. She had fainted on the spot, she recalled. And in the middle of the night, for weeks afterwards, the pain and sense of loss seemed almost to be tearing her apart. Only thus was her brother prised away from her. Those weeks were a confused nightmare and she could recall little from them now. Somehow, she acknowledged with a resigned sigh, thoughts of Mike had all fizzled out whilst he was so far away. She couldn't now think why, but it had happened and Tony had been there to comfort and console her and her life had taken a strong new direction.

Now, as she turned again to the window half dreamily, Mike straightened up and squared his shoulders a moment, his body slightly arched, head erect. Mary turned quickly away, sensing a physical stirring which alarmed and confused her with its sudden strength, and she hurriedly busied herself again with domestic matters in an effort to regain her serenity. She had many times resolved, both from her own conviction and after talking things over with Joan, that she would be exceedingly slow to get involved in any new relationship with a man. She had no intention of committing her affections to the risk of the sort of mauling they had recently experienced. Her mother too was most anxious that Mary shouldn't rush into a new affair that could prove as disastrous as the first and tried urgently to impress this on her daughter. She need not have worried. Mary was very much of like mind, for although buried deep beneath all the sorrow and hurt there may have been dreams of happiness, she put them well away into the future, telling herself that it would take a long time to recapture her confidence sufficiently to entrust herself wholeheartedly to another man, adding always that it may in fact never happen again.

She was therefore disturbed that her emotions had been so suddenly and strongly aroused by the sight of Mike working. She didn't try to understand this or come to terms with it, still less to give free rein to those emotions. She sought to put an immediate block on any further thought on the whole subject, telling herself firmly that this would not do, she mustn't be and wouldn't be a poor weak fool. She must put such things right out of her mind and concentrate on practical matters.

As he guided the tractor up and down the field that April afternoon to finish rolling the oats before milking time, Mike pigeonholed his musings about Mary. Though he was, of course, aware that he was far from disinterested in her fate, his resolve was unchanged to let matters take their natural course, unwilling for reasons of personal pride and self protection to lift a finger to encourage for a second time those feelings within him which were slowly gathering strength in spite of himself.

A few days later potato planting was in full swing on Manor Farm. This was a big operation, one of the farm's important occasions and a good source of income. The acreage of potatoes planted was, with government encouragement, almost as high as the wartime peaks of production, as the nation, still striving to overcome the continuing shortage of food which had dragged on for so long after the war, urged farmers to produce as much as possible.

Mike on the tractor, with the bouting plough behind to dig the deep planting trenches, had previously prepared the large strip. Now he and Nick and Terry with Mary had come down to plant the potatoes by hand. A couple of dozen or so hessian sacks of their own King Edward seed potatoes had been brought down on the trailer and they were busy placing these along the trenches ready to start the planting. Several sacks of superphosphate fertiliser were also placed out, as this was dribbled in by hand from a bucket at the same time.

The soil was a fine and rich brown loam above blue clay and, as Mike walked across it to where they were working, he trod it as often, conscious of the generations who had worked there before, back in a long unbroken line to the days of the nearby medieval manor and earlier, ploughing, manuring, cultivating, harvesting. He imagined the teams of horses and before them of oxen, there where the tractor now stood, and he tried to picture the bearded and moustachioed men in waistcoats and gaiters or in smocks who had toiled for a lifetime and gone their way back into dust, leaving no sign of their having been upon this unchanging soil. Once again this same earth was being planted up and he had no doubt that once again it would bring forth an excellent crop, one that he was very conscious of playing a part in producing. He too would leave no monument upon this soil, but that was not to deny the vital nature of the task nor detract from the keen pleasure of the living moment. It still seemed little short of miraculous to him that seed was buried in the earth on such a vast scale and that with sensible care and average luck it gave a marvellous return. It was fantastic when he really thought about it that this thin skin of good soil, averaging only a foot or two deep world wide, should support the earth's huge population, and he looked at it as he crushed it beneath his boot, almost with reverence at man's dependence upon it, a dependence most often taken for granted and scarcely ever given its true worth. Was it just by chance that the good earth is here making all life possible, all civilisation, all progress? If so, how very fortunate indeed, how happy the accident, how apt to man's precise needs!

"Surely it is no outlandish thing," he thought as he tramped the furrows, "to spend my time working on this soil, playing my small part in this most basic industry of them all?" He looked around him at the field of young green corn nearby and the large clover field next to it. Beyond the brook were tree-lined meadows with cows grazing them, their udders heavy with milk, and further up the gentle slope the orchards fringing cottages, trees still dark and leafless but soon to open their pink and white blossoms, forerunner of the bounteous fruits to come. Everywhere he looked there was food growing in one form or another and all of it not only useful but beautiful. It was a beauty which extended to the enclosing hills, so that the whole view was as of a vast productive yet ornamental garden.

The gang of four worked very harmoniously together. Being mostly within earshot of each other as with buckets of potatoes they bent to plant them, they managed to carry on snatches of conversation all morning to ease the tedium of the task. Terry and Nick were very pleasant fellows, Mike considered. He had come to like and respect them very much over the months they had been there. The five years or so that they were younger than him set them a little apart perhaps, but they all got on well together. They were an easy going pair, strong and intelligent but not ambitious apparently and were no doubt like many farm workers of previous generations in that respect. But this generation had a different destiny with higher expectations and, when this pair started having regular, steady girl friends, this differing outlook began to show itself.

Mike noticed that their talk dwelt more frequently than at first on their friends who worked in local factories and of the cars and houses they were buying. He wondered how long they would stay in farming, especially now both their fathers had retired when Turvey's Farm had increasingly gone over to mechanisation. How would Mary manage, he wondered, if Nick and Terry were to leave? They probably would leave one day, perhaps quite soon. The temptations of factory work with its higher wages, regular hours, five day week and longer paid holidays were great, but nothing had been said so far and Mike put the danger time at when they should decide to get married and so far that date hadn't been fixed, as far as he knew.

The pair were the ideal antidote to Mike's, by his own admission, rose tinted view of farming and country life. Brutally matter of fact in their reaction to hard, unromantic work and in their opinion that machines couldn't take over quickly enough for them, they kept Mike's feet more or less on the ground on work matters and, when Mary wasn't around, eased themselves of frustrations by free flowing invective. And yet they kept going and were in fact excellent workers and Mike did sometimes idly wonder if they might get to that decisive point one day beyond which they would settle happily into the classical farm worker mould, paid at decent union rates. "Someone has to do the work," he thought. "What little work there will soon be left to do."

That morning the talk, as often, was of local sport, of Luton Town's current football team and their prospects of gaining promotion from the second division which seemed to be their natural home, and of Vauxhall's team which had done particularly well in the local league. Mike had been over to see Luton play several times, since he no longer played himself, and he took enough interest in their progress to be able to talk knowledgeably and at length with the two young men about this most passionate of sporting subjects. "Of course, I can see them going up to the first division this year," Nick said, as he pushed potatoes into the earth alongside.

"Well yes, they're very well placed, it's true," Mike agreed. "What are they, third from the top at the moment? If they can keep up their current form they may well do it this time."

"You didn't see the game against Charlton last week, I suppose?" Nick asked.

Mike shook his head.

"It was fantastic," Nick went on, whilst Terry straightened his back and listened. "Three goals they rattled past Sam Bartram and it's not many sides have done that lately."

"They had a good cup run this year, didn't they?" Mike said.

"Oh yes," Terry enthused. "They could so easily have gone the whole way if it hadn't been for that damned penalty miss in the last minute against West Ham."

"That's true," Nick said. "But it's promotion they really want, I think. Though whether they'll be able to stay in the First Division if they get there is another question."

They went on to discuss darts and billiards and badminton, which Nick and Terry played in Dunstable and in several village pubs, which themselves provided much material for talk. With all this Mary joined in when she could, so that although the work was undemanding and monotonous, their conversation made the time pass agreeably. By mid-afternoon, with backs holding up well against all the bending involved, the task was completed and Mike was left with the job of putting the plough through the ten acres or so again to cover the rows and leave them well ridged up.

When he drove back to the farm the milking had been done, Nick and Terry had gone home and two full churns stood by the gate ready for collection by the milk lorry. As he put the tractor in the shed for the night Mary came out to ask if the covering and ridging up had gone well. He assured her that it had.

"We did quite well today, I thought," she said.

"Yes, very well," he agreed. "The conditions were just right."

"I suppose we're dreadfully old fashioned," she said, "doing it all by hand like that. I've been looking at mechanical planters in 'The Farmer & Stock Breeder.' They would be much more efficient, as well as taking the backache out of the job."

"Oh, I daresay," Mike said. "But for the acreage we plant I shouldn't think it's worthwhile, is it?"

"I'm not so sure," she said. "And of course we could plant much more with a machine."

"Thinking of getting up to date, are we?" he asked, lightly teasing.

"Well," she said with a smile, "There's no doubt, I think, that that's the way things have got to go sooner or later. But I'm no expert."

"No, nor am I," Mike admitted. "And I must say I tend to have a healthy mistrust of so-called experts of all sorts."

"What would you think, though," she asked him, "if we did start modernising a bit?"

"Oh, I'd be all for it, I think, in principle anyway," he replied, meeting her gaze frankly, thinking that she must feel confident if she was considering making changes. He felt flattered to be asked his opinion.

"We'll have to have a chat about it all soon," she said thoughtfully. Then after a short pause she added, "Why don't you drop in for a bite of supper, say tomorrow if you've nothing better to do? Then we could chew it over a bit," she concluded, putting into words her recent thoughts about actually doing something towards making plans for her farming future.

"Okay, thanks," he replied willingly, pleasantly shaken to receive a personal invitation about such a potentially serious subject, but of course he had to insist to himself as he walked home that it was only motivated by politeness and was a natural and civilised follow on to what they had been discussing.

That was what Mary said to herself too, indoors minutes later, as if answering the unformulated assertion that there might have been rather more to it than that. Later that evening after Mike had eaten, Mac called in and they walked the meadows again with one of the four tens that Norman had let Mike have on more or less permanent loan now. There was nothing more soothing after a hard day's work than to patrol the fields at leisure as the sun dipped low on the horizon, when the budding hawthorns were full of chaffinches in noisy dispute before settling down for the night, and the rooks were winging in to their nests in the neighbouring tall elms. Sometimes he might be lucky enough to surprise a flock of pigeons preening in some oak or sycamore after their last feed of the day, and he occasionally got one before they exploded out of the branches and away. He was happy enough with his own company at such times and usually came home with a feeling of deep satisfaction at being so close to nature and with time to notice the subtle, changing beauty of sunset and twilight when all life sank calmly to rest. It made a nice change however, to have company, and the two friends wandered in mostly silent companionship, their minds more finely tuned to their quarry than Mike's usually was.

After an hour or so they came out onto the road, Mac carrying the rabbit he'd been lucky enough to bag. They weren't far from his house, so they went in for a cup of coffee. There Mike was shown the brochure of the housing development Mac was interested in between Luton and Dunstable. "It looks pretty good," he said encouragingly.

"Not bad for a start, I suppose," Mac agreed. "Two bedrooms, bathroom, fitted kitchen, lounge-dining room. It's as much as we have any right to expect. There's a small garden, as you can see. I'm sure Jeannie will approve."

"And it's not too far from work, I presume?" Mike said.

"No, I can be there in less than half an hour on the bus."

"So that's you just about settled down."

"Yes, it looks like it," Mac agreed. "With a mortgage, of course. It comes to most of us sooner or later, I suppose."

"If we're lucky," Mike added, wondering if he would ever be so lucky.

The following evening he cycled back from the Memorial Hall after only one leisurely game of snooker with Mac. It felt strange to be knocking on the farmhouse door in the dark, but he did so and Mary came out beaming to greet him. She'd got a log fire blazing in the huge grate, the curtains were drawn across and it felt warm and cosy within.

They chatted for a few moments, then Mary offered him a glass of cider and excused herself for a couple of minutes to finish off cooking the supper in the back kitchen. Mike sat in one of the comfortable old armchairs and looked around at the room which he hadn't seen much of in recent months. Little seemed to have altered in it. Save for the big rolltop desk which had gone to the bungalow, all the things were there which he knew and loved so well - the old china and pewter laden dresser, the book case on the wall by the dartboard, the big old wall clock still ticking away loudly and the jumble of walking sticks and a twelve bore in the corner by the treadle sewing machine.

Mary soon came back bearing their supper tray and they sat down to enjoy a meal of lamb's liver and onions with thick, rich gravy and mashed potatoes. Mike complimented her on it but she said dismissively, "Oh, it's only a simple offering, I know, but I haven't had much practice in cooking anything decent lately."

"This is perfectly decent," he objected. "But no, I suppose you have been rather busy these last few months."

"I should say so," she said with feeling. "Not that I've minded. In fact it's been my salvation." She paused and they both pondered the background to her remark.

"But you're enjoying yourself now?" he enquired.

"Oh, yes," she replied with enthusiasm. "It is rather strange, I suppose, unusual anyhow, for a woman to be trying to run a farm like this one, and to be honest I've been lost many times. But yes, I've enjoyed it on the whole."

"It was asking a lot," he commented, "to jump in at the deep end as you did, but it hasn't exactly been disastrous has it?"

"I hope not," she said. "You've all been very tolerant, I'm sure."

As they chatted on in this vein for some minutes while they ate, Mike was aware of how pleasant it was to be talking to her again. Really talking at ease and leisure as opposed to purely working, jargon talk in field or yard. Gone now from Mary, he realised, were all her young posturing, the striking of attitudes and affectations that are inseparable from youth. She was now a mature woman, wiser and certainly sadder by her recent experiences but also certainly more rounded and secure in her personality and as with all such truly adult women it was a pleasure to be with and talk to her.

She poured him more cider and took a little herself. "Do you know, this is a sort of celebration," she said surprisingly, raising her glass. "I hadn't realised myself until this morning that it's six months exactly since I took over the running of the farm."

"Is it really? Oh, well done," he responded, lifting his glass. "Let's drink to that, then shall we? Six months under your belt and here's wishing you many of them and successful ones too."

She went out to the back kitchen again and soon returned with a dish of stewed apricots and a jug of custard. "You've really done me proud, Mary," he said. "I'm thankful I only had a light tea."

"I always think a man needs feeding properly," she said simply. "Especially if he's been working."

"Oh, you're right," he said laughing, "so right."

As he tucked in, he speculated silently on what it must be like for her, living there alone in that largish house amid the ashes of her broken marriage, as it were. Six months she'd had to think about it all, to suffer and now perhaps to emerge into a new life. She might well be, probably was, very lonely in spite of her whirl of activity and that was why she had invited him in. Certainly they'd had no talk so far of farm improvements or modernising, which was what she said she wanted to discuss.

They cleared the table together but left the washing up and came back with coffee to the front kitchen and its comfort.

"Were you thinking seriously of going in for more modernisation?" he asked as he stirred his coffee, thinking that he'd better try to justify his being there in some sort of consulting role.

"Yes, I'm beginning to think of it, in theory at least. It seems to me that farming is ready to move ahead again after the war, if ever it did stand still, that is. All the young farmers I've spoken to recently have been keen to modernise. We are at the end of an era, I think, and we probably can't afford to be left too far behind in the new modern farming world to come, can we?"

"No, I'm sure you're right," he said. "You've only got to think how many more combine harvesters there are around here now, compared to when we were kids. It's a mechanical revolution in farming that we're entering on, I don't doubt."

"And of course," she went on, "mechanisation entails a big investment and that will mean big bank loans. So we've got to know exactly what we're doing. We can't afford to make too many mistakes."

"Yes," he agreed, "finance will be crucial, I'm sure. You've got to do your sums right and get down to fine detail. I'm sure your dad will have some good advice to offer there."

"I've no doubt that is so," she said. "But for one thing I don't want to burden dad with these matters if I can help it. It might cause him to worry more than is good for him. And the other point is that this is to a large extent a generation thing. We seem to be heading towards a situation that dad simply didn't have to deal with."

"That may well be true," he agreed. "But you know, if we're going to touch on the philosophy that lies behind all this modernisation drive in farming, there are one or two things that worry me, I must admit. You know Len Dollimore, don't you? He plays for Eaton Bray cricket team and he was telling me the other day that his dad has had to lay off their three chaps since they bought their big new combine and at the same time went over to machine milking. Now the whole farm, nearly four hundred acres, is run by Len and his dad with just one part timer. And he's mortgaged up to the hilt."

"That's hard luck on the three chaps laid off, I can see that," she admitted. "But I suppose they can get other jobs."

"They may well do," he agreed, "but I should be very surprised if it's in farming. If that's the way things are going to go it makes me wonder what farms will be like in a few years."

"Yes, I see," she said. "I remember dad talking sometimes about when he was a boy when they had as many as six village chaps helping at harvest work. And he said once his father was saying they had as many as a dozen men scything the corn and as many women binding it by hand."

"That's right," he said. "Farming involved a large part of the village in those days. It's all going to look very different when machines take over more or less completely, isn't it? They'll be ghost farms then, I reckon. And what's it going to do to villages? What jobs will be left in your average village? What, I wonder, will be the price of all this progress we're hearing so much about?"

"Well, following on logically," she proposed, "I suppose villages will become more like dormitories, with most people travelling to towns to work."

"What, villages with no honest to goodness life of their own!"

"Ah, you're getting into the realms of pure speculation now," she said. "Into the realms of prophecy. I can't see that far ahead."

"No, nor can I," he admitted. "But it's not too hard to build up a depressing picture, is it?

"The part I don't like is the thought of no more horses working the land," she said with feeling. "Tractors may be more efficient but they're pretty soulless."

"I agree," he said. "But there you are, now mechanisation is really getting going, what chance do horses have?"

"I'm certainly not getting rid of our four," she insisted. "They can live here in splendid retirement for the rest of their lives, for I'm not selling them off for cats' meat. I might easily be tempted to put one on a grass cutter now and then and have the thistles down in the orchard."

"Good for you," he nodded enthusiastically. "I'd personally hate to see the countryside become less colourful, with no horses and no gangs of working men and women in the fields."

"We sound like a couple of reactionaries," Mary half whispered, with a giggle. "A sort of modern Luddites of agriculture."

"Well, since you mention it, I just happen to have a nice little bomb in my saddle bag and I know Horace Henley's combine harvester is in an unlocked shed."

They had a good laugh at that before Mary proclaimed, "So the general feeling of the meeting is that perhaps we'd better stay as we are for the time being?"

"No, I doubt if it will be possible to do that and stay in business," he said, returning to seriousness. "The pressure will be on everyone to keep up, especially if mechanisation means more profit, which it will undoubtedly. Efficiency is set to become the god now, it seems, and we shall all be required to worship it. The old idea of farming being a partnership with nature is in eclipse, perhaps it is going for ever. I hope not and we may well come to regret it if it is."

"Mm," she murmured pensively. "Farming does look as if it is becoming ever more of a business like any other and I for one will be sorry to see it go that way. But anyway, there's no great hurry to do anything. The whole matter needs a great deal of serious thought. Who knows, there may be some more reasonable way we can proceed."

"And another point is," he threw in lightly, "how Nick and Terry and I would fit in with any modernisation we might suggest?"

"Oh, I couldn't contemplate losing any of you," she replied with a smile, gathering up his coffee cup. He weighed her remark before pronouncing, "That's all right then."

They left the subject there and after a little more general talk he took his leave and cycled the short distance home, musing on a very pleasant evening. Mary too was very happy with the evening and, as she tackled the dishes, reflected on how easy they had been together, without strain or awkwardness, and on how much she had enjoyed their talk. She considered once more the strange fact that, although she had known Mike for so many years, she was only recently surprised to find such depths in him and to acknowledge this as a very attractive feature. He certainly wasn't all surface and superficial like so many she'd met. He was a thinker and she liked that. She was also forced to acknowledge, as she had on that previous occasion some days before, that emotions long dormant had been stirred by his physical presence.

In bed later that night, Mike realised that for him a line had been crossed, his own personal Rubicon. In spite of his oft repeated cautionary watchword he knew that his affections were once again becoming deeply involved with Mary. Being with her for a couple of leisure hours as he had just been, he sensed that all his previous doubts would be of no avail. It was as though the intervening years had never been, when he had not permitted himself the luxury of dreaming of her, when he had told himself she was gone forever and that he must seek his happiness elsewhere. All that was swept away as he lay in bed going over the time they had just spent together. Was he right to think that she was fond of him, he asked himself. Really fond? Anything more than fond? She had invited him into her home, cooked for him, been very attentive and lively in her talk with him. He was inclined to think that he was right this time, that she did have feeling for him, though he was very cautious with this notion. The shadowy remnant of his old heartbreak still lingered to dampen any renascent ardour. What was sure was his feeling for her, though he tried to resist luxuriating in this, telling himself firmly and repeatedly that he may once again prove mistaken, that their talk had, after all, been general, nothing even verging on the personal and intimate and that he was merely being treated as a valued employee and a friend, nothing more.

"It's strange," he murmured to himself in the darkness, "she only has to lift a little finger and I come running. Only invite me into her house and speak kindly and I lie awake all night, unable to sleep for thinking of her, wanting her."

After a fitful sleep Mike was up at dawn, surprising Marjorie who often had to call him to prevent him being late for milking. She heard him downstairs making tea and grilling toast and wondered what he had on his mind. "Some woman, I expect," she muttered to herself as she settled down for a few minutes more in bed.

She was indeed right, although the passage of night had blunted slightly the sharpness of his earlier reflections and conclusions. In the cool morning light his hopes had subsided into sober objectivity, where his instinct counselled continuing caution against unjustified optimism.

Impatient to be active, he let himself out of the cottage quite a bit earlier than usual to go to work. The sun would soon rise to flood the fields and orchards with its level golden rays making the dewdrops flash like diamonds in the grass. High above, the sky was bathed in a glorious pearly hue, rapidly warming before changing to clearest azure whilst the whole scene of sleeping cottages, gardens, trees and wide verged lane had that stillness and a breathless air of being new-made that forced him to stand and stare in admiration at the world's early morning loveliness. It was not difficult to believe in a Creative Spirit of the universe on such a morning, its presence was almost tangible. He gave silent thanks once again to that spirit as he looked around him, for the destiny that had brought him to that lovely corner of England and given him a love and appreciation both of nature and of man's best efforts in the landscape which, as with all natural growth, were both harmonious and useful.

As he walked along the road to the farm, thinking of the day ahead, Mary let herself out of the house and crossed the silent yard to the stable. She too had slept less soundly than usual, having many engrossing matters on her mind from the previous evening. She also knew that she had to give a further dose of medicine to Captain who was suffering a mild attack of colic. So, as she was awake and mentally active, she decided to get up early and see to the big gelding before milking began. She let herself into the stable and with the aid of a hurricane lamp peered into the dim far corner where Captain lay spreadeagled on his deep bed of straw. The vet had been the day before and pronounced himself satisfied that the horse was in no real danger, although colic always has to be watched with care. He had left her the necessary medicine in a large lemonade bottle. Knowing of Mary's lifelong experience with horses he knew full well that she would have no difficulty in giving Captain his required drench, especially given his equable temperament. "Captain," she called from the doorway, "Captain, are you awake, boy?" The horse raised his head from the straw and looked up alertly. "Good morning, Captain," Mary said, putting the lamp down and walking towards him. She was relieved to see that he appeared to have improved overnight from his previous lethargic state. She examined him closely to make sure that she was right, that he did indeed seem better. As Captain struggled gamely to his feet, Mary looked closely at his stomach to see if it was still distended as it had been. "That's better, Captain old chap," she pronounced. "That's much better," and she patted his shoulder affectionately.

She uncorked the bottle, grasped the bridle and tipped the contents into his mouth. Whether it was from some sudden twinge of pain or some imaginary fear in the shadows there is no telling, but Captain gave a sudden loud whinny and reared up, his head catching Mary, who was a little off balance anyway. She staggered back slipped and fell, striking her head on the manger, then collapsed unconscious to the floor, as she did so knocking the lamp over and breaking the glass. It rolled across the floor and in a few seconds the straw in which it came to rest was alight, the flame low at first but soon rising as the fire took hold on the dry bedding in the neighbouring empty stall.

As Mike turned off the road into the yard he saw smoke billowing from the half open stable doorway and heard the uproar inside as Captain, held prisoner by a stout rope, reared and whinnied in panic. He dashed across the yard and stood in the doorway for an agitated second, taking in the situation. Seeing Mary unconscious on the ground but clear as yet of the flames, he rushed forward, quickly releasing the lunging horse which clattered out into the yard, then he snatched Mary up in his arms with the flames licking near and, almost crouching with his burden, dashed through the swirling smoke, outside to safety.

As he was making for the house he heard a shout, and Nick and Terry arrived at the top of the yard on their bicycles. They rushed to the water trough and buckets as he went indoors and put Mary down on the chesterfield in the dining room. He stood back a moment, looking anxiously at her, then, seeing her eyelids begin to flutter, he quickly fetched a glass of water and came back to find her conscious. "Drink this," he ordered and she sipped and sank back again with a sigh. "How do you feel?" he enquired with deep concern. "All right now," she murmured, smiling wanly. "What happened, I...?"

"Stay there and don't move," he interrupted sternly. "I'm going out to help Nick and Terry. I'll be back soon."

He seized another bucket from beside the well, filled it and dashed into the stable and the three of them very quickly threw several more buckets of water on the seat of the fire before they were satisfied it was finally out, relieved that it was before much damage was done beyond charring one of the stall partitions and blackening the walls.

"Could have been nasty given five more minutes," Nick commented laconically, after they had inspected the blackened mess. "How's the boss?"

"She's come to." Mike said and he explained the situation as he'd found it. "I'll leave you two to look after things here and go and see how she is now."

"Yeah, you do that," Terry urged with a sly smile.

He found her sitting up on the chesterfield, sipping her water, the colour somewhat returned to her cheeks. Taking the handkerchief which she held he moistened it from the glass and gently dabbed away a trickle of blood from her forehead.

"Tell me what happened," she asked in a low voice. "I reek of smoke."

He briefly told her what he'd seen and how it had ended. "It was that lamp that was the trouble," he concluded. "You can't be too careful with them."

"You came just in time," she murmured falteringly. Then she held out her hand to him and he took it. "Sit down," she said, her eyes gazing intently into his, "here, next to me."

"Are you feeling better now?" he asked, still greatly concerned.

"Oh, yes, much better now," she murmured, as she leaned towards him, her lips only inches from his. In that instant he knew all he needed to know about their feelings for each other. All doubts and hesitations instantly evaporated as he gently met her lips with his and gathered her into his arms in a long and tender embrace.

"Why has it taken us so long to come to this," she murmured, "when it is so right, so inevitable and right?"

"It doesn't matter," he offered in response, smoothing her rumpled hair. "Perhaps we had to travel different roads awhile, to grow maturer in our experiences, to make our mistakes even. It doesn't matter, I'm sure we shall be all the more ready for each other now."

"Yes, I feel so too," she agreed. "It's no use regretting the wasted years, is it? They're gone and finished with, I know that for sure now. The future belongs to us, that is what is so exciting. Oh Mike, dear Mike, you don't know how happy you've made me."

They kissed again and sat a while in silence, holding hands and gazing into each other's eyes, content, if it were possible, to stay like that forever.

How he passed the rest of that working day Mike couldn't clearly recollect in detail. He knew that he had eventually torn himself away and gone outside again, leaving Mary comfortably tucked up with a cup of tea to rest and recover from her painful experience. He remembered checking up that Captain was none the worse for his fright, then he supposed he must have spent most of the morning clearing up and repairing the damage to the stable. The truth was that his mind was not so much confused with the suddenness of his coming together with Mary - he accepted that easily and naturally as if part of him that had been long hidden and silent now surfaced, having known all along that one day it was bound to happen one way or another - it was more that he was so completely in a whirl over the reality and the rapture of those few precious moments he had so far lived through with her. He was constantly reliving their embrace and their kisses, dwelling over and over on the deep satisfying thrill of their oneness, of their coming together in that divine prelude to a life of close companionship.

At lunchtime he had gone into the house and found Mary just awakened from a sound and refreshing sleep. She smiled and gestured to him to come in as he stood in the doorway. "Sit down by me here," she said, smoothing out the blanket on the chesterfield. "Look, there's a plate of sandwiches on the little table. Help yourself, I'm sure you're hungry."

So he'd sat there holding her hand, eating with a will as they had talked sweet nothings, savouring to the full the new and vital pleasure of mutual intimacy. And what a heavenly intimacy it was! The electric thrill that ran through their joined hands and radiated from their eyes transported them for that eternity of precious minutes into a private haven of pure joy. Eventually he had returned to work, refusing all Mary's protestations that she was all right now and could do some useful work outside. "That bump is still nasty," he declared, leaning over to examine it. Please rest this afternoon. Read a book or have a nap," and he kissed her lightly on the lips and left.

By evening Mary was completely recovered from her ordeal, as Mike ascertained when he called at the house before going home after the milking was done. After embracing her tenderly he said he'd be back as soon as possible, for Mary wanted them both to walk down to her parents' bungalow to tell them their good news.

Over his evening meal at the cottage Mike blithely recounted the day to the astonished Marjorie, who listened with bright eyes and exclamations of surprise and pleasure. At the end she came round the table to him, put her arms around his shoulders and hugged and kissed him joyfully on the cheek. "I'm so pleased," she said, her eyes brimming with tears of happiness. "What a fairytale outcome to what is truly an amazing story, although really I suppose this is just the beginning of a new chapter rather than the end of the story." She paused to gather her thoughts, almost overcome with emotion. "I can hardly take it in," she went on, "it seems so incredible. Who would have thought on the day you fled the blitz and arrived here a pale and thin little city lad, that you'd end up as you have. Wherever it might lead to from here."

"Well, wherever it may be, I owe it in no small measure to you, Marjorie," he said, squeezing her hand. "I shall never forget it. Even if I'd never had this good fortune with Mary I'd still be deeply in debt to you. Don't ever believe that I don't realise it."

"It's your happiness that I'm really pleased about," she concluded simply. "That's what really counts."

Mike paused again in his long train of recollections, almost ready to stop altogether as he felt a sleepiness coming upon him. "What a mass of memories I've run through," he murmured. "How much could I in fact tell grandson Paul? Some of it in bits and pieces perhaps. Or perhaps one day I could have a go at writing some of it down? We'll see. And what comes out of it all beyond the personal story? Well, one man's lifetime is a pretty short affair in the evolution of a nation or a countryside. Looking back, it seems but an instant to my young days but in fact just about everything has changed, much of it beyond recognition. Now as a nation, in spite of universal education, we have the evils of affluence to afflict us, drugs, crime, vandals and hooligans. Everywhere around us the degenerate, depraved and third rate is on the increase. Is it all inevitable? Can no one lead us out of it? But what I suppose I've observed closest of all is the decline of the countryside into what risks becoming a sort of glorified theme park for the enjoyment of city people. Is farming coming to that, with Paul destined to be no more than a park keeper? I hope and pray not, but I actually believe that the life of the countryside, which politicians have no understanding of, is in danger of being fatally weakened, and the rich life and traditions of centuries risk being ground down into bland suburbanisation.

"At least I have no personal complaint about life," he reflected. "I'm so lucky in the way my marriage has worked out. How the years have passed in almost perfect harmony and contentment - in all the main aspects of a marriage anyway. How Mary has been just right for me, has been a perfect partner, in fact". His mind slipped back to the close of that momentous first day of their coming together…

He'd gone with Mary to meet her parents and astonish them with their news. He found Emily and Norman deeply sympathetic to their daughter's choice, showering congratulations on the pair and drinking their health in a generous tot of good Scotch whisky.

As Mary explained to her parents, "Maybe it took an accident to provide the final push, but this is no lightly taken nor superficial decision on either of our parts. I know for me it is as though a door from which a chink of light has long been showing was suddenly flung wide open and I see what has been there all along but somehow hidden until today."

Mike smiled in agreement, knowing that for him too it had taken her sudden flash of recognition, that flinging open of the door in such a dramatic way, to sweep away all his past fears and doubts and set him confident and positive in his love for her.

"I'm so glad it has turned out like this," Emily said, with characteristic candour. "I used to think once, long ago, that I could wish for nothing better than you two coming together. That was just my silly fancy, so I told myself, but lo and behold! it has happened and you don't know how pleased I am." She kissed Mike and hugged Mary with deep affection.

Norman's warm handshake spoke volumes, as did his eyes in sincere goodwill. "I couldn't wish for anything more fitting," he exclaimed. "It's only a pity it was so long delayed, I suppose. But anyway, let's forget past sadnesses and concentrate on a bright future, for that's what I am sure is in store for you. So let's fill our glasses again and drink to your lifelong happiness."

Through all the friendly talk that followed and went on for some considerable time into the evening, Mike was aware of the presence of Dennis hovering around the perimeter of his thoughts. As he reflected in quiet moments on his beginnings with this family that he was finally making his own, he couldn't help feeling that Dennis would not have been displeased at the way things had eventually turned out. Although these thoughts were inevitably tinged with regret he knew that Dennis would be an ever present part of him in the years to come, a presence and an influence that he would carry with pleasure.

They talked a lot about the farm and its future and Norman pronounced himself very happy to make over the ownership of Manor Farm jointly to Mike and Mary in the certain knowledge of Mike's lifetime commitment to Mary and to the land, and he assured them that, as far as he was able, he would back them with any advice they might care to ask for. Mike received this gesture of great generosity with lively but serious gratitude. He regarded his new status very much in the nature of a sacred trust and he had every confidence in his future relationship with Norman.

Afterwards Mike and Mary parted very affectionately and went their separate ways. Theirs, they mutually and happily decided, was going to be an old fashioned courtship, still much in keeping with village ways.

The due process of law eventually made possible Mike and Mary's legal union which, thanks to a sympathetic vicar, they were able to celebrate with simple dignity at the ancient village church in the presence of their many friends. As a result of their unhurried courtship they were as certain as two people can ever be before the exchanging of vows, that theirs was a relationship which in its physical, emotional and intellectual aspects gave promise of a full and satisfying life together.

The couple honeymooned in Scotland as a consequence of their brief but very happy visit there for Mac and Jeannie's wedding, and Mike achieved his ambition of being among and walking upon mountains. It was an experience of rugged grandeur, of communing with a wilder, more glorious nature nearer to its primeval origins than in the softer south, and it came fully up to his hopes and started off a lifetime passion that expanded gradually to Wales and to the Lakes and brought them very great pleasure.

But however grand those higher hills they never for a moment detracted from the unique and undying pleasure he felt as he climbed his own grassy chalk Knolls and gazed out on all the familiar shapes of hills and valleys receding into the blue distance. Never did he tire of gazing down below at the delightful vista of fields, orchards, farms and villages that was his own known and loved territory. With Mary and their first small son and soon with more, he would survey their own productive fields, their very own domain and wonder at and always be deeply grateful for the destiny that had led him there from London's East End and so showered him with blessings. Whatever the problems he would meet with as he farmed, and they were many and of late years alarming in their increase, he knew that the love of his own blessed plot, together with the companionship of the woman he loved, would be for him the basis for a life of deep fulfilment and true content.

THE END

Gleanings Revisited
Nostalgic Thoughts of a Bedfordshire Farmer's Boy
E.W.O'Dell
The original small town of Barton has gradually spread and grown over the years. Very few of the current residents can still recall the way of life there in days gone by. However, here one of the few collected his thoughts and embellished them with his own sketches, plus early photographs.

Farm Of My Childhood
Mary Roberts

A way of life in the countryside that has almost disappeared – a young girl on a remote farm near Flitwick in Bedfordshire some fifty years ago.
A free and happy childhood centred on a rambling old farmhouse – much of her time spent with the farm workers and the animals she loved so much. Sometimes in her wanderings she would pass the artist Sylvester Stannard happily preserving such scenes for posterity in his well-loved watercolours, as Mary Roberts now does in her truly evocative word-pictures.

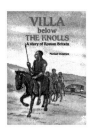

Villa Below the Knolls
A story of Roman Britain
Michael Dundrow

Ten year old John was a lively boy, full of curiosity. He was in possession of a copper brooch given to him in the Iron Age fort on Totternhoe knolls. With this brooch he'd been promised he could travel back in time to any period he chose. Little did he know that in a few seconds' time his curiosity about life in Roman Britain was to plunge him into deadly danger and hair-raising adventures with new-found friends.

The Ravens
One boy against the might of Rome
James Dyer

It is 54 BC. The Romans have landed in Britain. The men of the great Iron Age fort of Ravensburgh have gone south to fight them. Two young Britons, Adam and Marik, get the chance to follow and to save their families and friends. All the time the ravens, the ominous 'birds of death', circle overhead…